What readers are saying about
Steve Mosby's gripping thrillers

'Steve Mosby is one of the finest writers in the UK . . . Mosby takes the serial killer genre and provides something new and exciting . . . This is a book – and author – I will endlessly recommend'   Luca Veste

'Intense, creepy and deeply disturbing'   Sharon Bolton

'Shattering. Profound. Wildly innovative'   Ken Bruen

'Strange and powerful'   *The Times*

'One of a handful of writers who make me excited about crime fiction'   Val McDermid

'Mosby has become renowned for thrillers that reach into dark places where most British crime writers are afraid to go'
Sunday Express

'Those who know their crime fiction have long been aware that Steve Mosby is one of the most idiosyncratic and ambitious of current UK practitioners, and this new book is well up to his customarily impressive standard'   Barry Forshaw, *Crime Time*

'Exciting and well written – Mosby excels at catching you off guard. This is a highly recommended read but you may have to leave the light on afterwards'   *Sunday Mirror*

'One of those crime novels that lingers in the mind long after the final page'   *Daily Mail*

'Up there with the Mark Billinghams of crime-horror'   *Metro*

Steve Mosby was born in Leeds in 1976. He studied Philosophy at Leeds University, worked in the Sociology department there, and now writes full time. He is the author of ten psychological thrillers, which have been widely translated. In 2012, he won the CWA Dagger in the Library for his body of work, and his novel *Black Flowers* was shortlisted for the Theakston Old Peculier Crime Novel of the Year. He lives in Leeds with his wife and son.

To find out more, visit Steve's website or follow him on Facebook or Twitter.

www.theleftroom.co.uk
🐦 @stevemosby
f /theleftroom

THE THIRD PERSON

STEVE MOSBY

ORION

An Orion paperback

First published in Great Britain in 2003
by Orion Books
This paperback edition published in 2019
by Orion Fiction,
an imprint of The Orion Publishing Group Ltd
Carmelite House, 50 Victoria Embankment,
London EC4Y 0DZ

An Hachette UK company

1 3 5 7 9 10 8 6 4 2

A CIP catalogue record for this book
is available from the British Library.

ISBN 978 1 4091 8878 0

Typeset by Deltatype Ltd, Birkenhead, Merseyside

Printed and bound in Great Britain by Clays Ltd, Elcograf S.p.A

www.orionbooks.co.uk

For Mum and Dad, John and Roy

Thanks for some of the ideas in this book are due to Matt Ridley and Richard Dawkins. More personal thanks to: Suellen Luwish and Simon Logan for comments on early drafts, along with much online entertainment; Jonny, Tilly, Neil, Ken, Ben, Cassie, Tom, Gaz, Nicole, Keith, Steve and Simon for various friendships and encouragement over the years; Marie, Debbie, Carolyn, Keleigh, Sarah, Jodie, Liz and Nicola and everyone else in the sociology office for taking enormous amounts of piss but generally being excellent; a fair few teachers along the way, including Mr Walker, Ms Charles, Mr Horobin, Mrs Hadley and Sally Roberts; my agent, Carolyn Whitaker; Sarah Such, for helpful comments; Jon Wood, Nicky Jeanes and everyone else at Orion; Katrina and Sal and Emma, for being great; Becki, for aiding my commitment to editing with her atrocious choice of television programmes (and being really, really, great); Angela, for being my best friend in the whole world; and Mum, Dad, John and Roy for all of their encouragement and love over the years.

Most of all, thanks to Janny, who always had more faith in me than I ever did or deserved.

PROLOGUE

The writing is always done by hand.

There are a couple of things you need to know, and that's the first.

He's gently flexing his wrist as they bring the girl in: warming himself up. It should take about half an hour from start to finish, and that's a long time to write for, so you need to be prepared. Loose and relaxed. He gives his shoulders a roll and watches the girl. The bed, covered in straight sheets of glinting polythene, is on the other side of the studio. When she sees it, her step falters, but they push her from behind and she starts moving towards it.

The door is locked behind them.

'Fucking *behave*,' Marley tells her. He's the one that pushed her. She glances at him, scared, but he's not even looking at her now: just grinding out the remains of his cigarette on the floor. The smell of the smoke drifts over, catching his attention just as the girl sees him.

He sees her right back.

For a moment, it's as though she's standing on her own, with all the other figures in the room fading into the background: Marley disappears; Long Tall Jack melts out of view; the others go; even the bed seems dim and far away. It's like the girl is spot-lit: a fragile, scared thing illuminated to the exclusion of everything else.

He wants to smile at her and tell her that it will be okay,

but it won't. And he's not here to make her feel comfortable, or help her.

So instead, he picks up his pen.

And without taking his eyes off her, he begins to write.

CHAPTER ONE

Did you know that it's possible to watch rape, twenty-four hours a day, in the comfort of your own home? I bet you didn't know that, but it's true. You can just sit in front of your computer screen – with a cold beer in one hand, clicking a mouse with the other – and watch rape after rape after rape. The scenes vary, but the reality remains the same. And that's what I was doing, on the evening when the end of it all began: I was watching rape, drinking a Bud.

There are certain ways to do it. I've found that the best is to abstract yourself from what you're actually watching and listening to: you quit hearing screams and, instead, you hear pitches and tones; and you don't so much see *skin* anymore, as you see pixels: patterns of colour that remind you of things. Pink flesh; a black open mouth.

It's the best way, but still not good.

I've grown up in a generation where reality is constantly mediated, though, and so it's really not that different. When you see a war on television, for example, you're not actually watching a *war*. Get close to the screen and you can see the little blocks of colour shifting, and that's really all it is: a lot of second-hand light. It's not really people dying at all. Reality, mediated. You're not seeing what happened, you're just seeing an effect it had on film in a camera. In every way that matters, it's no different to someone describing it to you afterwards: someone whose eye is a lens; someone whose

3

memory is camera film. Purely and simply, what you are seeing is hearsay.

The hearsay on the internet varies, depending upon where you go to listen. If you enter the word *rape* or *snuff* into a search engine, you'll find the tip of the iceberg. Seriously – it's that easy. The first few porn sites you'll visit will be mostly – if not totally – legit. They offer violent, hard-core porn for download, generally for money but there are ways around that, and you'll know, from watching them, that they're fakes. There'll be a plot structure that gives the whole thing away. Sometimes, there are even credits at the end. These are stories: fantasies designed to give you a thrill, acted out by paid, willing models.

I had a few hours' worth of this type of movie on my hard drive: some good quality and some bad. I'd seen enough to know I wasn't interested. I wouldn't find Amy here. These staged travesties weren't an abyss, merely a gutter, and I knew from the beginning that I was going to have to look deeper to find her.

Here's something else I'll bet you didn't know:

The deeper you look, the darker your house gets.

It's a strange thing. You start to feel very lonely, sitting in front of the screen. The heating starts clicking; pipes creak. The ticking clock in the other room starts to sound like cover for movement downstairs. You feel things standing behind you. The shadows become gloomier and the light less sufficient. The first time I felt this – and it felt like cold breath on my neck – was when I was looking at the carcass of one of Jeffrey Dahmer's kills: a medium-sized jpeg image of a corpse, resplendent in streaks of red and white, propped up beside a stained bath. And suddenly, I felt watched. The silence in my house – our house, I mean – started to ring, and I slept with the light on later, lucky to sleep at all.

The death sites and the rape sites go hand in hand. Do you

4

want to see dead people? You can. More specifically, you can view them by category. Do you want to see burn victims or hanging victims? Do you want to see gunshot wounds and people smashed beneath fallen rubble? You can see all these and more: rotting corpses; naked women, murdered and in various states of dismemberment; rape victims, discarded like torn bags of old clothes beside forest paths; deformities, both congenital and deliberate. The sites are often white text on black, adorned with skulls and candles, and the tone is generally humorous and genial. If you don't like it, you can leave. These sites are not illegal.

Some skirt close, though. I found one site which showed photographs taken by two killers as they raped, tortured and murdered a young girl. They had also audiotaped it, and the track was available at the site. I listened, deliberately hearing it as pitches and tones: fluctuations in sound. The site claimed, incorrectly, that it was the closest thing to snuff available on the internet. I've seen closer. Other sites are devoted to animals, both sexually and otherwise. A woman being raped by a horse (real). Cats being flayed alive, their skins coming off like sellotape unsticking from a parcel (real). During the time of the Waco siege in Texas, FBI agents played tapes of rabbits being tortured to death into Koresh's compound in order to wear down those inside. I have that sound file, and it wears me down, too.

But like I said: none of this is *actually* real. It's all just hearsay after the event, like a newspaper report, or the Bible. And that's the best way to think of it: maybe the only sensible way, if you're going to think of it at all.

Just dots of colour or beats of sound.

Just words on a page.

'You have one message ... Message One.'
Beep.

I recognised her voice straight away, and pictured her face as she started talking to me from the pocked, steel-grey grid of my answerphone.

'Jason? It's me. Charlie. I was just calling to find out how you are. I mean, I know that you're not great, but ... you know. Williams is going spare about you not turning in this week.'

Charlie had just turned eighteen and was cute as hell. Short blonde hair, trim figure, pretty face. She had a pierced nose: a little gold stud, as though someone had banged a painless nail into the perfect skin on the side of her nostril. Whenever she spoke, she didn't seem to have a bad word to say about anyone. For me, for some reason, they were all good.

'He's tried to ring you a couple of times, but there was no answer. He's left messages, though. Have you not got them?'

I nodded to myself, picturing Williams behind his desk. White shirt, dark tie. Neat hair and glasses. He always had little red flushes in his cheeks, as though he was constantly embarrassed about something. I think he was slightly paranoid that the other guys all took the piss out of him when they were out of ear-shot, but in reality they couldn't give a shit about him, and I felt the same way. He was my direct superior, and he'd left increasingly angry messages on my answerphone for the last few days. I'd deleted them as soon as I heard the first few nasal notes. A lot of times, you don't need to hear people to know what they're saying.

'Well, whatever. I mean, I know that you're having a bad time, and you don't have to talk to me if you don't want. *Obviously*, but – you know. I just wanted you to know that I'm here for you. If you want to talk, that is. We can have a chat. Hey – I could buy you a coffee some time.'

She always made sure I had a coffee each morning at nine. Bless her. Over the weeks, she'd even kept track of my increasing lateness, with the coffee starting to arrive on my desk at nine-fifteen, and then nine-thirty.

I smiled, and clicked stop, but I didn't delete it. Instead, I shrugged off my coat onto the chair and headed through to the kitchen.

There was beer in the fridge, as there should be in every decent, civilised home. I collected a bottle, and then went upstairs, to the study, clicking the computer on at the plug and settling in for the night.

The Melanie Room.

Not a room in the normal sense that you might think of a room, but I'd say it still had a good claim. It had two walls, a floor and a ceiling – of a kind, anyway – and rooms branching out in all directions that you created as you went. It was a Chat room: white space filled with text, divided into two vertical sections. The section on the right listed usernames; the larger section on the left was the chat space, steadily scrolling away upwards as users typed in messages that appeared at the bottom. The Room was named after Melanie Shaw, a five-year-old girl who had disappeared in Central England a few years ago. She was still alive somewhere. The Room had been named in her honour after a user named JACKJILL posted a picture of what was claimed to be her: a bound, naked girl, with her head wrapped entirely in black electrical tape, breathing through straws in her nostrils. That was two years ago, and he'd posted a picture a month ever since.

There were thirty-seven users in the Room that night, which was about average. Sometimes there were more and sometimes less, but it hardly mattered. As always, the main room was almost entirely empty. Little in the way of real conversation ever went on there – the real action took place privately. By double-clicking on someone's username you could enter into a private room with them – just the two of you, unless you invited others – and chat one-on-one. You could cyber or discuss cases in the news, or exchange favourite photographs and links, all out of the way of prying eyes.

I'd logged on as Amy17, and it took all of thirty seconds for the first private message to come through:

HARD4U: [u like it in ass bitch]

Invitations to 'private' – however primitive – almost always came up in a separate window, and you could choose to *chat* or *cancel*. I took the first sip of my beer and pressed *cancel*. That thing about my boss? It goes for perverts on the internet, too.

A few more windows flashed up over the next twenty seconds, but none of them were that much better than just plain annoying.

SEXXXYFUCK: [i'll tie you with ur panties]
M-BRACE: [hi – asl?]
likeyoungirls: [r u wet Amy?]

I pressed *cancel* on each of them in turn, all the time scrolling down the list of users until I found the one I wanted. I'd been talking to this guy for the last couple of weeks, hiding behind the Amy17 name, and trying to get a little closer to him. Recently, it felt as though I'd been succeeding. Now, I peered at the screen, moving my head closer and closer. His name – <~KaREEM~> – did not dissolve into dots the way the gifs he often sent me did: the lines remained solid and connected. It was just text on a screen, this man's name, but you still couldn't see through it; it didn't break down. It gave me the sense that this really *was* happening now, and that – somewhere nearby – he was looking at his own screen, perhaps running a finger over the text I was hiding behind, and thinking something similar.

I took a sip of my beer, and waited for him to come to me.

A few facts about Amy17. She was seventeen years old, five feet and three inches tall in her bare feet. She had short, blonde hair, cut off in a line just before it touched her shoulders, blue-green eyes and clear skin – a pretty girl. Generally, she wore plain white tops, sometimes a skinny-rib, and a skirt to mid-thigh. Both items showed her off well, because she had tanned, toned legs from her thrice-weekly gym visits, and firm 34C breasts. Amy17 was sexually experienced, and had discovered the boys very young. Her favourite position was missionary, held down firmly by that lovely hair of hers, but she was always open to suggestions. Kareem generally had a few.

I sat and waited for him, wondering how long he could hold out. A few more revolting hopefuls approached me, and I cancelled them all. Mr Hard4U tried me again, and I responded by telling him to fuck *himself* in the ass, and try his mother out first for practice. I was beginning to despair until, after five minutes, I felt his breath on my neck and the room went that little bit darker. The window appeared.

<~KaREEM~>:   [(whispers) Where are you?]

Got you, I thought, taking another sip of my beer. As always, my heart was pounding and my palms felt sweaty: slightly shaky. That feeling of connecting with someone over the net has always made me feel strange. It's a feeling that's never gone away.

I clicked *chat*, which opened up a private window. When I typed in my reply, it appeared underneath his:

<~KaREEM~>:   (whispers) Where are you?

9

Amy17:	I'm walking through a wood.

There was a brief pause. The white background of the window seemed to buzz with possibility. Somewhere, Kareem was busy typing his own reply: the next line in our own little play, a long way past first night nerves. I took another sip of beer.

<~KaREEM~>:	I'm walking behind u can't hear me

I typed quickly, hitting [RETURN] to post the messages and then immediately writing the next one.

Amy17:	I'm a little frightened
Amy17:	It's dark
Amy17:	I hitch my bag up slightly
Amy17:	adjust my skirt

There are probably a few facts you should know about me, too. I didn't know what Kareem was imagining, sitting at his computer, talking to me. I didn't know if he figured that Amy had told him the truth on the first night we met, but she really hadn't.

<~KaREEM~>:	i can see u. i'm walking closer. catching u
<~KaREEM~>:	a stick cracks

I wasn't five foot three; I was six foot two. My hair was blond – true – but it was cut short, shaved at the sides and back. I never used to wear it that way. In the old days, before Amy disappeared, I'd had it longer, and in a far more friendly style. These days, I looked like a thug, but that was no bad thing and, more to the point, it was an efficient cut. Reality over appearance. I shaved it once every fortnight, and didn't have to think about it again, which suited me just fine. One less thing to worry about.

Amy17:	I turn around and see you. I'm very scared
Amy17:	I cry out HELP!
Amy17:	start to run as fast as I can

I weighed fourteen stone. At the other end of the study, which had housed our main computer suite ever since we moved in, two years before, I kept a bench and some weights and a punchbag. Generally, I did a few hours a day on both, listening to music so loud it almost made my head bleed. Unlike Amy17, if Kareem had ever started to chase me through a dark forest, I wouldn't have been running away from him.

<~KaREEM~>:	i'm gaining on u. my cock is so hard
<~KaREEM~>:	i'm gonna stick it in u until u scream
Amy17:	I can tell. I'm running so fast, but know it's not enough. no-one around!
<~KaREEM~>:	i've almost caught u
Amy17:	I'm falling over. I scream for help
<~KaREEM~>:	i've got u fuckin bitch
Amy17:	HELP! HELP!
<~KaREEM~>:	(slaps AMY17 hard)

I could never know for sure what Kareem imagined Amy's motivation was for coming here and subjecting herself to this. I'd never known any woman who *really* wanted to be raped, although I knew there was a male myth that they existed. I guess Kareem knew that, too – or wanted to believe it, anyway. I mean, maybe he figured I was just another bloke, like him, doing the decent thing and enjoying the fantasy in my own way, even as I helped to create it – but I doubted that. I'd sent him a picture of Amy; we'd chatted at length. I'd invested time and effort in making her seem real, giving her a credible background, getting her name posted at websites, generally making her presence felt in places I knew he could check. After all this time, she seemed real to me, and I was hoping that she would to him, too.

My guess? Kareem thought he'd struck lucky. He'd found a beautiful, young girl who got off on the idea of being raped. Risk-free, trouble-free: his dream come true.

That was what I was counting on, anyway.

I sipped my beer and continued to type. On screen, Kareem was describing how he was raping Amy. Like a good little girl, I made sure I (SCREAM)ed in all the right places.

Cybersex takes place in every Chat room on the internet. Due to the ephemeral nature of the web, most of these Chat rooms are open twenty-four hours a day, seven days a week. They never close. Members vary, of course, but a good Chat room could expect to have an average of at least one hundred people logged in and talking at any hour of the day, and some of those people will be having sex in private rooms. There are thousands of Chat rooms on the internet. What this means is that there might well be as many people fucking on-line at any given moment as there are people dying, or being born.

You meet someone in a Chat room – usually by a random message inviting you to go private, and you chat for a while, sizing each other up. It works best if you're both fast typists, and there's no point at all unless there's a chemistry there. In that sense, it's the same as a physical meeting. Think it's boring and clinical? You're wrong: it's not. It's amazing how much personality shines through in the way you type. People fall in love on-line. It's exactly as real as any other conversation, and often more telling: you can always scan back through what you've said to clarify meaning. It's not like spoken words, which just drift away. Nothing on-line can ever be properly forgotten.

The act itself, then.

Some people cyber with strangers: others prefer to be in a relationship. And there are as many ways to do it as there are with physical sex. Some people talk through an actual, imagined sexual encounter, complete with (bracketed physical instructions) and <u>hyperlinks</u> to on-line pictures, while others just talk about what they're physically doing at the time: undressing; masturbating; being masturbated. Maybe it's real and maybe it isn't. The cybersex ends when it ends – usually with both partners having reached orgasm, however many miles apart from each other. Sometimes, the whole procedure will progress to phone sex; more often, though, the two people involved will never encounter each other again. Such is life. At least on the internet it's nice and clean, you can break it off at any time, and there's no risk of disease. No shrieking, unwanted kids for the state to support afterwards.

That's how it usually is, anyway.

But sometimes, on-line lovers will actually meet.

Kareem had taken a break, presumably to clean up. He'd fucked Amy hard, before turning her over and – eventually – coming in her backside, with her neck locked in the crook of his elbow, half-choking her. His mother would no doubt have been proud.

I took down the dregs of my beer and immediately wanted another one, but knew it would ruin me. I wanted ten three-minute rounds on the punchbag before turning in that night, and so a second beer would just have to wait. I played absently with the neck of the bottle, waiting for Kareem to return to the keyboard.

After a couple of minutes:

```
<~KaREEM~>:    back
```

Conversation was usually thin on the ground before we cybered, but he tended to be far more prolific afterwards. It was as though he'd released the tension and could relate to me as a human being again. I suppose that made sense. Talking to me beforehand would have killed his fantasy dead, whereas now he could light up a cigarette and kick back a little.

```
<~KaREEM~>:    u like that?
Amy17:         not so much tonight
```

A little disappointment for him, there. I could almost smell the palpably wounded male pride in the next message, which arrived on-screen quickly.

```
<~KaREEM~>:    why?
```

I guess no man likes to leave his woman unsatisfied. Kareem was probably worried that his dream girl was about to bale on him, and I figured he'd do just about anything to stop that from happening.

A few quick messages, punctuated by the [RETURN] key.

```
Amy17:         not enough anymore
Amy17:         need more than that
Amy17:         need more than just words on a screen
Amy17:         :-( x 1000
```

I was surprised by how excited I felt. There was a fluttering in my guts: the thrill of the hunt. Anything could happen in the next few minutes, and it would all be played out in a handful of sentences dropped onto a screen: black on white in neat, meaningful little scars.

14

```
Amy17:            :-( x 10000000000000000
<~KaREEM~>:       sorry.
<~KaREEM~>:       sorry not enough 4 u.
Amy17:            not ur fault
<~KaREEM~>:       (pauses) so what do u want?
Amy17:            (pauses) brb
```

Be right back.

Amy17 was going away to think about something. I leaned forwards in my chair again, bringing my face closer to the screen. Watched the blank space for a second or two, and then turned my attention towards the last frowning emoticon that Kareem had left me.

```
<~KaREEM~>:   Amy17?
```

I zoomed in on that simple, unhappy face until it seemed to fill my head from one side to the other. So simple and straightforward: just a couple of lines, really. But the human expression is universal. We see the frowning, unhappy face, and we feel sad for it. Or at least, we're meant to.

Something that Kareem had said to me on the first night we met.

Lots of Amys hang out in here

That had been the wrong thing to say. I would learn, from subtle enquiry, that Kareem and I lived quite near to each other, and that was one coincidence too many. From that point, it would always have come to this. It had just taken a little bit of time to soften him up along the way.

```
<~KaREEM~>:   Amy17???
```

I started typing, before I lost my nerve. I didn't look up the whole time.

15

Amy17:	back now. listen.
Amy17:	tomorrow is Saturday
Amy17:	there r woods nr my house
Amy17:	Swaine Woods. between morton and ludlow
Amy17:	lonely woods nobody ever around
Amy17:	i walk from lacey's beck entrance to ring road
Amy17:	i start at 4pm. i'll be there by 4.30pm

And then I paused, just for a second, and glanced up at what I'd written. That pause seemed like it had the potential to last a while. But there was no time for doubting. I'd made up my mind about what I was going to do days ago. Without this, it had all been worthless.

So I finished up quickly.

Amy17:	im easy tofind there
Amy17:	so find me

As soon as I'd pressed [RETURN] on the last message, I closed the private window and disconnected from the internet. My desktop appeared; the conversation vanished. Of course, the words would still appear on Kareem's monitor, wherever he was, but now there would be a footnote running underneath them in red:

(*Amy17 has logged off system*)

'Jason, it's me. Charlie. I was just calling to find out how you are. I mean, I know that you're not great, but . . . you know. Williams is going spare about you not turning in this week.'

I picked up the phone and checked that Charlie had been the last caller; she had. I hit redial and waited, turning gently on the spot to wring some of the stiffness from my lower

16

back. As it rang at her end, I wandered through to the kitchen, selected a pint glass from the cabinet and took it over to the sink.

Click

'Hello?'

'Charlie,' I said, 'it's me. Jason.'

'Oh hiya.' She sounded pleased that I'd called. Maybe a little surprised, too. 'I'm glad you rang back. We've been worried about you.'

I held the receiver between my head and shoulder and poured water into the pint glass.

'I'm okay. Just finding things ... hard-going. You know?'

'Yeah. Well, you know – not really. But I guess I can imagine what you must be going through. I wish I could help, or do something.' She paused. 'I mean, you're in trouble here.'

'I figured.'

'Not that it matters.'

'Not much,' I said. 'No.'

'I guess you've got other things on your mind at the moment.'

Hearing her voice, it was like Charlie was in the room with me; I recognised her slight accent. I mean, it was *her*. But at the same time, it wasn't – couldn't be – because it wasn't as though she was shouting down a tube and I was hearing her. The sound wasn't her at all. It was Charlie mediated. A load of electrical signals transformed into pitch and tone and volume.

It was an artificial voice. Made-up. Created.

But then we never really do hear people do we? We experience the vibration of air molecules in a certain way, and come to associate that with the individual people around us. It struck me that – in a weird way – I'd never actually heard Charlie at all, just the effect that she'd had on the world.

Other things on your mind.

'Yeah,' I said, closing my eyes. 'A thousand things.'

'Is there anything I can do? Anything at all? I'd like to help.'

I sighed. Opened my eyes.

Don't do this.

But I'd thought it through before this, and I was pretty sure that it would be okay. No – strike that. I was just plain sure.

'You want to go for a drink tomorrow?' I asked. It came out a bit too quickly, as well, but I figured she'd take that as my reluctance to ask her for help. Male pride. Whatever. 'I mean, I'd like that. It'd be nice. We could talk.'

'Sure.' She sounded pleased. 'Where would you like to go?'

'Um.' I pretended to think about it. 'What about the Bridge? You know – the one on the ring road?'

Charlie lived on the other side of Swaine Woods. A patch of houses just across from Lacey Beck, in fact.

I closed my eyes; forced myself to carry on with the conversation.

Really sure.

It *will* be okay.

'Sounds good,' she said. 'It's nice in there.'

'Yes. It is.'

'So, what time?'

'About half-past four?' I suggested. 'How about that?'

'Still sounds good.'

'Well okay, then. It's ... well, it's not a date.'

'No.'

I'd meant it as a joke, but realised – as she replied – that I'd said entirely the wrong thing. That used to happen with Amy all the time, before she disappeared. We'd both be happy, having a lovely conversation and the sun would be out, and then one wrong word from me would turn the whole day on its head. Make the sky go dark; make us both not know where

18

to look, or what to say. It was good to know that I hadn't lost the knack.

'Okay,' I said softly. 'Well, I'll see you there.'

'Yeah. Thanks for ringing.'

'Take care,' I said, and pressed [CANCEL] on the call.

The kitchen was suddenly very quiet. The enormity of what I'd just done was hanging in the air; I could just make out the shape of it, and saw enough to know that it was wrong.

The year before, when I was still hung up on material things and the idea of being part of something that mattered, I would have stood and agonised about my actions. I would have fought with my conscience over it. But that was all past now. I'd learnt the best way to deal with these things. A two sentence thought which was hard to face but seemed increasingly easy to take to heart.

It's done now, and you can't change it. So deal with the consequences.

And what I'd found was: that thought is like a box. That's how I imagined it, anyway: a black box up in the loft. Whenever you're facing anything you want to save until later, or don't really want to face at all, you open the box and drop whatever it is inside. And so that's what I did. I put my conflicting emotions about what I'd done that evening in the black box, allowed the lid to seal itself, and forgot all about them.

And then I went upstairs to exercise.

My punchbag was the shape of a man's upper torso, minus the arms: a strange, jet-black sculpture, resting on a strong, metallic pivot in the same way that a work of art might rest on a plinth in a museum. There, however, the similarity ended. It had square indentations for eyes and mouth, a rough block of a nose, and not so much a neck as a curve from non-existent ears to rounded shoulders. From certain angles it looked angry; from others, the expression seemed more pained. When I'd first bought it, Amy had referred to it as The Scream.

While I talked to Kareem earlier, I'd also been downloading a six-minute dance track from Liberty, and I put it on now, looping the play function and knocking the volume up to three below maximum. One less sense to worry about while I trained. In fact, it was so loud that, when I started work on the bag, I couldn't even hear the punches land. I like my music that loud; I like to feel the cobwebs being blown out of my head.

My routine was pretty standard. One hundred jabs with each arm. One hundred jab-crosses, leading with each arm. By that point, my shoulders would be trembling. One hundred hooks, alternating body and head shots, generally at random. And then a combination: jab, jab, hook; jab, jab, cross. Whatever, really. I'd throw in a few kicks for good measure, but only when I could get away with it realistically, and maybe even add in elbows, knees and – rarely – a headbutt or two. Twenty minutes later, I'd be warmed up – ready for the main event.

I warmed up hard that night – so hard, in fact, that I was dripping with sweat and almost unable to throw a punch by the time I'd finished. I didn't know whether it was the correct way to train or not, only that it was the way I'd found worked best for me. Start at the bottom, feeling as drained as possible, and then try to make it through the workout. If I was in a real fight, fresh and full of energy, then all well and good, but if I was caught on my last legs, I wanted a precedent to work from of how it might feel.

This time, I was cut off before I could even begin.

Maybe the banging at the door had been going on for some time. I don't know: I only recognised it when I went over to the computer to change the track. I wanted something heavier: more industrial. Instead, in the silence, I got a hammering fist on the front door downstairs. I threw a towel over my shoulder and went to answer it.

It was raining outside, and there were two guys in black raincoats waiting on my doorstep, hunched against the cold. The first one showed me his badge and said:

'Inspector Wilkinson.'

But I didn't need that to know he was a cop. The i-Mart logo was all over the left breast of the raincoat. I watched a few droplets of water fall off the edge of his hat, heading down past a slightly pained face.

'We're looking for Jason Klein,' he said.

'That's me.'

'We'd like you to come down to the station,' he told me. And then eyed my upper body. 'Preferably with some clothes on.'

'What's it about?'

He looked at me. Rain was slashing down on the road behind them, but closer to it sounded more intimate. It was tapping on their hats.

'We've found a girl's body,' Wilkinson told me. 'We need to speak to you.'

CHAPTER TWO

It was a McDonald's moon that night: two great big, golden arches staring down at me from the black sky, with stars twinkling beside and around. I've always hated that one the most: a big M – M for Moon – as though we're all so stupid that we need everything labelling for us. The Nike tick annoys me, too. *Everything's okay*, it seems to tell you, when you know that – really – it isn't at all. I guess that my favourite, aesthetically speaking, would have to be Pepsi, but Benetton could sometimes be quite inventive.

No, fuck it – my favourite was old-fashioned plain. The night I'd met Amy it had been that way: three-quarters waxing, which was still slim enough to be free from advertising. Not exactly the stuff that poetry's made of, I grant you – a kind of half-fat and unremarkable moon – but you need to take what free space you can get these days, and so that's what I'll take.

Amy.

Wilkinson wouldn't tell me any more information than he'd told me at the house. They'd found a girl's body, and they wanted to speak to me. But what else could it be? I couldn't think of anything. My body rocked with the motion of the car. I was aching slightly from the force of the exercise, but my mind felt very calm and passive.

Amy.

The police car headed quickly through drenched streets. There were a few people around, black as the shadows between the buildings, and the pavements looked so dark it was as though it was raining oil and not water. I supposed that it could have been. Clouds, sponsored by Esso. Bright lights turned to blurs through the front window, before the screeching wipers smeared away the rain; water pattered on the roof, like pins dropping. We tail-ended a pair of bright red lights for half a block, and then headed onto the freeway. The city dropped away to the side, and the driver sped up a little.

The in-car radio was tuned to i-Mart's main station, and they seemed to have Will Robinson caught on a loop. I could have screamed: if there was one thing I didn't need right now it was shitty pop music, but I didn't have long to suffer. In ten minutes, we were there.

The Bracken police centre was floodlit in amber, with enormous, upturned lanterns bathing the building from all four sides and making its naturally orange brickwork all the more pronounced after nightfall. With its black canopies and foyered entrance it was often mistaken for a hotel – all twenty storeys of it – and I figured that more than a few late-night travellers had turned off the freeway over the years expecting a Holiday Inn. It had been built a decade earlier, when the police service was privatised. Bracken was one of three national hubs, connected to a spider's-web of regional, and then local, offices. Following the i-Mart business model, the police force farmed out their officers to areas where 'sales' were lowest, setting up clusters of shops in key target areas and taking them over. In this case, the product on offer was a low crime statistic – coupled, of course, with some exemplary computer produce. i-Mart – to protect and to serve; Microsoft never even saw it coming. Where do you want to go today? Directly to fucking jail.

Wilkinson opened the door to let me out, and then we walked over to the main building while the driver parked the car up, tyres slashing away across wet tarmac.

'Miserable night,' Wilkinson said.

I nodded, never really that good at small talk except when it was faked on a computer screen.

He pulled up the collar of his coat and did a silly little half dance as he got beneath the canopy over the main entrance, as though he couldn't stand another second of rain. I was barely noticing it. My hair was short and the rain couldn't do any more damage than my face already did. And clothes dry, after a while. I had other things on my mind.

Amy.

I supposed I'd been expecting this eventually, and now it was happening I felt an empty kind of calm. I wasn't really upset or angry. It was more like nothing was going on in me at all.

'Come on through.'

The foyer was silver: kitted out from the feet up in the best shiny-metal™ that i-Mart could provide. Everything looked as though if you touched it, it would leave a smeary fingerprint, so nobody had yet. A bank of blue-backed Powermacs faced out at the incoming public, with a row of pretty receptionists taking 999 calls through headsets, fingers chattering commands to local offices. A pair of cops stood near the mirrored elevator doors to the right, while blue carpeted stairs led up to the left. Wilkinson headed for these, and I followed.

'Good for the circulation,' he insisted, as I looked around. The walls of the stairwell were decorated with old i-Mart advertisements: freeze-frames from computer commercials and adBoard stills. 'I never take the elevators, anyway. Can't stand the music.'

I nodded.

'All they play is Will Robinson,' he told me as we reached the first floor and he pushed through some double doors. 'Like in the car. You know that kid? They pipe that shit out day and night. I didn't know he had so many songs.'

'He's got a bunch.'

If I remembered rightly, the last few had adorned i-Mart's recent ad campaign, which I figured might have had something to do with something.

I said, 'But they're mostly the same song in a different order.'

'Is that right?' Wilkinson raised an eyebrow at me. 'I didn't know you were a musician. You a musician?'

'You don't need to be.'

He looked away.

'Yeah, well. They all suck like a vacuum cleaner, if you ask me. His current single makes me want to fucking kill myself. My daughter loves it, though. She loves all that kind of shit. Here we are.'

He opened the door to an interview room.

'Take a seat,' Wilkinson said, closing the door behind him. 'If you're nice, the décor won't bite.'

I had my doubts, but sat down anyway. The silver desk extended out from one wall, blocking two-thirds of the room, with a raised computer panel on Wilkinson's side. The i-Mart Eye™ logo looked at me from the back. He took a seat in front of it, opposite me, and started running a nicotine-stained index finger over the screen. It beeped in protest, but a keyboard flicked up out of the desk. He sniffed.

'State of the art,' he told me, without looking up. 'Means it takes half an hour more than pen and paper used to. Bear with me.'

'Okay.'

I looked around some more as he started tapping keys, starting to have a weird feeling that this wasn't about Amy at all. Surely, it would have been different if they'd found her – not like this, anyway. A camera was watching me from the far corner of the room, above the door, and there was a plexiglass division running down the centre of the steel desk. I figured that Wilkinson had a button his side, and if he pressed it the plexiglass would raise, and maybe the table would extend out of the wall, caging me in. I thought I'd seen some kind of documentary where they'd shown it happening. I looked up.

There was a gas grill on the roof, slightly behind me.

I looked back at Wilkinson.

'Can I ask what this is about, please?'

He tapped the keyboard once more and looked up.

'Yeah, I'm ready now.'

And then, suddenly more serious, the question, coming out of nowhere:

'Can I ask you, Jason, do you know a girl called Claire Warner?'

Now here was something. She sent me a jpeg of herself, once, and she was as beautiful as she'd always made out she was. *I can get any man I want*, she'd bragged to me at one point, except that it hadn't been a boast as much as a plain statement of fact. Not something she was proud of, exactly, more something that bothered her. Because getting exactly what you want is only good when you know what that is.

I took the jpeg into Fireworks and magnified it up to 800%, until her crimson lips filled the screen and were reduced to red squares, darker red squares and dots of black – until it wasn't recognisable as a face anymore: just a hotchpotch of blocky colour. And I looked at the edges where they touched, imagining that she might emerge from the non-space there, in hiding behind her own bitmap. The same way that I ran my fingers over [claire21] when we chatted at Liberty-Talk, and wondered at the million other words that were hiding between the letters of her name, the ones she didn't give me in the hours we spent typing messages to each other.

Looking for traces of her on the internet: typing her name into ten search engines at once. They ticked through a hundred thousand sites between them and threw hopeless pages back at me. Not one was of her, or even close. There were a whole bunch of *her-names* in the phonebook, and any one of them could have really been her, but I couldn't find out which without ringing them each in turn. And even then her voice would have been a stranger's, and yet not.

Here was something, indeed.

I don't know why I bothered stalking her so unsuccessfully, when she would have told me anything and everything I wanted to know – even from that first accidental meeting on Liberty-Talk. She would have met up with me in half a second, fucked me blind with a smile on her face and then whirled away out of my life without a second thought or a backwards glance.

She was single, after all. It was me that was in the relationship.

'Is Claire dead?' I asked.

Wilkinson was implacable. 'So you did know her?'

I nodded.

'Yeah. Kind of.'

'We knew that you knew her. How did you meet?'

He typed something in.

Suspect admits knowledge of victim, I thought.

Best just to tell the truth.

'I met her in LibertyTalk. We got chatting.'

'How many times did you get chatting?'

I shrugged.

'A bunch of times. You probably know that already, too. Is she dead?'

Of course she's dead.

Wilkinson was still typing.

'We need to talk through some stuff,' he told me. 'But, yes, Claire's dead. She was found earlier this morning. I'm sorry.'

'It's okay.' I didn't know whether I felt anything at all. I thought of the pixels in her lips. 'We hadn't been in touch for a while.'

'How long's a while?'

I thought about it.

'A fair few months.'

'Since before your girlfriend vanished?'

A beat. He didn't look up at me.

'I guess so. Yeah.'

'But you can't remember. You might have seen her since.'

'No,' I said. 'Not since then.'

'You sure, now?'

'Yeah.'

He looked up at me.

I looked away from him, thinking about the train station in Schio. It was the last time I'd met Claire – the only real time I'd met her at all, in fact, outside the internet. How did I know it was before Amy disappeared? Because I'd come home afterwards and crawled into bed beside her, that's how, and then spent the next day chasing her round to reassure her that I loved her – doing a hundred little things to make her smile even though none of them felt like enough. But I decided that I didn't want Inspector Wilkinson to know about the train station at Schio.

'I'm just sure,' I said.

'Well.' He looked back down at the screen. 'We can come back to that in a bit. Let's talk about how you first met her.'

It's easy to meet people. Bracken City Market holds at least three thousand shoppers at any one time. I could walk through it, from one end to the other, and brush against a hundred strangers. It's limited and irrelevant, perhaps, but so what? The amount you know somebody is always subjective and limited, and so every contact you make is valid, no matter how small it seems and no matter how little you think it reveals. It's easy to meet people. Easy to meet anyone.

Harder to connect, though.

LibertyTalk was a little bit like the Melanie Room in its basic format: just a bog-standard, generic Chat room. Where you choose to chat on-line is usually pretty much accidental: you find somewhere, you start talking to a few people, you begin to feel at home. It's like becoming a regular at a pub in a lot of ways. They serve the same beer as everyone else, and people are people – but you get to know these particular people, and the beer starts to be ready for you when you walk in the door. So you stick around. It's no more – or less – complicated than that.

I ended up there out of a random mix of internet kudos and hyperlinks, both of which I know mean very little in the everyday world. Liberty was the official site of Dave Pateley, who was rumoured to have pioneered the original free code that made places like the Melanie Room possible. The idea was that you downloaded specific software from another user, someone you knew, and it linked you up to a random selection of neighbouring computers – sometimes three or four, sometimes a hundred, and you never knew how many – all around the world. And you shared a folder on your computer with those other users, putting whatever files you wanted in it – music files, text files, government documents, pornography. You gave it a universal key name, which you could also post at the main Liberty site, and left it there. If you wanted to get hold of a particular file – say your favourite song – you just entered the key name in as search criteria, and the program searched through all the computers you were connected to. If it didn't find it in those, it set them searching through all the ones *they* were connected to. And so on. When it did find it, it copied it back to you, leaving an additional copy in all the computers along the way.

This achieved a number of things. Most importantly, it got you the file. But there was no way – from looking at your computer – that the authorities could tell whether it had got there by accident or design. You were clearly either a criminal or a victim of crime, but it was impossible for them to tell which. Secondly, there was no way that – from you – they could trace more than a handful of other users. They could bring down a cell, but never disable the entire network. Thirdly, it meant that you had to clear a few gigs of shit off your hard drive every evening, or else install some software that did it for you. A small price to pay for total freedom of information? People thought so. Even the politicians whose private documents were being circulated on a daily basis recognised that it was pretty cool, and attempted to ally themselves with it. Nothing ever changes.

That's why I ended up there, anyway, wandering through the hundred or so hosted Chat rooms as [JK22], looking at the throb of conversation scrolling up before me: SHOUTs and (whispers); multi-coloured text; emoticons; roses and kisses being passed around like spare cigarettes or bought like free drinks. It was an alien world to me, and every time I saw a new name entering the room, or slid sideways through into another one myself, I felt a thrill of excitement in my gut that I hadn't felt for a long time.

People as text.

I'd sip coffee after coffee, or sometimes a beer, and have random conversations with complete strangers.

I was never on for that long. By that point in time, Amy was spending a great deal of the evenings on the internet herself, looking at sites she didn't want me to see, and so I was always grateful for any time with her that I could get. But sometimes – when the clouds came over – I was also glad for somewhere else to go: somewhere I could be whoever I wanted, talk to whomever I please and feel that there were no consequences.

None at all.

And one late evening, with a simple invitation to private, Claire Warner had found me. I knew, because she told me while we were talking, that she was sitting in her bedroom, naked, with the bedclothes wrapped around her a little. (It was cold that night.) Throughout it all – until towards the end, anyway – she was sitting cross-legged on the edge of her bed with the keyboard resting across her bare thighs, and there was a bottle of wine on the bedside table. She had a glass in her hand, and there was hard dance music playing in the background – only she'd turned it down so low that it had the volume and ease of a soft, comfortable ballad.

She always typed to music, she said. It made her fingers feel as though they were dancing.

'You had cybersex with her?' Wilkinson asked me.

I tapped my fingers on the table a couple of times, wondering where exactly this was going. All the time, I was remembering things that I'd done my best to bury and forget. Unhelpful things.

[CLAIRE21]:	why do you want to know that?
[JK22]:	?
[CLAIRE21]:	well why are you asking?
[JK22]:	(getting all embarrassed . . .)
[CLAIRE21]:	aw – blushing boy!

'Yes,' I said. 'After a while.'
'That night?'
I stared at the top of his head.
'Yes,' I said. 'Later on.'

[JK22]:	I don't want to offend you.
[JK22]:	. . .
[CLAIRE21]:	you think you could offend me?
[JK22]:	maybe
[CLAIRE21]:	lol

[CLAIRE21]:	*doubt it*
[CLAIRE21]:	*feel free to try!*
[JK22]:	*lol*
[JK22]:	*(still blushing tho)*
[CLAIRE21]:	*y r u so worried about offending me?*

Wilkinson was still typing, but now he was frowning slightly.

'So you had cybersex with her that evening.'

'Yes.'

'Just the once?'

I almost laughed.

'Of course.'

He looked up at me, not really smiling.

'Jason, I don't know anything about this kind of thing.'

And, although he said it in a neutral voice – deliberately neutral – I could tell that it was a loaded sentence. *This kind of thing.* This kind of *disgusting* thing, was what he meant. I checked out his hand. No wedding ring. I figured that Wilkinson was a real man: he picked up his ladies in bars or clubs. Never anywhere so sad as on-line, even though it was exactly the same.

'You generally only tend to do it once,' I explained.

He started typing again, his voice more normal.

'Did you meet her again?'

'Yes.'

'On-line?'

'Yes.'

The excitement, fluttering in my stomach as the train pulled into the station at Schio. The people milling around. My fingertips were pressed on the glass, with a phantom hand touching them from the outside and a slight reflection of my peering face almost cheek-to-cheek with me. Looking for that white dress in the crowd.

'Yes,' I said again. 'It was always on-line.'

He tapped a key.

'How many times did you meet her?'

I thought about it.

'I couldn't say for sure. Maybe eight or nine times, over a period of about . . . I don't know. Two months?' I shook my head. 'But I'm not sure.'

'You didn't keep track?'

'No.'

A few more keystrokes.

'And did you continue to have cybersex with her throughout that time?'

A loaded question – again – fired like a blank.

I said, 'A couple of times, maybe.'

'So, yes?'

'I suppose so. Yes. But not always.'

'Sometimes you just talked?'

'Yes,' I said. 'That's right. Just like in any other relationship. Sometimes we just talked.'

[CLAIRE21]:	y r u so worried about offending me?
[JK22]	because you're nice
[JK22]	you know?
[CLAIRE21]:	I think you're nice, too.
[CLAIRE21]:	you're not like the other bastards on here
[CLAIRE21]:	r u gonna blush now?
[CLAIRE21]:	whaddyou think?
[CLAIRE21]:	lol
[JK22]	no. I'm glad you think I'm nice
[CLAIRE21]	(shocked) what would your gf say?

Wilkinson tapped in a few more lines of text, recording the strange fact that – from time to time – two people had actually managed to talk without having sex. I shifted in my seat a little. He looked up, then, catching my movement.

'You okay? You comfortable?'

'I'm fine, yeah.'

'You want a coffee?'

Of course I wanted a coffee. But not as much as I wanted to be out of here.

'No,' I said. 'No, thanks.'

'Okay. You know – this is just routine.' Suddenly, he leaned back in his chair and seemed more relaxed. 'Your name was on her computer: a bunch of old transcripts and stuff. She'd erased a load of it, but some were still left. Not just you, by the way.' He leaned forwards again. 'A whole load of guys. She was on the internet a lot, huh?'

I shrugged.

'I don't know. Not that I know of.'

He just nodded, dismissing it.

'She was on the internet a lot. Look, are you sure you don't want a coffee? I mean, I want a coffee. Do you want a coffee? I'm going, anyway.'

'In that case, sure,' I said. 'Black, no sugar.'

'Virgin coffee.' Wilkinson stood up. 'That's the way I have it, too. I don't like people fucking with my coffee.'

'Lol,' I said.

'What?'

'I'm laughing out loud.' I gave him a smile. 'That's all.'

'Okay.' He turned around, nodding to himself. 'Laughing out loud. That's very clever. That's a computer thing, right?'

'Yeah.'

'Well, that's very clever.'

He returned five minutes later with two coffees. While he was away, I tried to get my thoughts together. Claire was dead, and I didn't know whether I felt much about that or not. I mean – she'd always seemed like a sweet girl, but when

34

it came down to it, I'd hardly known her. She'd been there for me at a difficult time: that's all. And because Wilkinson hadn't told me anything about it, it seemed somehow less real – as though it wouldn't have actually happened until I'd heard all of the grim details. Maybe I was just numbed from all the stuff I'd seen on the internet. Murder? Give me photographs and tape recordings, or don't expect me to feel anything.

But that wasn't true.

By the time he returned, the only thing I'd really figured out was that I wanted to go home and forget about this. Forget all about Claire, as bad as that was, and prepare myself for tomorrow. The police didn't mean shit to me. They didn't figure in the cycle of my life at all these days.

'Here you go.' Wilkinson passed me the coffee, taking his seat again. 'It's hot, be careful, etcetera. Now, where were we?'

It wasn't directed at me. I turned the cup around on the table between my fingers, and waited for him to catch his place, trying to remain calm and patient.

'So, all of this – this was all before your girlfriend disappeared?'

'Yes.'

'Amy?'

'Yes.'

'I mean, what we're talking about here is an affair.'

'Yes,' I said again. 'I suppose that it is.'

'Brass tacks, that's what it is. An affair.' He typed something in. 'Did Amy Foster, your girlfriend – did she know about Ms Warner?'

The coffee cup stopped turning.

[CLAIRE21]:   *(shocked) what would your gf say?*

                 {pause in proceedings}

[JK22]   *that doesn't matter right now*
[JK22]:   *does it?*

35

'No,' I said. 'She never knew.'

Wilkinson looked at me for a second or two, judging me. I think those few seconds held a great deal for both of us. For him, they held a murdered girl who had conducted an affair with a man whose girlfriend had then disappeared two months later. For me, they held all that and more, but from such a different and darker angle that I figured Wilkinson could never even have contemplated the view.

'I guess she wouldn't have known about it, though,' he said. He was speaking more to himself than to me. 'Would she?'

There's a certain kind of hole that your heart can plunge into, and you only really find out about it when you care for someone very much. Nobody ever teaches you about it, and nobody talks about it much, either: it's one of those things that you have to learn about by yourself. The first time that you fall into it, you feel as though you'll never stop falling and, when you do, that you'll never escape – that you could never climb out of anything this deep and this black: you can't see the handholds, and there are probably too few, even if you could. After a few trips down to this place, though, you figure out the truth: you just need to relax, and forget about how far down you are. You float out by yourself, given time.

It happens mostly because of communication breaking down. I don't mean that in some kind of talk-show bullshit way, either; it's just what it is. You'll be talking to each other, and a word will go wrong. Or you'll argue over a trivial sentence that neither of you care about and that, after three more lines of dialogue, neither of you can even remember properly, and so neither of you can ever really win. If one of you sees this coming and tries to end the conversation, the other resents it. And if you follow it through, you hate each other for a few black minutes, as a thousand buried irritations come flooding out. They're like demons spilling out through

36

an argument that, on the surface, has nothing to do with them, but deep down has everything.

All that matters is not saying you're wrong. That's what keeps you down there in the pit, and you only float back up when enough time has passed for you not to care about the argument anymore. It sounds kind of hokey, but it's love that pulls you out: the knowledge that what you have is too good to let go of, and that the other person is too good to let you go. So, the truth is this. You only end up in this place when you love somebody very much. Clouds don't matter much at night-time – only when there's a sun for them to cover.

But while you *are* in there, you have to be careful. It's dark and cold, and while you're down there you can't even remember what love *feels* like. Worse than that, you don't want to. And there are things down there with you that will whisper things, and suggest things – that have an upside-down logic to them, and which seem quite appealing and sensible in the cold dark of day. *Come deeper*, they say. And it sounds so right. You never want to feel love again, and damaging it feels good. But they're things that you really don't want to listen to, and when the clouds come over forever you'll wish that you hadn't.

Wilkinson asked me a few more questions about my relationship with Claire, coming back more than once to the concept of us having met outside the internet. I denied it, and then denied some more. At one point, I looked at my watch and saw it was after midnight. *We'll be done, soon*, Wilkinson told me. But we weren't.

'I want to go home,' I told him, as it reached one o'clock. 'We've talked about everything there is to talk about, and I just ... want to go home.'

He sighed, leaning back in his seat. I stared at him, not letting him off the hook. Yes, I'd known her; yes, I'd had an affair with her; no, I wasn't proud of it.

Yes. I wanted to go home.

'Okay, Jason,' he said after a second. 'I'll have an officer drive you back.'

'Don't bother,' I said. 'I'll walk.'

'You'll walk?'

'That's right. I like walking.' Which was true, especially at night when there was nobody around. 'And I hate your fucking in-car music.'

'But it's pouring down.'

'Then, I'll get wet.'

He slapped the table gently.

'Okay, then. I guess that's okay. We're done, here, anyway.'

Wilkinson showed me back to the main entrance. Outside, in the amber glow around the nearest floodlight, I could see the rain spitting through: invisible beforehand, up in the night, and then invisible afterwards, as it smacked into the pavement. When he opened the door, the cold hit me like a splash of sea-water: refreshing but slightly cruel. It was a bad night.

As he opened the door, Wilkinson was wincing. Briefly, I wondered what he would be like if someone ever shot him, or something.

'Take care, now.'

And then he said something which made me realise that this wasn't over yet – that we weren't *done here*, at all. My private world, which I'd cultivated and focused, was no longer mine alone; my isolation was an illusion. Society had come knocking.

He said, 'We'll be in touch.'

CHAPTER THREE

I was drenched by the time I reached the end of the car park, never mind my house, but I find that there's a certain level of rain that takes away worry. You get as soaked as it's possible to be and think: *fuck it*. It had always struck me as a pretty good motto for life in general, and it had served me ... not well, exactly, but at least I'd never been disappointed. And so that's what I said to myself as I reached the edge of the freeway and turned down the footpath beside it. *Fuck it*. I was soaked already, and anything that didn't include me slipping and falling on my ass in the mud could only be considered a bonus.

The footpath followed the canal, which snaked under the freeway and fed back into the city centre, skirting within a few hundred metres of my house along the way. The actual water was stagnant and old. Ten years ago, when I'd been a boy, I remembered riding my bike along the footpath, the gravel crackling beneath my tyres and disturbing all the fishermen who were waiting patiently, like tents, on the banks. Nobody fished here now, though; and the only bikes that came along the footpath were motorbikes on an evening. It was a desolate, sad little route, made all the more so by the city in the distance, like an enormous cybernetic limb where one old vein still remained, unbeating and unused. Soon, they'd concrete it in and build over it. Or maybe just above it, instead, leaving it to solidify beneath: mythic and forgotten.

That night, as always, there were a few shapes beneath the

pillars of the freeway, sheltering. A dozen ghosts of Tom Joad, slumped around fires flickering in gigantic, rusted drums, casting hunched shadows over graffiti and fractured rock. The skin of the concrete was coming away in places, like the wallpaper in an abandoned house, revealing layers of older graffiti underneath. Beneath the surface of the city, like so many of the people who lived and worked there, everything was shabby and untended. After the comfort of the police station, it felt like coming home – but maybe that was just wishful thinking. Everybody likes to feel like an outsider at heart, and you can feel that way pretty fucking easily walking along under a road-bridge, but it's an illusion. They can still hook you up whenever they want to, and then drop you back when they're done. You're still their fish, in their pond. It's all a matter of social physics.

It was a twenty minute walk back along the canal, but I did it in forty. I was thinking about a lot of things – although not in any focused way: rather, I was letting my emotions and feelings wash over me, wave after wave. Sometimes, it's difficult to separate out the threads that have led to you feeling a certain way, and all you can do is wallow in it: the same way that you can often only taste the end meal, never the individual ingredients. So that's what I did now, and my life tasted black to me: as ruined and tatty as the underside of the freeway; and as dankly unpleasant as the water beside me. A while ago, there was Claire, and the fact of my affair with her soured my search for Amy, which I'd pretty much dedicated my life to ever since she went missing. That was four months ago.

I've always been big on the grand, meaningless gesture, and so at one point I stopped on the edge of the canal and took everything in like a deep breath. The flecked, golden M of the moon's reflection in the water, spotted and shattered by rainfall. The glow at the horizon, and the black, starless expanse of the city to one side, and then Uptown above it. The slight rush of air. The sound of the rain on the water, and on the path, and on me. And I whispered *I love you, Amy* so quietly that I hardly said it at all.

A meaningless gesture, though. They always seemed to work that much better in the movies, with soaring music and audience identification, but never so well in real life. I listened to the same sounds afterwards, looked at the same things, and nothing had changed. And it didn't make me feel any better, either, because with everything that had happened tonight it felt like a lie.

The rain was getting in my eyes by the time I arrived back at my house, pooling there. Stinging slightly. Clouds sponsored by Domestos and Imperial Leather; air sponsored by FreeZee. Even moving my body made me feel cold, and I was shivering as I got my keys out of my pocket. For all my stoic bullshit, I was only human. I wanted to feel independent and tough, of course, but also – a little bit more than that – I wanted a towel.

The house seemed quiet as I closed the door. Quiet and contained. Nothing, as it turned out, could have been further from the truth.

'Don't move.'

It was a man's voice. I heard the sound of a safety being clicked off.

I stopped immediately, and then started shivering.

' "Freeze" might be more appropriate,' I said.

A towel was flung at me from the living room.

'Here. Dry yourself off.'

'Thanks.'

The guy stepped out as I was doing so, pointing a gun at me rather casually. He was dressed too neatly to be a burglar: I could see a nice, black suit underneath his beige overcoat, which was spotted darker brown in places with rain that had yet to dry. He looked like Dick Tracy without the hat, except his face was pock-marked and his hair receded to behind his ears, making him seem more like an ageing doorman. To complete that image, he had a vicious-looking cut above his eye. The light in the hallway was gleaming on his balding head.

I'd had a gun pointed at me before. When I was nineteen, I was caught up in an armed robbery at the convenience store around the corner from my hall of residence. It was one of those weird things that you beat yourself up about afterwards – Tyler, one of my flatmates, had asked me to pick up a pack of rizlas for him, but I'd forgotten them until after I paid. So I had to hang on for an extra few seconds, and if I hadn't done that then this bouncer in my flat would have been my first proper gun experience. Instead, I had a shotgun pointed at my head for a full minute, as three other kids took the cash-drawers from the till and scared the counter-girl shitless. The guy who was drawing on me was so fucked up that his eyes were bright red and he could hardly even stand up straight. It was unreal. I mean, the gun didn't look like they do in the movies: it was wooden and metal, and so alien to me that I figured it had to be a toy, even though I knew it wasn't. In the movies, guns shine; they're sleek, not dull and real. In the movies they fetishise these things, but in real life it wasn't all that sexy. In fact, it wasn't all that anything until about five minutes after they'd gone.

Now, I dropped the towel on the floor beside me. Upstairs, I could hear the sound of people going through my things. Above me, in the study, I heard something smash and someone swear.

'Come in and have a seat,' the guy told me, twitching the business end of the pistol towards the living room.

I made my way through, somehow unsurprised to find that

there was somebody already in there, waiting for me. He was an old man – probably in his early seventies – but looked spry and commanding, and he was sitting in my armchair, over by the bay window, with one leg resting over the other, and one hand resting on the bulb-end of a mean-looking iron cane. He looked like some kind of porn king, in fact, with his full complement of silver hair still tinged through to a fake black in places, and skin that was as tanned as the bouncer's raincoat.

'Jason Klein,' he said, as the door was closed behind us. 'You live like a pig in shit.'

Pigs in shit are supposedly quite happy, but it seemed a foolish point to argue over. I noticed that he was sitting on some kind of blanket, and realised that, whoever he was, his ass was clearly too good for furniture as neglected and woeful as mine. Ours.

'Sit down.'

He nodded to my other armchair; I walked over and sat.

'Now,' he said. 'We have a couple of things to talk about, you and I.'

'Right.' It felt oddly as though I was at some kind of job interview. I supposed that I was, in a way. The post I was applying for was the rest of my miserable life.

'You don't know me?' he said.

'No.'

'You don't have any idea who I am?'

'No.'

'What you *do* know, though, is that you want us out of here as soon as humanly possible. Am I right?'

'Oh yes.'

He nodded to himself.

'Well, we're going to make this nice and easy for you, because we're busy men. Answer quickly and carefully, and we'll be gone before you know it.' He gestured with his free hand and looked around my pig shit palace almost hopefully. 'As though we were never here.'

'What do you want?' I asked. 'I've had a long night.'

My abruptness seemed to surprise him almost as much as it did me. God only knew where it had come from but – now it was here – I tried the feeling on and found that it felt good. All of it – Amy, me, Wilkinson, Claire – was like a dark room inside me, and anger felt like a small but vital light. One I could burn myself with and enjoy the heat.

'Seriously,' I said. 'I've been through the fucking mill this evening, and I'm not in the best of moods.'

The man studied me for a few seconds, as though trying to decide if I might be edible and, if so, whether I could be fed to his dog. Then, he leaned forwards. His eyes were very white in the brown skin of his face; their centres, a perfect sea-blue. The kind of colour you have to have surgery to get.

He said, 'I want to talk to you about Claire.'

Okay, let me tell you about Claire: about the truth behind the jpeg, as far as I know it. And I don't know much. There are a few average, everyday statistics which we can dispose of first. She was twenty-one, when I met her. She had curly brown hair, hanging as far down as the tops of her arms; blue-grey eyes, fair skin and a few freckles. A slim figure, but not especially attention-grabbing. The sexiness with which she carried herself – and she was sexy – came from something much deeper than looks, and perhaps also a step sideways from personality. But, whatever it was, you saw her and you just couldn't look away again. You chatted to her – let her dance with you – and there was no signing off.

After our first conversation, I felt bad. The argument I'd had with Amy was a few hours old by then, and orgasm has a way of removing urgency and replacing it with guilt. I went straight to bed, and fell asleep facing Amy's back, with my arm around her, hand cupping her stomach, my face in her hair. My last thought was *that was a mistake*, but what I figured was that I could just put it behind me and not do anything so stupid again, despite having taken Claire's e-mail address and promising that I'd write. And of course, I *did* write. The next time the clouds came over, it seemed less like a mistake and more like a good idea. To mail her again; to chat again; to do what we did.

We carried on like that for a couple of months. I'd send her e-mails from work, and we'd get together on-line in the evenings from time to time, when I stayed up late. She sent me a picture of herself. Every time we met, I felt bad afterwards, but not that bad – and less bad on each occasion. I think you can fall into step with the bad things you do: the dance seems mad and impossible at first, and then you get swept away and realise the moves are a lot easier than you thought. You begin to invent motivations and excuses, and then start to believe them.

I learnt a bit more about Claire. Her parents died when she was little, and she was raised by her aunt, who instilled in her this incredible love of life and rejection of the mainstream and the ordinary. She had a hedonistic youth, and had grown into a young woman who adored sex and everything to do with it. She was the most physical person I'd ever encountered: I could close my eyes and imagine her dancing to work, flirting with strangers on the way, doing whatever she wanted. She had freedom written in her DNA. The instructions that had built her body and soul were coded in her genes: make something wonderful, they said; make something that will sweep through other people's lives and remind them what colour is and what it's like to be alive. And when the clouds gathered at home, I came back to her, because it felt like I needed to know.

Every day, I trudged into work, and then trudged home.

Amy was there in the mornings, and there in the evenings. Sometimes it was okay; sometimes it was great. A lot of the time, though, it was plain old bad. And Claire symbolised something more positive for me. When you're young, you think you can do whatever you want with your life, and your parents lie to you and tell you that it's true, but then you grow up and realise that you have to be like everybody else – or at least that you're going to be, whether you like it or not. You're not going to be that astronaut they always told you you could be. And you slide into the groove, and that's that. Claire struck me as being someone who'd never done that, and never would.

I'll be wearing a white dress, she told me, on the day before that one time.

What time does your train get in?

'I have friends in i-Mart,' the man told me. 'After speaking with them, they gave me the impression you might be able to help me. That you might be able to tell me about Claire.'

'What about her?' I asked.

Thinking: *what on earth is this about?*

'About what happened to her.'

'Anything I knew, I would have told the police.'

He looked at me, and I felt press-ganged into carrying on.

'I guess what I'm saying is that I don't understand what you're asking me.'

He said, 'You met her.'

'No.'

He ignored me.

'You met her. We know this for a fact. She travelled to Schio on the eleventh of August at nine-thirty am. I have the ticket she used – which she kept, incidentally – and I have had people cross-reference listings of her on-line boyfriends with rail records. You arrived twenty minutes later on a train from here, in a seat you reserved over two weeks earlier.'

'Jesus.' I shook my head. 'Your people have too much time on their hands.'

'So. You met her.'

'Yes.'

I was thinking: *the ticket she used – which she kept, incidentally*.

There are no incidental details in my life.

All this because of a railway ticket.

'The police know, too,' he said. 'But they don't care. They don't think you killed her, and they have better things to do. I don't think you killed her, either.'

'I didn't kill her. I haven't spoken to her in months.'

He seemed interested by this.

'When *exactly* did you last speak to her?'

'In Schio,' I said immediately. 'That was the last time I had any contact with her at all.'

He leaned back. It was impossible not to see the look of disappointment on his face, and I knew that I was going to have to work hard to convince him that it was true. And although it *wasn't* strictly true, as far as I was concerned it might as well be.

'Why?' he said.

'Why what?'

'Why *then*? After you'd met her for the first time. Why was that the end of it?'

Her pretty face, giving me that look. That look that was half-affection and half-pity. The one that said: you fit into the groove too well, no matter what you say, and if I offered to launch you into space on the adventure you always wanted, you know what would happen? You'd run away screaming.

You're a nice guy, Jason. And I'm not into ruining lives.

After I met her, I went home, arriving back quite late. Amy

was already in bed by then: three-quarters asleep and only vaguely aware of me slipping in beside her. She was naked. She was facing away from me, and I moved up against her, pressing my chest to her thin back, putting my arm around her and cupping my hand on her slight stomach. All I could smell was her hair. I'd come so close to making the worst mistake of my life, and I'd never been more relieved than I was right then.

'I love you,' I told her, kissing the side of her neck.

She didn't say anything, but she moved slightly and took hold of my hand where it rested on her stomach and she gave it a squeeze. And she pressed back against me, giving a noise that might have been contentment.

Why hadn't I seen her again?

I looked at the old man.

'Because I love my girlfriend,' I said. 'That's why.'

I saw her through the window of the train: an odd moment, but fitting in a way – that my first real-life glimpse of her should be occluded slightly by the sunlight on a streaky window. I recognised her face from the picture she'd sent, and would have known it was her even without the white dress. The way she was standing. It's like everyone else in the station was forty per cent less real than she was. Crowds, sponsored by Stand-In.

She didn't know me to look at, but I caught her eye before I'd reached her, smiled, and she smiled back and knew it was me. Amazingly, she didn't look disappointed. I walked over to her feeling nervous, not knowing how to greet her or what to say. In the end, it was easy. We said *hi* to each other softly, and she kissed me on the cheek, her body like air in front of me. *Would you like to get a coffee?* And I said *yeah, please – this is really weird, isn't it? Isn't this really weird?*

Claire looked beautiful, and I was tongue-tied for a few

48

minutes, but then I loosened up. I already knew her, after all: her e-mails and chat-voice had given accurate readings of her personality, and before too long we were talking easily and freely. She bought me an espresso. *Knock it back*, she said. *Like a shot of spirits.* When she did that with her own, I saw her throat and felt my stomach lurch. There was something half-wild about her – about the way she laughed so unselfconsciously, the way she touched me gently on the shoulder, the way this whole encounter seemed so easy for her. It seemed mad that we were in a train station, talking. Flirting, even – because that was what we were there to do, after all. That was what we both wanted. Ever since I'd booked the ticket (and I'd had to book it, just to be sure) I'd been anticipating it. The night before, we'd cybered for what would prove to be the last time. She'd described taking me into the toilets at the station and fucking me in one of the cubicles, wrapped around me and desperate. That was why we were here. But:

'I don't think I can do this,' I told her.

'Do what?'

'You know. *This*. I don't think I can do it.'

More than that, I could barely even look at her. The table was so very interesting. She frowned slightly, her chin resting on her hand, her elbow resting on the table, so perhaps my look got to her face in a roundabout way.

'Have sex with me?' she asked. 'Is that what you mean?'

I shrugged, feeling awkward.

'Yeah. I guess that's what I mean.'

She shrugged herself.

'Well, we don't have to do that. Don't worry about it.'

'But that's why we're here. We've both been on the train for over an hour.'

'Sure,' she told me, standing up. 'But we'll have a coffee instead. Another one, anyway. Same again?'

'I'm sorry,' I said. I don't think I'd ever felt so pathetic in

49

my life, but at the heart of me there was this strange kernel of light, and I think it came from knowing that I'd made the right call. Suddenly, all the excitement I'd been feeling over the past couple of months felt like tension, and what I was experiencing now felt more and more like relief.

'Don't be sorry,' she said, and then looked at me with that expression – the one that said she liked me but was slightly disappointed at the same time. She touched my shoulder gently, and then gave it a squeeze. 'You're a nice guy, Jason. And I'm not into ruining lives.'

'Maybe I should go,' I said.

She shook her head.

'Why? Come on – let's have another coffee. We can talk.' She gave me a nice smile. 'You can tell me about your girlfriend. Okay?'

I thought about it. As weird an idea as it should have seemed, suddenly it didn't. In fact, I realised that I really *did* want to talk to Claire about Amy – that it seemed right. The feeling of relief was getting stronger and brighter. I figured that I had a lot I needed to say.

'Okay,' I told her, nodding. I even managed a smile. 'That'd be really nice.'

'We talked for a couple of hours,' I told the old man in my flat. 'And that's all we did. She bought me another coffee; I bought her one later on. We wandered out into the city square for a little while. Weird, I guess.' I laughed. 'It was a nice day. And then we went our separate ways. And that's it.'

And that *was* it, too – stripped down to minimal detail, anyway. But it had been an important afternoon for me: I'd told her about Amy, and the distance that was growing between us. I'd said that it felt like a light that was going out, and she'd listened and been sympathetic. Like a best friend – or the closest thing to it, with Graham seconded. As my train pulled away from the station that afternoon, I watched her from the window – standing there in much the same way as she'd been standing when I arrived. The whole afternoon felt like a beautiful holiday, or a dream, and it made me feel sad to see her move backwards away from me, reduced to a tiny white blur, and then swung out of sight by the corner of the track. I was never going to e-mail her again or chat to her. It wouldn't have worked. It was just one perfect day. The End.

'You never saw her again?' the man asked.

'No.'

'Never spoke to her?'

'No.' I looked at him steadily. 'Never saw her again, on-line or off. Never exchanged a word with her. That was it.'

He kept looking at me, almost as if he could smell the lie but couldn't tell which direction it was coming from. So, I furnished the lie with a few final truths.

'I loved my girlfriend,' I told him. 'I still love her. My relationship with Claire, as much as it even *was* a relationship, was a mistake. We both knew it. We both left it at that.'

I didn't feel like saying anything else, so we just sat and stared at each other for a second. The old man seemed about to say something, but then we both heard the sound of footsteps on the stairs. Two guys walked into the room. They were both dressed the same as the bouncer with the gun, but they didn't look half as mean. One had glasses, foppish brown hair and seemed to be about eighteen; the other was all pasty-faced and mid-thirties. They looked like nothing so much as a couple of half-harried computer geeks, and they seemed nervous about whatever it was that they'd found:

'Nothing.'

'You checked everywhere?'

The younger guy nodded, pressing his glasses back up his nose.

'His hard drive's clean. And there's nothing in the deleted

data that could be recovered. If there was, we'd have found a trace at least. No sign of it on his disks either. I think he's clean.'

The old man stared through him, looking disappointed and suddenly distant. Then, he nodded to himself, and started to ease his old body out of the chair.

'Never mind.'

As the bouncer moved over to help him, the old man turned to face me.

'Don't get up, Mr Klein. We'll see ourselves out.' He seemed suddenly contrite. 'I'm sorry for any ... inconvenience.'

'Don't mention it,' I said, wondering how many pieces my computer was currently resting in. 'Any time.'

As if as an afterthought, he reached inside his suit and retrieved his wallet; from that, he produced a business card and passed it to me. I took it, and turned it over.

Walter Hughes, it said, along with an address uptown, telephone and e-mail details, and a stylised eagle watermark.

'If you should hear anything,' he said, replacing his wallet, 'I'd like to hear it, too. I can be contacted as it says there. And if you drop my secretary a note on Monday morning, I shall arrange to have any breakages paid for and replaced.'

'Okay,' I said.

The situation seemed to have gone from one extreme to the other, and it had been a long night: my brain was having trouble keeping up with the swerves.

Hughes nodded to me once, and then turned to his accomplices.

'Gentlemen.'

The four of them swept out of my living room, and I heard the front door close behind them. Within a few seconds, a car engine began gunning outside. I waited for it to drive away and then – when the sound had become a distant whine, barely even audible – I let out an enormous breath and went to find that second beer I'd been dreaming of, so long ago.

I had a dream that night, or a vision.

Sometimes, Amy used to wake me up, when she'd had a bad dream – it happened less and less as our relationship became stronger, and then more and more as it weakened again. Often, I'd already be awake; she'd be fighting with the bed, and you couldn't sleep through something like that. I'd lie there, watching, wondering whether I should touch her or not. I wanted to; I wanted to reassure her. But I knew it would probably frighten her more than anything else, and so I had to wait for her to lurch awake, turn to me in the dark and cling there, shaking. That was how it always ended. Sometimes my back would bleed, she'd hold on to me so hard.

And that was what I dreamt about. I dreamt that I woke up and she was there, lying beside me on the futon – more of a dark shape beneath the covers than a real person – with blue dawn light coming through the curtains and brightening her edges. She had her back to me this time, not clinging at all, and she was quietly sobbing. Her hand was over her face; the futon was trembling beneath her. In the dream, I moved up against her, pressing my front to her back, and put my arm around her, curling it into the warmth of her belly. She ignored me. I whispered that I loved her, but she just kept crying. And that was when I realised the truth.

She was dead: not really here with me at all. I was alone on the futon, and it was like someone had opened a window beside me that allowed me to see into the world where she was. She was crying, oblivious to my touch, because somehow she'd found out about Claire. In my mind, the room she was in became a cell. The blue light was streaking through a food slat high in the door, and Amy was curled upon cool flagstones, crying inconsolably because she was dead and betrayed.

I don't know how the dream ended – only that at some point it was finished and I was sitting up in that blue light of dawn, covers pooled around my waist, totally alone and crying. And I stayed that way for a while, wishing she was home, while all the time the memory of Claire's voice was intruding into my grief.

Jason, if anything ever happens to me, she was telling me, sounding both scared and exhilarated, and I didn't want to hear it then any more than I wanted to hear it now. The phone call had come out of the blue; I didn't even know where she'd got my number from.

Why are you ringing me?

Because you're nice, she'd said quietly, and then carried on, as though it was a difficult task that needed marching through. *If anything ever happens to me, I just want you to remember one word*, she said.

*I want you to remember **Schio**. Just that.*

Click

CHAPTER FOUR

There's no easy way of projecting a brand logo onto the sun, which meant that the light coming streaming into the bedroom the next morning was a roughly natural amber – albeit stained a couple of shades closer to piss by the tepid tone of the curtains. I sat up, rubbing my face, aware through my feeling of rested nausea that I'd slept in. Ever since I was a little boy, I'd never slept much, and in adulthood – or as close as I'd gotten to it – I still tended to get up early and do my own thing. It has its benefits. The roads aren't filled with traffic; there aren't bunches of irritating fucking people around; even the adBoards are generally quiet apart from a sort of low-key buzzing. Shit-all on the television to even pretend you want to watch. It almost felt like the world was unspoilt.

I pulled on a dressing gown and made my way downstairs, figuring it was about ten-thirty, or so. That was bad, in a way. My dream had made me feel empty and miserable enough as it was, and now I got to feel lazy as well.

I had a ritual.

Every morning, what I'd do was get up early, come downstairs and put a pot of coffee on. I'd slip bread into the toaster, get the butter and milk from the fridge, and maybe even put some music on quietly: something that wouldn't disturb her. And then I'd sit at the kitchen table and wait for breakfast to be ready, and for a few brief minutes I'd be able to pretend that Amy was still upstairs, half-asleep, ready to come down in a bit when she was properly awake. A few minutes of denial? Sure: guilty as charged. But it was too late to go through that today.

I made the coffee and toast and sat down to eat, but this morning I wasn't thinking about Amy; I was thinking about Claire, and the phone call she'd made to me. *Schio*. I remembered it, of course. How could you forget a phone call in the evening from someone like that?

I finished off my toast, licked melted butter from the tips of my fingers and thought about it. Maybe she'd got the right number after all – I'd remembered the word, hadn't I? And something *had* happened to her. Since it stretched credulity a little far to imagine that she'd rung me up in a moment of existential anguish, that left only one option: she'd trusted me with something, and I didn't know what it was.

And . . .

And my fucking computer was smashed.

The kitchen suddenly seemed more real around me, and an awkward truth settled in: I already had one woman to worry about. I already had a woman to care for, search for and be responsible for and to, and the last thing I needed right now was another. Especially Claire. I mean, one unwanted phone call in the night from her, and here I was: cheating on Amy again.

I wanted to slap myself in the face.

Instead, I took my plate and knife over to the sink, where they could wait with all their friends until I was ready to attempt a wash. Then I took my coffee upstairs and began to gather together today's selection of clothes from the more promising heaps on the bedroom floor.

It had stopped raining, but only just. Everything was freshly wet. The road looked like it was made from jet-black rubber, and the cars shining along it seemed bright and newly washed. People's hair was in sodden tufts of disarray, and the sky was a blue-grey watercolour smear: misty and full of cloud, as though it might boil back into a rainstorm at any moment and soak us all again.

My trainers squeaked on the pavement as I walked, heading into the centre of Bracken. As you went from the suburbs to the centre, there was quite a transformation. The gentle noise – laughter; promotional jingles from the increasingly prevalent adBoards – grew louder and gradually more irritating as suburban streets segued into more industrial avenues. Houses became shops, and the shops became taller, until finally they morphed into these enormous, glass-fronted office blocks – the tenets of evolutionary capitalism. Within twenty minutes, I was truly among giants.

Actually, I didn't know how Graham could bring himself to live this far into the centre, where everything was way too big, noisy and busy for me. The one thing I supposed he had going for him was that he lived quite far up, in one of the more prestigious apartment blocks, slightly west of dead centre. It was the kind of place where, if you opened the window, you were more likely to hear helicopters than cars, and they generally didn't bother with adBoards that high up – most of the people who lived there invented either the campaigns or the products, and they wouldn't want to take their work home with them. Can you imagine a twenty-four hour jingle? You'd go insane. Well, city centre life had never appealed to me anyway, but I figured I was in the minority. If they had money, it was where people naturally gravitated to: the best bars; the best theatres; the best restaurants. I mean, in some parts of the suburbs, city centre life was actively advertised, to keep you in line – keep you pointing in the right direction.

Graham had money, all right, and he was one of those vaguely unfocused people who, lacking any impetus of their own, tended to go with the crowd by default, and so it was natural he'd end up there eventually. But I looked at him sometimes, and I'd see this slight look of confusion on his face, as though he was nervous about going the whole hog and actually embracing the emotion he was feeling for what it really was: dissatisfaction. It's a word you can hiss, and you should feel free to try. In their heart-of-hearts, everybody knows that the life-path is just another branded commodity these days, and that fact can bite you from time to time – when you're looking around and thinking *what's next*? But everything you've been taught is telling you that there *is* nothing next: that you've hit the peak and now all you have left to do is balance.

A sad fact: nothing ever looks as good on you as it does in the catalogue. For a pound, you don't get the juicy steak that's beaming out of the adBoard at you like some kind of meaty ambrosia. You get a flat fucking burger in a miserable fucking bun. In life, as in fast-food chains.

I had to pass through one of the main shopping precincts to get to Graham's building, and it was heaving with people. It always was on a Saturday. All those weekday-workers came out window-shopping. Couples went strolling. Kids hung out in baggy, coloured posses, with nothing to do and nowhere to go. And there was this genuinely unpleasant, slightly threatening undertone to everything. It was as though, despite the smiles and hum of conversation, at any moment somebody might buy something.

A few minutes' walk took me to a quieter section of the city, where the canal snakes through at the edge. Graham's building backed onto the canal, which is why the three lower floors remained entirely unoccupied. When the industrial skies open over winter, the abandoned canal overflows, filling nearby buildings to an admirable height and washing away any derelicts that have managed to squeeze in through the cracks. Of course, it doesn't make any difference to the high-flyers on the floors above: for them, the canal is just this picaresque thing from another era; it's no different to having an old, golden barometer on the wall, or a three-hundred-year-old wooden chest to put their dirty laundry in. When the banks flood, it just gets a few metres closer and they can see it better. That's all.

The intercom on the front of the building looked like something you'd put a cigarette out on – and, if you did, it probably wouldn't have left a mark. Cars shot past behind me as I tapped in seventeen-twelve and in the pause that followed, I turned and looked around. Busy road. Perfectly-styled park over the other side. A deli further up, painstakingly recreated. There was probably even a nice little church around here somewhere: a church without a door. When we were teenagers, Graham had told me: *life's just a lot of fakery and bullshit, and I hate it*. What had happened to my friend?

I heard the voice come out of the intercom and turned back.

'Hello?'

His voice, and yet not. All the intercoms in the city centre sound exactly the same: it's a lightly amplified, disguised male voice. Imagine a vaguely pissed off robot. For all I knew, it was Helen answering the door, but I took a gamble that it wasn't.

'Gray,' I said, leaning in. 'It's Jason.'

A pause.

'Hijay.' Our old amalgamated greeting told me it was him. 'Come on up. Wait; hang on.'

The intercom was muffled for a few seconds. I could hear that he was talking to Helen, but couldn't make out the actual words. Of course, I didn't really need to.

A moment later, the intercom cleared.

'Come on up.'

The latch on the steel door buzzed loudly for a couple of seconds, as though in warning, and then clicked open. I pushed it and went inside, and was immediately hit by the smell of fresh pot-pourris that filled the stairwell. This was such a nice apartment block.

The elevator was already on its way down for me. I waited

for it to arrive, already sure that this was going to be a tense morning.

A couple of picture portraits.

Graham is	Helen is
very quiet	very quiet
doesn't smile much	false smiles
	false laugh
tall and solid without being muscular or fat	little and thin without being attractive or fit
always clean-shaven	buys into everything she is told to believe she
brown hair	
blue eyes	also has brown hair (to her
wears glasses	jaw line)
clear skin	clear skin

Those are the facts – but even there they've come out uneven, because the facts about Helen are more difficult to pin down. Nobody would ever deny the things I've said about Graham – what you see is what you get – but Helen's a far more subjective prospect: it's difficult to pin down anything concrete and personal about her, because she's totally absorbed in the relationship.

Certain things are true, of course. She is small (five foot) and thin (probably about seven stone), and she does have clear skin, in the same way that a baby has a clear conscience; these aren't things she's ever had to work at. In fact, she's never had to work at anything, as far as I know. Her parents are both very rich and very protective: a lethal combination. They paid her way through University, and then supported her for a while afterwards, all the time assuming that their investment in her gave them overall control on any decisions she had to make. If you wanted to see Helen as a company, you might see her parents as two silent partners who between them have the casting vote. You would have to see her as a small company, of course, but keep that a secret from the silent partners: they see it as a world-beater.

What would this company do? It's simply not streamlined for business and knows it. So it merges. There is strength in numbers, and it makes sense for the weak to ally themselves with the strong. The silent partners – who, having organised it themselves, don't understand how weak the original corporate structure is – see it the other way around.

Merge by all means, they explain, *but never forget* who is the *most important and dominant company in this merger*.

I'd been friends with Graham since we were little kids; our families lived next door to each other and we got on from day one – peas in a pod, and all that. Except he was always more brilliant than me academically, while I outshone him socially. When I was already happily esconced with Amy, he'd never even had a girlfriend. *What about Helen?* Amy asked me one day. Helen was a childhood friend of Amy's, but the revolutions of our social circles were such that Graham and Helen had yet to actually meet. *What do you think about them as a couple?* I thought it sounded cool. I wanted Graham to be happy: he'd been growing increasingly insecure and introspective as time went by, and it was starting to worry me. Helen seemed nice. *Is* nice, really, in her own way.

So we introduced them and encouraged them.

Madness.

On the one side, Graham: a genuinely nice, shy guy who – despite his notable success in several key areas of life – had begun to feel like an abject failure because he didn't meet the marketed standard of shagging hundreds of women and having relationships which, the movies had assured him, would provide him with that all-important reason to live. On the other side, Helen. She was desperate for a relationship in much the same way, but her subconscious feelings of inadequacy – so well-covered by those false smiles and that cheery disposition – were bubbling up, convincing her that she would never get one.

The way I saw it was this: when you're falling through the air, you don't pick and choose your handholds; you grab onto the first branch you can get your fucking hands on, and you cling to it with grim determination. And they were both falling. Putting them together was only ever going to end one way: in a kind of awful, successful failure.

'Hi, Jason.'

Helen peered around the edge of the door like an anxious child, giving me a big smile. She was one of those people who had to say everything with a laugh and a joke. The subtext every time she opened her mouth was always the same: *things are spiralling out of control*, she was saying, *but you have to laugh, don't you?*

'Come on in.'

'Cheers.' I wandered into the hall. 'How are you doing?'

Being quite small, Helen was also quite weak, and she had to push the door quite hard to get it closed. The effort was there in her voice:

'Oh – just pottering. You know.'

She laughed.

'Gray in?' I said.

'Through in the study.' She raised her eyebrows by flicking her head back: a Helen tut. 'Working. As usual.'

'Keeping you in the manner to which you've become accustomed,' I said, smiling. It was half a joke, with neither half being particularly funny, but she laughed anyway.

'Well, yes.' The arms went out in a shrug. *What can I do?*

I gestured with my thumb. 'I'll just go on through?'

'Sure, go on. He's expecting you. Coffee?'

'That'd be great, yeah.'

I meant it, too. Look – don't get me wrong about this. As a friend, I didn't dislike Helen. In fact, in a lot of ways she was lovely: anybody who offers you coffee as a matter of course is okay by me, and – in general – she was personable enough. I just didn't think she was right for Graham. Nobody thought that, even, I suspect, Helen and Graham, and – coffee and smiles aside – that's a pretty fucking significant detail. You can have a relationship with anyone, after all, but despite what the books and the movies might tell you, a relationship is not, in itself, what you need. What you need is to add some qualifiers. '*Good*', in the middle of that phrase, for one. And while we're on the subject, '*that you really want*' at the end is also an idea.

I made my way through to the study, where heavy industrial music was grinding away quietly in the background. In the kitchen, Helen would be listening to glitzy, gloss-sheen pop – slightly despairingly. On the cupboard above the kettle there was an A4 sheet listing the names of friends and how each friend liked their tea and coffee. By my name, it would say *white, two sugars, black, no sugar*. She'd run her finger over it and tap. *Ah ha*.

Whereas I'd known Graham for years, but he still had to ask me – and I don't know why that's better but for some reason it is. Maybe I'm just suspicious that if you concern yourself too much with little details, there's no mental space left for the more important stuff.

He leaned back in his chair as I entered the study, putting his big hands behind his head, yawning and stretching. Then, he gave me a smile.

'Hi mate. How are you doing?'

'I'm okay, yeah,' I said, wandering over and taking a seat

beside him. In front of him, his computer was chugging through what was, no doubt, another mindless search. 'How's tricks?'

'Ticking over.'

'You're busy?'

'I'm always busy. Is Helen making you a cup of coffee?'

'I think so, yeah.'

'Nice to know the bitch is good for something.' He closed two search windows down with a click of the mouse, and then set another three tumbling. 'She's been doing my head in this morning. All morning.'

Every morning.

I remembered parties where Helen would talk to Amy and Graham would come into the kitchen to talk to me, and they'd both say the equivalent of the same thing: *goddamn, my juicy burger is squashed and wet and fucking miserable. I can't believe I paid a pound for this shit.*

I said, 'Getting on your case?'

'Exactly. I mean, I have work to do. She wants to play house.'

'Want me to get out of your hair?'

'No, it's okay.' He clicked the mouse again. 'I can talk while I work. I just can't Ikea. Or at least I won't.'

He typed in a few words, his fingers as lightning fast as ever.

cola boy coat shoe light [RETURN]

'Just give me a minute. On top of all the work I have to do, I'm also trying to download the new Will Robinson single from Liberty. To keep her happy.'

'That would keep anyone happy.'

'Well, obviously. So just give me a minute.'

'Okay.'

I looked around while he worked. The study was incredibly old-fashioned, especially given the industry he worked in. As a contrast to the spare, metallic feel of the rest of the flat, this room was decked out in dark wood, with crammed bookcases lining three of the walls, while the other was taken up by the console he was working at. The books themselves were old – classics mostly – with modern reference texts and manuals dotted around, their vibrant spines standing out. You could buy bookcases like these from lifestyle catalogues – I think there were about twenty or so on the market – and save yourself the bother of collecting and reading a lifetime's supply of literature: you just ordered the bookcase and it came ready-stocked, making your study look authentic and used. I could have been on a ship, or in a Victorian drawing-room.

In the centre of the room was an old table with battered, bowed legs. A series of printed paper sheets was spread upon it, with more paper slipping out of the printer hatch in the wall no doubt soon to join it. This was Gray's job: professional web gopher. He was one of the most respected information-ferrets in the business, employed by a number of well-known companies and individuals to hunt down details of rival products, research projects, other individuals and then produce easy-to-read reports on what he'd found.

And he was good at his job. The approach he had to the internet was one of Zen interconnectedness. All the information is linked together in a web, he figured, and every little bit of information affects all the others. According to chaos theory, a butterfly flapping its wings can eventually affect weather systems on the other side of the planet. Graham had taken this to heart, and he'd applied the science of it to the web, at first by trial and error and then – as he learned more – by developing systems and approaches. Nowadays, with the internet, he was that butterfly. He flapped his wings in significant little ways that only he understood, and the information he wanted came blowing in from the east. One day, he told me, he was going to write a book and become enormously rich.

After a minute or two, Helen brought a mug of coffee in

and passed it to me, along with a cork coaster. I smiled and said thanks, and she left. Graham looked a little resentful.

'I guess I don't get one, then?'

'Guess not.' I tasted it. 'It's good, too.'

'Of course, it's good,' he said, turning back to the screen. 'What are you trying to imply about my coffee? And what can I actually do for you on this fine morning?'

'Status report?' I asked. 'Just the usual.'

'Pull up a pew.'

I edged my seat a little closer, so that I could see the screen more clearly. We did this most weekends, and every time I got a feeling of excitement as I moved in next to him. He was reassuring. With Graham on my side, it felt like I stood a chance.

'What have you got for me?'

'Maybe nothing,' he said, shrugging.

He clicked the mouse, searching for something on-screen. 'But maybe something.'

There was a playground near where Graham and I grew up, formed in a concrete bubble on the edge of this park which wasn't really a park at all – just grassland, really, with a couple of chalk-white pitch shapes stained thoughtlessly into it, and the ring of a path for older people to stroll around in summer. There was a maze of trees and bushes which people from the nearby pubs would lose themselves in on an evening, in order to fuck drunkenly. In fact, I lost my virginity there one night to some random girl, shivering and cold. The playground was at the top. Every morning, the park keeper would come, and you'd hear the steady swish-sweep as he pushed the previous night's debris over towards the waiting sanitary truck. The needles, broken beer bottles, empty pill boxes and used condoms. A few children would play there during the day, depending on the weather, and then in the evening it would be ours again.

I had my first beer there, too, and smoked my first joint. We shared the place out between about thirty of us, mixed in every way – from age and race to gender and sexual preference. It was a weird thing. That lasted for about two years, all told. Nobody had used it before and, as far as I know, nobody's used it ever since. Our generation blew in like a tornado: like the life of the party, spinning through and dancing with people at random, whirling from one partner to the next before spilling out of the back door. And that was it. The park keeper swept up for the last time, and then the next day there was nothing for him to sweep.

I'd been back there twice since then.

The first was after a phone call from Helen. *He's gone out drunk, Jason, and I'm worried about him.* Graham had stormed out after an argument, hours before, and it was dark now. Helen was going out of her mind.

Leave it to me, I told Amy as I pulled on my coat. *You wait here. I know where he is.*

I remember the way he looked when I got there: this hunched black shadow perched at the top of the slide. I could hear him slugging spirits back from a litre bottle, but other than that it was almost eerily silent. It was as though the playground hadn't been used for decades. I got him down from the slide, and we sat on the climbing-frame instead, sharing memories and sour shots of Kentucky bourbon. He never told me what was wrong, but he didn't need to. When I suggested this terrible, taboo thing – that he left her – he didn't even get angry: he just shook his head and said it wasn't that easy and I didn't understand.

And then, I guess, he saw a few ghosts in the corner of the playground – his shared mortgage; his joint bank account; his coagulated pool of mixed friends – because he threw the bottle over in that direction, and it smashed against the wall.

The second time was the opposite of the first, except that I wasn't drinking that night, and I was already on the climbing-frame when he found me: perched there, hugging my knees, looking up at the sky. It was surprisingly bright that night – a shade of light blue with the contrast turned slightly down – and it felt open. I was figuring that everybody had the same sky, and so I was sending thoughts up into it, hoping that they'd somehow make their way to Amy.

I miss you. I love you. Please come home.

I'm sorry.

Please come home.

There was a desperation to it. It felt like if I stopped thinking these things then I'd start crying, but if I continued then they might come true. In the end, neither thing happened. Strong emotions that you think will destroy you never do. It always *feels* like you're going to burst, but in the end they just fizzle out and you keep going. I wasn't thinking about anything much by the time that Gray arrived: this dark figure wandering slowly over across the tarmac to sit down beside me.

We didn't say much. We didn't have anything to drink, and by that point our relationship was becoming slightly strained. His days with Helen were getting longer at dawn and dusk, and his nights with me were dwindling away. We just sat there for a while, and then, after a bit of time had passed, he clapped me on the shoulder like the good friend he'd once been.

Don't worry, he told me.

I'll help you find her.

With no alcohol to drink, and cold air falling from that open sky, we didn't stay there long. Instead, we went back to my house, where there was beer and central heating. After we'd drunk a couple of bottles in relative silence, Graham asked me if I had any clue where she might have gone, any idea at all, and I told him the truth: none. I showed him the note that she'd left, which he read a couple of times through, and then I found it was all spilling out of me: everything about the arguments we'd had, the difficulties. The nights spent sleeping apart. I told him *why* she'd gone – I knew that much. I just didn't know *where*.

Graham listened to this without really looking at me, nodding occasionally, frowning the whole time, and then when I'd finished he gave me a look. I don't know how to describe it, except that he looked very sad: it was worse than that, and I think I'll remember it for a long time. Then, he shook his head and the look seemed to go away a little. He asked me about Amy's behaviour: what she'd been doing on the occasions I'd gone to bed alone; whether she'd gone out and, if so, where she'd gone. Who she'd gone with. Perhaps he thought she had another boyfriend. She spent her nights on the computer, I told him. For hours on end. Sometimes, I said, there would be soft yellow light in the curtains by the time I felt her slip in behind me, careful not to touch me. But I didn't tell him that, when that happened, I turned and put my arm around her and she didn't even move.

The computer, he said. *Let me look at it.*

There was nothing obvious to see when we went upstairs and switched it on. I wasn't stupid: I'd checked the browsers we had installed but Amy had totally blanked the histories and navigation bars. I told Graham this, and he just said: *wait*.

Mechanics. It's like this: when they're out on a job, mechanics carry toolkits filled with everything they might need, but even on a casual day out chances are they have a pen-knife with a few attachments, or a screwdriver, or some shit like that lurking around. A kind of minimal toolkit, carried as naturally as someone else might carry their wallet or glasses-case. Graham had a nerdish equivalent: a slim case of about five compact disks, together containing the absolute minimum amount of software he could survive with. You never knew when you might need to unzip a compressed file in the chemist, I guess. Or defragment shattered information lying around on your best friend's hard drive.

This is a variation on some sneaky cookie software I developed, he told me. *I adapted it to work on computers like this, as well.*

It took about two minutes, and as the list of sites appeared in Graham's makeshift navigation window I found myself staring, surprised, growing colder inside as each one was listed. The addresses were never obvious dotcoms, but their content was obvious from occasional words appearing in the path. These were rape sites, death sites, murder sites. Of course, at that point I didn't know what those things were like; I didn't know quite how deep she'd gone, or how awful it was going to be to follow.

Jesus, Graham said.

That was where I started. I found that I could get to about a third of the addresses listed, and they turned out to be the shallows. You had to wade a lot deeper to find the real blackness, and there were strong undercurrents misleading you along the way: washing you quickly to more shallows, to the shore itself. The majority of the sites that Amy had visited were simply inaccessible. Graham explained that it was likely the addresses had been abandoned. This was common with illegal sites: the owners would shift servers often, sometimes moving every few minutes. They were like street vendors, alerted to approaching police, stuffing their briefcases closed and hurrying off to another corner to start again.

There would be others though, Graham told me. There would be sites protected by specialised software – the type he occasionally dallied with – that would have left no traces of themselves on a visitor's hard drive. There was no way around it: I would only find them by following Amy and discovering them for myself. And so that's what I would do. In the meantime, Graham would do what he did best: search the internet in his own inimitable way; do a little hacking here and there; try to put together, as best he could, information about where she'd gone on the day she left me.

So: over the last four months I'd collected hardcore pornography, chatted with paedophiles and rapists and wormed my way into their community. Graham had been hard at work too, but his collection was more innocent. On his hard drive we had a few different videos that, when pieced together, showed Amy's basic trajectory on that day. The first CCTV cameras were a few streets away from our home, and there was a lot of footage to sieve, so it took quite some time to locate her, but once we knew she was heading for the city we found things easier. We didn't have tracking shots or anything, but we had rough continuity for much of it.

Amy had taken the same route into the city as I had on my way to Graham's, only she'd waited for a bus and taken that for three stops. I could watch her get on and get off. Nobody was following her. In fact, as far as I could tell, nobody followed her at all until we came along. After a brief, purposeful walk, she went into a café called Jo's and sat in the window. She was there for half an hour in all, and drank two cups of something, taking her time over each. Between the drinks she sent a text message. We don't know why she was there, or who she contacted. After she left the café, we lost track of her. The streets of Bracken can get pretty busy, and a lot of the film we had was low resolution, making it difficult to separate people and differentiate between them.

But Graham kept looking.

The video that he'd found from the station that day was stuttering and incomplete: as much evidence as you could

71

possibly want that film footage is about as real as Jesus. He had four frames. All four were of the station floor, filled with a bustling crowd of blurry figures, but if you set them to play then they might as well have been distinct photographs, because they had different people in each. First one crowd, then another, then a third, and then one final group. She was in the third. Nowhere to be seen in the first or second, and nowhere to be seen in the last.

Graham zoomed in on frame three. I moved closer to the screen, leaning over.

Amy?

I couldn't be sure, but I touched the image anyway.

It felt like her.

'It's a pretty good resemblance, isn't it?' Graham said.

You could only tell what he meant if you blurred your eyes – otherwise, it was ridiculous. Her head was maybe twelve blocks of colour. Her body, which was visible to the waist, was another thirty or so, if that. In many ways, she was nothing but a pattern, but if you blurred your eyes then some kind of Amy appeared: an Amy obscured by tears. She was wearing that pale blue blouse with the sleeves rolled up to the elbows: the one that wasn't in the closet anymore.

'She tied her hair back after leaving the café,' I said.

Graham was more cautious.

'It looks like her, doesn't it?'

'It's her,' I said.

I touched the screen and murmured:

'Amy.'

Please come home.

The timeframe in the corner of the video told me that I was looking four months into the past. Four months ago, she'd been at the train station.

That was quite a head start.

'Have you looked at the passenger listings?' I asked.

72

I saw him nodding out of the corner of my eye.

'Most of them. There's nothing in her name.'

'Nothing on any of the other cameras?'

'Not so far. The platforms are all covered, so she must be there somewhere. If I can find her, I will. But you've got to understand that I don't have unrestricted access to these cameras. I've had to scrabble for these.' He shook his head. 'It might take time.'

I nodded to myself, and then caught a thought: Walter Hughes had access to those cameras.

Maybe we could trade in some way. I could tell him what Claire had told me.

'I might know somebody who can get you access,' I said.

'Who?'

'I don't really know. It's too complicated to explain.'

Of course, he wasn't going to help me out just for one word.

Graham said, 'When can you find out?'

'Monday. But it's not as simple as that. He won't just help me. I'm going to need some leverage.'

The picture of Amy flicked into the next frame: a random jumble of black at this magnification. Graham clicked a button and she came back to me.

If only.

'What do you need?' he asked.

I was thinking:

She was on the internet a lot ... a whole load of guys.

That was what Wilkinson had told me.

'I need some bargaining power.' I was still staring at the image of Amy on the computer screen. I couldn't look away.

The computer beeped. A window popped up informing Graham that the Will Robinson single had been successfully downloaded from Liberty.

I blinked.

73

'I need you to do a search on Liberty for me,' I said. 'I need you to look for just one word for me.'

'Shoot.'

If anything ever happens to me, I just want you to remember one word.

That's what she'd said to me.

'*Schio*,' I said. 'Just one word. Run a search for *Schio*.'

'Are you all right?' Graham asked. 'I'm worried about you.'

'I'm fine. Well—' A little incline of the head; a raise of the eyebrows. I sipped Helen's perfect coffee. 'You know.'

He nodded.

'But you don't need to be worried about me,' I said. I tried to make it sound as reassuring as possible – as though all this was some hobby I was vaguely committed to in my spare time, and not the only real purpose in life I had left. 'Look. I've got to get going.'

He took the mug from me. I glanced down at the screen. Reports were coming flooding into the program window as the search ran its way through a thousand computers on Liberty, and then ten thousand more:

[*schio* not found]   [*schio* not found]

[*schio* not found]   [*schio* not found]

[*schio* not found]   [*schio* not found]   [*schio* not found]

[*schio* not found]

[*schio* not found]   [*schio* not found]

'I'll leave it running,' he told me. 'Should have something in an hour or so.'

I nodded.

74

He clicked the [Reporting] button off, and the messages disappeared.

'I'll call back. Is it okay if I call?'

'Of course, Jay,' he said. 'Always. It's always okay.'

But I didn't believe him.

I thought about Helen's list of tea and coffee, and about Graham's perfect bookcases and computerised intercom voice. Their uptown address. They had so much money that they almost didn't know what to do with it – except buy what they'd been told to. Maybe they'd even be starting a family soon: a frightening thought.

In a way, though, it was weird for me to think that their relationship was so fucked up. My love for Amy felt like something pure and wonderful in comparison, but the only evidence of our relationship at the moment was an image on the screen, and me – currently staining an unwanted shadow into their bright apartment. I could almost feel Helen washing up in the kitchen, wondering when – now that Amy was gone – their duty to me as friends would be finally discharged. When she could cross me off her coffee list. When they could trade me in for a better model and just have done.

The only times I ever saw them these days were times like this.

'I've gotta go,' I said. 'Say goodbye to Helen for me.'

I wandered out and, like I was a blackmailer come to visit in the night, he watched me to the door without saying a word.

CHAPTER FIVE

Lacey Beck.

It was at one end of Swaine Woods – the Ludlow village end. Ludlow was pretty small: basically just a road of country houses backing onto the wood, all of them carefully reconstructed. They had bright white walls – many with black cartwheels nailed to the sides, for some reason – troughs filled with flowers, and they all sported tiny, random windows you couldn't see shit out of. You could see into some of the kitchens, though, and they all looked the same: herb racks and wooden-handle knives; pans hanging from hooks above the work surfaces; an olde cookery booke. Outside, you could breathe in the smell of grass and trees, and listen to birdsong, assuming you might want to.

At one end of the road, a ginnel led to a footpath through the woods, which went all the way through to the ring road at the far side, skirting Morton. It was a lonely walk, but a nice one; Amy and I used to wander along it sometimes, and it would take about half an hour to get from one end to the other. The sun came streaking in through the tips of the trees, and the embankment sloped down to the left: a mess of dusty roots and dips. The beck was at the bottom, diverging away from the path. Half a mile into the wood you could barely even hear it anymore.

I wouldn't have wanted to live there. It was where a lynch mob hanged Edmund Lacey, an eighteenth-century highwayman, and although I don't believe in ghosts I've always thought that there was an atmosphere to the place. Most of the time, it felt peaceful and pleasant, but occasionally it was almost threateningly still. All you could hear was the stream, which – in its way – was all that was left of Lacey: his name, rushing endlessly past.

Sometimes, it made me think of screaming spirits blowing through abandoned buildings like the wind. Most of the time, it just made me think: *oh – so there's a stream here*.

I'd carefully followed Charlie from her house, waiting at the far end of the road until she emerged and then watching her all the way to the ginnel. When she'd turned the corner onto the footpath, I'd started to make my way down the road. By the time I'd started to hear the stream, and then reached the corner myself, I was figuring that she'd be out of sight. And she was.

In spite of my days of careful planning, I wasn't entirely sure how this was going to go, or even if it was going to go. It was more than possible that Kareem was many miles away right now – more than likely, in fact – and if that was the case then, although it meant another dead end, at least I didn't have to worry about Charlie getting hurt. If he was here, though, I had at least two concerns.

Firstly, and most importantly, protecting Charlie.

Secondly, protecting myself.

Kareem really shouldn't have written that, *A lot of Amys hang around in here*, because what it now came down to was this: I was here in these woods, expecting him. If he showed up, then the likelihood was that only one of us was leaving, which was a pretty big thing.

I set off along the path.

There would be a fair amount of luck to this, I realised. After all, I had no idea what Kareem looked like, in terms of his age, race, height, build, dress sense – anything, really – and although these woods were quiet, that didn't mean I was about to leap on someone the moment I saw them. It could just be a guy out for a walk, and so I needed to be certain it was him before committing myself. That meant giving him enough rope to hang himself with, à la Edmund Lacey, which – in turn – meant exposing Charlie to more danger than felt entirely comfortable.

Ideal situation?

Aside from us all being at home, tucked up in bed, it was this:

Kareem was deep in the woods, watching for a woman of Amy17's description to come walking along the footpath. I'd be far enough back for him not to see me. Then, he'd see her and move onto the path behind her, and that was when I'd move in, running up to catch him. In an ideal situation, Charlie wouldn't know anything about it; I'd take him down before he reached her, and she'd carry on, none the wiser.

How likely was this ideal situation? Let's say I didn't exactly have my hopes up. But I didn't think he would have waited on the road and followed her in, like I did, because he wouldn't have known where she was coming from, and so waiting in the woods was probably a good bet. Another possibility was that he'd come the opposite way, and then turn around and go after her, but I didn't think that was likely either. He had his fantasy to think about, after all: whenever we cybered, he didn't like Amy17 to see him until he was chasing her. I was figuring that would hold here, too.

I moved as quietly and quickly as I dared, trying to recreate the pace I'd seen Charlie moving at. A quick walk, keeping my breathing in check so I could listen as carefully as possible. For a twig snapping, or a shoe scuffing the dirt up ahead. Worst case scenario: a scream. And all the time keeping an eye out on the woods to the left: looking for colour, for movement, for anything.

I'd been walking for about ten minutes when I heard the scream.

I started running immediately, twitched into motion by the sound. The woods around me seemed intensely real; I took in every shade of green, brown and yellow as I ran, hurdling over looping roots, tapping trees as I passed them, partly to propel and partly to steady myself. Too busy to notice the adrenalin. The path twisted around to the right. Too busy, until the last moment, to realise that the scream I'd just heard had come from a man. That fact occurred to me as I rounded the corner and saw them, a few metres ahead.

They were almost in a rugby scrum, forming a bridge, with Charlie holding on to the shoulders of a much bigger man and yelling in anger as she launched kicks into his flabby stomach. The man was panting uncontrollably: although he was much taller and heavier than she was, he seemed to have been bent double by the force of her attack and was now hanging on for dear life. As I started to move forwards, she stamped down hard on his shin, and he screamed and stepped back, letting go of her and covering his face just in time as she launched a series of punches at him. Quick, snappy left jab; hard right cross that smacked the back of his hand and must have broken something, and then a solid left hook that knocked him a step sideways. From nowhere, her foot was suddenly in his stomach again – she'd spun around on her heel and launched a blistering kick that seemed to go a full metre through him.

Kareem disappeared backwards into the wood. I watched him tumble down the embankment, with little punches of dust and cries of pain following him on his way.

'Holy shit,' I said.

'Jason?'

Charlie was flushed.

I ran over. Kareem had come to a halt in an ungainly heap

79

about thirty metres down from us. He seemed to be deciding whether to attempt to get to his feet or not.

'What the hell just happened?'

Charlie said, 'Son of a bitch jumped out at me.'

We both looked down at the son of a bitch in question: a mildly overweight man in blue jeans and a checked shirt. He was struggling upright, with the aid of the tree beside him, and seemed as stunned as I was. He looked up at us. He was shaking, and I saw an average face, filled with a kind of stupid, awful terror. Then, he turned around and began to flounder off in the direction of the Beck.

'Wait here.'

I started down after him.

Leave this, my mind told me, even as I was running. Or stamping, anyway – the embankment was forty-five treacherous degrees of dry mud, spotted with a slalom of trees. You couldn't run down something that steep; it was more like a semi-controlled, high-stepping fall that jarred your legs and hurt your stomach. As the ground evened out, the world juddered around impossibly quickly. I hit the woodland floor and was after him like a gunshot.

Leave this.

Kareem glanced back, saw that I was coming after him and found a higher gear. His shirt came untucked as he ran deeper into the woods. His arms were pistoning. In fact, he could move pretty quickly when he wasn't having his ass kicked by a girl.

I was exhilarated, but also feeling like I was a worm that had been let off the hook and had then jumped right back on again.

Leave this. What the fuck are you going to do when you catch him?

Kill him? Now that Charlie's seen him?

But I was still running in the wrong direction, regardless.

Straight after him, slapping past trees as I went. He veered right, heading deeper still. I could hear the stream and knew we must be getting close. He'd need to level out soon: just head straight right and hope he could outpace me to the ring road. But that was five minutes' run, or more, and he must have known he wouldn't make it.

I could hear his frantic breaths.

This feeling was the same feeling I'd had waiting at the station for the train to Schio on the day I'd gone to meet Claire. It was the shaking, stupid anxiety of a man who knew he was about to do the wrong thing; that he was going to disregard all the pleading, desperate advice that his mind was throwing at him, and go on and do the wrong thing regardless.

I put on a last jolt of speed as I reached him, punching into him from the side and driving him over towards the beck. Kareem went down; I heard a splash as my leg smashed into the water. Then grunting as I got my arm to the side of his head and pushed him.

He wasn't a serious contender. I punched him again – hard – as we were getting to our feet. His nose shattered, and suddenly he was flat on his ass again, with blood spattered onto his shirt. He brought up his hands to hold his face together.

'Shit,' he said simply.

I wandered back up the bank and checked out the woods. There was no sign of Charlie, so I figured that she'd stayed up on the footpath out of the way. Either that or she was wandering, unsure where we'd ended up. I backed down to the edge of the stream. Over on the other side, there were just green fields: empty and desolate. The grass was long overgrown and untended.

It was still possible to walk away. I really did know this. Instead, feeling sick, I pulled the stanley knife out of my jacket pocket, clicked the blade out three notches and turned back to where he was lying.

'Hey Kareem,' I said.

He stopped massaging his face and looked up at me. Confused.

And then with a little more understanding.

I'd well and truly boarded the train now.

I grabbed him by his hair and put the blade to his face. It was a weird thing. Like something out of a movie: not at all like I'd expected it to feel. It was too sunny, for a start.

'We've got some talking to do,' I said.

'Please don't hurt me.'

His voice was this stuttering, fragile thing. He couldn't even think about fighting back; couldn't think about anything right now apart from how he was suddenly all past, no future.

'Amy Foster,' I told him, tightening my grip on his hair. He winced a little. 'You tell me about her, and you get away from here today alive.'

The words came out in a gush.

'Who? I don't know any Amy Foster. I swear I don't—'

And so I cut his cheek. I'd never cut anyone before and I wasn't really sure how to do it. It was meant to be a warning cut – a taster – but it didn't turn out that way. The blade went through his cheek like paper, and with about the same sound. Blood spilled out of the side of his mouth.

He started crying.

My hand was shaking, but I told him:

'You know who she is. You met her in the Melanie Room about four months ago. And then you met her in real life. She took a train to come see you.'

I didn't know that any of this was true until he started crying harder, and then I knew that it was all true. Suddenly, it didn't feel too sunny for this anymore; something went out inside me. Some light. I cut him again, digging the stanley knife over his cheekbone, pressing down so hard that the muscles in my forearm bunched and my teeth gritted.

'You fucking killed her.'

'I didn't! I didn't! I swear to God! Jesus, ahhhh!'

The train leaving the station now: rolling out backwards. It was out of my hands.

'You met her and you killed her.'

Easier to just sit back now, as I carved his face apart.

'I didn't kill her,' he sobbed. 'Please stop hurting me!'

I let go of his hair, throwing his head back in disgust, and stepped away from him. Then, I went to the top of the bank and checked the woods again. In the distance, I heard Charlie calling my name. She was a long way away by the sound of it. If she'd been closer, I might have left it there.

Who am I kidding?

Back with Kareem, by the side of the stream. In the sun. With the breeze making the grass in the field shiver, and the trees above us nodding thoughtfully.

'What happened?' I said.

'I don't know what happened.' He was knuckling blood and spit off his chin. His cheek was bright red and looked utterly destroyed.

'Jesus. Oh, Jesus.' He looked up at me desperately. 'Marley took her. I owed Marley some money, and he fucking took her. That's all I know.'

I made to grab him again, and he flinched away.

'You *sold* her?'

He shook his head.

'Not like that. I didn't have any say in it. We were just talking about things.'

'About what?'

'About rape. About why I wanted to do the things I did. Why I like that stuff. We were just talking, I swear. We weren't doing anything!'

I pictured this man in a room with Amy. Just talking. Either side of a table, elbows resting there. Cups of coffee between them. Just shooting the breeze.

'What happened?'

'I owed this guy Marley. He's like this big underworld guy in Thiene, and I owed him money. I'd been gambling, and taking shit from him on loan, and I didn't want my wife to know. He was gonna tell her. Gonna beat me and tell her everything. Maybe beat her too.'

'So you gave him my girlfriend?'

White rage: I took hold of his hair again, ready to put the knife through his face a *hundred thousand* times.

'NO! He just took her, man. I didn't have any say in it, I swear. He had a couple of other guys with him – real big guys – and they just took her out by the hair. I tried to stop them, but—'

I attempted to picture him trying to stop them, but the image wouldn't come. I couldn't see it somehow. All I saw was Amy being taken away by her hair, and I knew exactly what had happened. Kareem had paid his debt by giving Amy to this man, Marley. Before I even knew what I was doing, I'd punched Kareem in the stomach so hard that the knife flew out of my hand and landed on the bank. All the air went out of him in a whoosh, and then I was dragging him up by the hair, pulling him towards the beck, then kicking his legs out from under him, and down he went, face first, into the water. He couldn't help sucking it in. Blood spilled away downstream in little tendrils.

And I held him there. Looking out over the field, and then glancing back at the bank behind me. Charlie was calling me: still quite a way away. Maybe if she was closer I would have stopped: I could keep thinking like that. My mind was calm now. The panic would come afterwards, I was sure, but for now there was only silence, as I carried out this unreal thing

84

that it had been telling me not to all along while at the same time knowing I was always going to.

He fought for a minute or so, but I was stronger than he was. And that's what life's about, isn't it? You fuck up, you fight with all your might, and then you die anyway.

I met Charlie halfway back through the woods. We saw each other from quite a way off and she waited for me as I walked towards her, head bowed. I scratched my nose, looked up at her and shrugged as I reached the place she was standing.

'He got away.'

'Too bad.' She noticed my clothes. 'Jesus – you're soaking.'

I looked down at my leg and my arms.

'Yeah. I took a tumble into the beck. My hand's pretty sore.' I looked at it, pretending that it hurt or appeared injured in some way. 'He took off over the field, and I figured I was done in.'

'Thanks for trying.'

She smiled at me, but looked a little shaken.

'You really beat the shit out of him,' I said, trying to make light of the situation. But my face just wouldn't smile. Every time I tried, it just slipped away.

She said, 'I think he had it coming.'

And then she shivered. 'The adrenalin's kicking in, though. I'm a wreck. Think I hurt my hand on him, too.'

'Let me have a look.'

Suddenly, I was this world expert on injured hands. I took up her small fist and examined it. Already, between her first two knuckles, the skin was darkening. It happened to me a lot when I went bare-fist on the Scream, and I figured she'd be okay.

'You'll live,' I said, letting go of her hand.

She rubbed it.

'Well – bit of excitement, anyway. Think we should report it?'

'I doubt it.' I looked behind me. 'He's long gone.'

'Probably think twice before he does that again, anyway.'

'I would think so.' I smiled at her, but it faded again. 'Where did you learn to do that stuff?'

She struck a stance.

'Second-dan gojo-ryu,' she said. 'I've been training since I was eight.'

'Jesus.'

She relaxed. 'You still want to go for that drink?'

'I think I really need it.'

'Okay, then. Let's go.'

So we walked back up to the path and together followed it all the way to the ring road. In better circumstances, it might have reminded me of walking with Amy. I don't know how I would have felt then, but it hardly even registered now. I was like a zombie, grunting in the right places to everything Charlie said. I'd left the thinking part of me back down by Lacey Beck, and it was still kneeling there now, squatting beside Kareem's corpse and keening like a frightened, abandoned child as the water washed over him.

CHAPTER SIX

When forensic experts want to recreate a murder victim's face from the skull, they stick little plasticine pegs at key points on the bone structure – at the right height for the ethnic origin and gender of the skull, which is determined by size, shape, and so on – and then they join those points up with strips and fill in the spaces in-between. My relationship with Amy was as complicated and intricate as a human face, but you could begin to see the shape of it in the same way: by picking out key points and then filling in the missing details later.

Year o:	We meet.
Year o.3:	I tell her that I love her.
Year 3.0:	I propose; she says yes.
Year 4.5:	She disappears.

Those might well have been four of the most important moments of my life, so they'll do as starting points.

We met by having sex, which is as good a way as any despite what your mother might have told you. The Fusee-Lounge was late licence by then: a student bar constructed out of the remains of an old aeroplane. I forget the exact model but it was one of those big ones. They'd taken out most of the original fittings, widened it, fitted a bar down one side and covered the rest of the area with seats, games machines and pool tables. It was a popular place. The DJ played loud punk and industrial, the lighting was dim, and you could drink and jump around until one or two in the morning, each and every night. For Graham and me, it was like a new playground, but with a better selection of booze.

It was Friday night when I danced into Amy: probably about half-past one. I'd sunk enough alcohol to kill a small village, and the dancefloor probably would have cleared around me if there'd been any room for people to move away. Luckily, Amy was as drunk as I was. Our bodies found each other, and it seemed easier to kiss each other than do anything else, so we did. It was late enough by then for us to make it last, and then we went home together and had sex that, given the circumstances, was pretty spectacular. Neither of us was sick until afterwards, anyway. Even better sex the next morning told of what might have been, and we just . . . sort of carried on. Saw each other the day after, and then the next. Went on a few dates; ate a few dinners. By the end of week two, we were in a Relationship™, and neither of us had a problem with it.

I bought a bog-standard pint of beer for me, and a bubble-gum flavoured bottled drink for Charlie. Mine was brown, whereas hers was an awful kind of murky green. As we made our way over to a table in the corner, it felt as though everybody was watching me and memorising what I looked like for the investigation to come.

Ugly fella. Tall. Kinda solid.

There was a camera above the main entrance, but by the time I'd seen it it had been too late. I did my best to look away to the left as we came in, but I don't think I really pulled it off.

Clothes looked damp – and kinda muddy, too.

We slid in around the table and ended up sitting beside each other on the corner. I was already wondering how long I had to stay, and whether there was a back entrance to this place I could escape through.

'Thanks for this,' Charlie said, touching the neck of her bottle with delicate fingers. 'My father would never approve. He's a real-ale man.'

'Is that right?' I was looking around.

'Uh-huh.' She took a swig, and the liquid chinked. 'He brews his own. Does wines and things, too. There're demi-johns in our attic that have been around longer than me.'

I smiled. Took a sip of my own beer.

Awkward silence.

It was dark and subdued inside the Bridge: everything and everybody was silhouetted by the bright white light of the day outside. Even the slot machines seemed muted, as though wary of making too much noise this early on. Blue smoke was spiralling up from ashtrays. You could actually see the air in here: like mist the colour of gun-metal. A television in the corner was showing horse-racing, but the sound had been turned down until the commentary was nothing but a low murmur. Everybody was watching brown animals pounding soundlessly over green grass.

'So,' Charlie said after a moment. 'How are you doing?'

'I'm doing okay.' I nodded. 'I'm not doing too badly.'

I looked at her, darkened by the window behind her. She looked different, I realised.

She'd cut her hair since the last time I saw her.

'You haven't been in recently,' she said.

Or she had make-up on. Maybe that was it.

'No.'

I was actually thinking that I'd just killed a man. An undertone of thought that rested below all the others. It was almost unreal.

I'd just killed a man.

She said, 'It must have been a few weeks by now.'

Perhaps I should just get drunk, I thought.

'It's been a month and a half,' I said, picking up my glass.

A month and a half of paid unwork. I'd received my payslip for the end of March and was half-anticipating one for the end of April. After that, I had a feeling they might start to dry up.

'People have been worried about you.'

I thought about it.

'I'm sorry that people have been worried. I mean, I never meant to worry anybody. I didn't think anyone would care, to be honest. It just . . . got to the point where I couldn't come in anymore.'

I didn't know how to explain it any better than that, even though that didn't really explain it at all. It really hadn't been a decision I'd made so much as an epiphany: something that happened to me. Somebody else made the decision, and I just realised how much sense it made. I think I did quite well, actually – for a couple of months after Amy vanished, I laboured into work on a morning, through work during the day and then out of work again in the evening: a good, solid pretence of normality. It's what you do, after all. I was carrying on; I was surviving. My mother would have been proud of me. And then, one day, I realised that I wasn't surviving at all: quite the opposite. I was being assimilated, and I was slowly dying, one day at a time.

'You couldn't come in?'

'No,' I said. 'It just didn't seem worth it anymore.'

I worked for an insurance company. Let me briefly explain how insurance works – in the lower levels, at least. Let's say you want to insure your house. The first thing you do is get a quote from my company, and in order to do this you have to fill out a breathtaking number of forms and provide us with an almost insurmountable mountain of personal information. This is only to confuse and lull you. What it boils down to is this. You live in a semi-detached house with x number of bedrooms in a certain post code (down to the street name). Now, we know – from our vast database of prior claims and police reports – exactly how likely you are to be burgled or for your house to burn down or whatever, which we read as: *how long will it take this person to claim one thousand pounds from us*? On average, let's say, it would take you five years, so we need to charge you two hundred pounds a year in house insurance to break even. It might take less time or it might take more, but the beauty is that they cancel each other out: that's the benefit of betting on average.

This is a simple matter of simple mathematics.

We charge you two hundred pounds a year to break even, and that's after your claim, if you claim. In reality, of course, we charge you more like three hundred pounds a year, but the amount is entirely variable. Whatever percentage profit we want to make, we make. There is no grey area. There is very little in the way of doubt, and we don't make many mistakes.

We're affiliated to several banks. They keep our accounts and, in exchange for our custom, they direct their own customers our way. They advise it, in fact. *What would you do if your house burnt down tomorrow?* they ask, frowning with worry. *What if you were burgled and lost it all*? They're quite blatant. The sensible thing to do is to take whatever quote we give you and store that much money away in a separate account of your own each year. That way, if you do get burgled, you have the money to act as your own insurance company; and when you don't get burgled and your house doesn't burn down, you haven't given all your hard-earned money to a complete stranger.

We didn't work at that end of things, Charlie and I. We worked at the end that tries to fuck you out of the money if and when you do eventually claim. We found clauses you never suspected were there. In a way, we couldn't lose – even if we ended up paying you, we knew the company was making a profit regardless. But we gave it our sportsman's best, anyway, because every penny counts. Customers often got angry when they realised that we weren't their friends, after all. That, at the end of the day, either they lost money or we did. And guess what?

'Do you still feel like that? I mean, are you going to come back to work soon?'

I thought about it, even though I didn't need to, and then shook my head.

'I don't think so, no.'

Even if I found Amy, I wasn't going back. I'd let my life unravel to such a point, now, that it would be all but impossible to tie it back together again. For once in my life, there were no plans for the future. I really couldn't imagine what was going to happen.

Okay, so what was she like?

Amy had brown curly hair, with streaks of gold that seemed yellow in the sun, and a warm, happy face that always looked flushed and enthusiatsic. Not exactly beautiful, but pretty – and far too confident and in love with life for it to be an issue anyway, at least to begin with. I know that's a cliché – but for what it's worth she was in love with life in the real way, not the fairytale way. Most of the time, she adored it; some of the time, though, she could barely face the day. That's love for you.

She was slim, but curvy. And she was sexy as anything, but you'll have to take my word for that. Imagine your ideal person. Amy probably didn't look like that, but she had the effect on me that the person does on you. There were days when I almost had to pinch myself. It seemed like a whole fresh side of me had opened up.

I told her that I loved her after a few months; I don't remember exactly when that was, but – if you really want to know – she told me first. In fact, she was very definite about it: she loved me from about the fifth week, and then, at three months, she was *in* love with me. It took me just that little bit longer to come out with it, but I tried it on for size eventually and found that I liked it. *I love you.* You should have seen her face light up when I told her that. She always looked happy, but when I told her that I loved her she looked like she was going to explode with joy.

I mean, have you ever seen joy in someone? Not just happiness, but actual joy? That was one of the only times I ever have, and it was like the sun came out inside her. Like everything just flipped right-side up. Suddenly, I couldn't hold her tightly enough, and she held me back just as hard, with the back of my shirt bunched up in her small hands and her knuckles digging into my shoulder blades. Have you ever had somebody grip you with a passion you never thought existed outside the fucking movies? As though they found you the most precious thing in the world? I felt it then, and couldn't believe that somebody would actually want me that much. I don't believe in Heaven as a place, but I sometimes think that if a person could write down how I felt at just that moment – if they could describe it perfectly – then that sentence would be something like Heaven to me. And as a final resting place, I'd be happy to have my name shrunk down and rested, invisibly, on the collar of the full stop at the end. That would be fine for me.

'What are you going to do?' Charlie said.

'You miss making me coffee?' I did my best to smile, but I could still feel the ice cold water rushing over my hands as I drowned Kareem. My bones hadn't quite thawed out yet.

She smiled back, playing with the neck of her bottle but then looked away.

'Yeah. I miss making you coffee.'

The way she said it made me realise I'd come off as sounding too playful.

'I kind of miss it, too,' I said. 'But that's all I miss, and most of the time I don't even miss that. It's moments like those that cloud everything over.'

'Cloud what over?'

I shrugged.

'The fact that we work for something intrinsically evil. In a benign way, if that makes any sense. We spend our days fucking good people out of their money. That's the reality. The appearance is that you make me coffee in the morning, and we have a laugh, and we take the piss out of Williams behind his back. We're okay people. I mean, we are okay people.'

'Well, yeah.'

'We take our cheques at the end of the month, and that's the only important thing.'

'Everybody's got to eat, Jason.'

'Yeah, everyone's got to eat. Exactly.' I sat back, listening to the cars shoot past outside. 'Everybody has to eat. So it's all okay.'

'Is that why you're not coming back? Because of this.'

'No,' I said. 'Well, not really. Maybe a bit. If Amy was here then I'd still be in work; still carrying on like before. But she isn't, and it's put things in perspective for me. It's a waste of our fucking time to be doing something so worthless.'

That was an understatement, but I couldn't describe it any better. The thing is, a working life is one of those things you're taught to respect and admire. Because a man pays his way. A man supports his family. There's no such thing as a free lunch. And so on. In reality, what you have are thousands of people doing the same thing, day after day, and it's not admirable: it's tragic. It's just a convincing fiction. So for a while after she disappeared, I shuffled back to work, all the time knowing deep down that the most important thing was Amy and the fact that she wasn't with me. It got harder and harder, as though I was tied by elastic to something in the past, and each day was one miserable footstep forwards. So I stopped going in – just made the decision one day – and it felt like an enormous weight had been lifted off me.

I felt like I had a purpose again.

I felt like I was looking at the scenery, for once, rather than just speeding past.

What I didn't feel was guilty, worthless, small, tragic or pitiful. For the first time in years, it felt like I'd taken hold of my life by the scruff of its neck, like a spitting, scratching cat, and turned its angry face around to have a good, honest look into its eyes. If I ever let go I'd have myself slashed to shit, but that didn't feel important: whenever you grab a tiger by the tail, you know you're going to get scratched eventually. You don't take it as a career path. It's not a long-term thing. It's just an awesome thing.

'Are you looking for her?' Charlie said.

'As much as I can. I have a friend who helps me. We've made some ground.'

'What about the police?'

'No.'

'No?'

'They won't help.' I sipped my drink. 'She left a note.'

We spent the next year of University doing exactly the same things: getting drunk, jumping up and down in time to loud music, grinning, fucking and hanging around, as though life was a bus we were waiting for that wasn't due for a while yet. Certainly, looking back, I have a tendency to see it as a time in my life when nothing felt urgent or pressing, and when everything seemed fun and new. The week would see casual study. The weekend would find us in pubs and in clubs, or propped up in single beds: logged on to illegal internet movie channels, the monitor flashing harsh light around the dark bedroom as we tucked into takeaway pizza and drank bottles of cheap Cabbage Hill vodka mixed with superstore cola.

The third year of University – our second as a couple – we moved in together and started The Collection. Crockery and cutlery. Pans and dishes. Furniture. Posters and paintings. Mutually agreeable albums, videos and friends. All sorts of things that didn't exactly belong to either of us, but to this weird new thing called both of us.

You start The Collection because you have to, of course, but it always struck me that there was more to it than that. It's like your relationship is a very beautiful, delicate cloth that either of you could accidentally blow away and ruin at any time, and the more stuff you pile on top of it – to weigh it down – the less likely that is to happen. So that's what we did. We put our new stereo on it. We put the signed Kimota hardback anthology down. And so on. We put a hundred things on top of it and then a hundred more, and with each came the knowledge that if we wanted to do anything so dumb as to blow that cloth away, we'd have to move our friends and our books and our casserole dishes first, and then we'd have to figure out where to put them.

We both graduated. Our parents' houses have very similar pictures in them on the mantelpiece: Amy and I, side by side, dressed in our black gowns and holding our degree certificates. Apart from our smiles, we look like we're in mourning. During the ceremony, along with a handful of others, we'd both worn A3 sheets of paper on our backs, denouncing the University's investment in various overseas arms companies, but our parents had made us take them off for the photographs. I guess it wouldn't have made for a nice picture. We did it to keep them happy – rebellion was okay so long as it was nice and controlled. The kind of rebellion that you can probably brand a pair of sneakers on, but not the sort that ever achieves much.

Jobs followed. Neither of us knew what we wanted to do, beyond paying the rent. Everybody has to eat, right? I got my job at SafeSide early on, starting off temporary in the mail room and ending up – lied to by all those capitalist fairytales – just one floor up, earning a couple of hundred more a year. Small town boy makes average. It's difficult to make a movie on the strength of that one, isn't it? Amy panned around a little longer, but still didn't find any gold. She worked for the post office, for a while, helping to facilitate the downsizing, and then drifted through e-centre work before finally settling into virtual secretarial support. The idea was that companies on the other side of the world could send you work to do – accounting, typing, website work – at the end of their working day (which was the beginning of yours), and when they arrived back the next morning, you'd have done all the work during their night-time. By the time I asked her to marry me, Amy had built up quite a respectable client base of Australian companies, and was thinking of expanding her business by farming work out. I was doing okay by then, too, in my own way, and so it seemed like a good time to make the commitment.

Hardly anyone got married anymore, and we really hadn't been planning it. I'm not Radically Opposed, the way that a lot of young people are; I knew it smacked of ownership of women, and outdated beliefs in gods we just didn't need anymore, and yet I still found it symbolically appealing. But I wasn't at the other end of the spectrum, either – the one where you get seriously married in the top-floor chapel of your chosen company. These days every major company has a licensed CEO, and all that changes from business to business is the logo in the corner of the certificate. I knew I could have got married as a SafeSide employee. But I didn't want that either: I wasn't a lifer. I just wanted to put a ring on Amy's finger, so that she could look at it every so often and know what it meant.

It's difficult, when you have principles, to know what the right thing to do is. We didn't want to get properly married – formally, in a registry office – but we both had friends who were getting married as some kind of retro-fashion statement, and we didn't want to be associated with that, either. So in the end we both agreed that it was no big deal. We'd wear a ring, and in our hearts we'd see ourselves as married. I got down on one knee, unclipped this pissy little green velvet box and asked her, literally, for her hand. She gave it to me. We smiled a lot, and made nervous phone calls to the people who cared. And that was that. We never said *husband* or *wife*. We were just us: Jason and Amy.

Two rings, not much more than fifty pounds apiece. Even together they weighed next to nothing, but when we put them down on top of The Collection, they felt like the heaviest items there, and when I looked at it afterwards – in my head – I thought it had never looked so steady and secure.

Of course, things hadn't really started to go wrong by then.

'The police figured that we'd had an argument, or something. I mean, we had, in a way, but not like they meant. I explained it all but they said there was nothing they could do. It's not a crime to leave someone.'

I remembered the conversation all too clearly. I'd felt like a child: desperate and panicked, and simply refusing to accept its mother's final word on a subject. The officer had told me over and over, maybe six times, that there was nothing he could do, and in the end he'd just told me to get out of his way. Not angrily, because he was too professional for that, but with enough of a threat in his voice to make it clear that this was the last time he'd actually ask.

Charlie said, 'That sucks.'

I nodded.

'Can't you go back to them? It's been how long? Four months?'

'Thereabouts. I suppose I could go back to them.'

Except I didn't want to. The same shift that had seen me quit turning up to work as the default setting had also altered my perspective on other things. A policeman was now just a man with a uniform on, no smarter or more important than I was. Society supports the police force and condemns vigilantes and, although this is often hidden beneath a cloud of moral respectability, it has nothing to do with morality at all: it's about logistics. As her boyfriend, I felt I had more right to search for Amy than they did. I didn't have the manpower, but that was another issue entirely. The point was that I had the responsibility. If the situation was reversed, I knew she'd be looking for me. That was what our relationship was about.

'But you haven't talked to them again yet?'

I shook my head. 'I'm making progress, though. I have a few leads.'

By her hair.

I looked at the table.

And then I started to shake. It felt like someone had kicked me in the heart.

'Excuse me,' I said, getting up so quickly I shunted the table and sent slops of beer rocking out of my glass. 'I'll be back in a minute.'

There was a note on the kitchen table and my house keys clattered down onto the wooden surface beside it. I'd already switched on the kettle. Behind me, on the work surface, it was beginning to rustle gently as the element set the water stirring. The house was quiet and bright. We'd never got around to putting a shade over the bare bulb in the kitchen, and the note was positioned almost exactly underneath, with light spilling down over it. The shadow of my hand reached it before I did.

Black biro on an A4 sheet: big letters, breaking through the faint blue lines and making the page their own.

Jason.

I love you very much.

I frowned, turning on my heels and moving through to the living room. The light was duller in there, and the page looked more solid.

and I don't want you to blame yourself for this.

I sat down gingerly on the arm of the chair. Starting to feel something lurching inside myself.

This isn't some kind of 'dear John' letter. I'm coming back again.

It was like the whole room was getting just a little bit darker by the second. There's nothing reassuring about the phrase *I'm coming back* if it needs to be said. It means it won't seem like it.

There are some things I need to sort out. You know how it's been between the two of us recently,

I closed my eyes.

Of course I knew. Sleeping back to back. Amy crying, and me not being able to comfort her anymore, or not willing to in some obscure, terrible way. Sitting in silence with some unspoken argument hanging in the air between us, ringing slightly. Not knowing what to do or say. Wandering past each other in the hallway without acknowledgement. Resentment. Discomfort.

It wasn't always like that, but our days could sink like a stone.

I opened my eyes and kept reading.

and it's not fair on you. I need to deal with the issues I have, just like you said.

It happened four years ago, Amy, I remembered thinking. You really need to sort yourself out.

I should have dealt with them already, but I really need to now.

Please wait for me. I promise I'll come home as soon as I can.

I love you so much (to the sky and back!).

Your Amy.

The bar's public telephone was padlocked to the wall in a dark annexe by the toilets. Two soft lights overhead reflected off the ruddy-brown wooden walls and gave the corridor a drawing-room effect. To complete the image, there was a spiralling, hand-crafted coat stand resting between the lavatory doors, supporting the kind of old green raincoat you might wear to place bets while propped by an ashtray in the bookies. I slotted a couple of coins into the phone, my hands trembling, and then leant back against the wall, somehow grateful for the protection the darkness gave me.

Helen answered after three rings.

'Hey-o?'

Well, I didn't feel like dealing with her right then.

'Hi, Helen. Is Graham there?'

'Oh, yes. Actually, he was hoping that you'd ring.' She sounded a little bit disappointed by this. 'Hang on.'

There was a pause and then a clatter, and I heard her shouting his name. A few seconds later, there was a buzz of white-noise and then the click of a phone lifting as she put me through.

'Hijay. How are you doing?'

I wasn't thinking straight, or I'd have noticed his voice wavering right then.

'Not great,' I admitted, leaning away from the wall and beginning to pace as much as the cord would allow me. 'I'm in a bit of a state here, actually, Gray. I don't know what I'm going to do.'

'Where are you, and what's happened?'

I just killed a man.

'I'm in the Bridge pub. On the ring road.'

'Want me to come and get you?'

'No.'

Graham was worried: 'What's happening there? You sound fucked to high Hell.'

I closed my eyes.

'I just found something out, that's all,' I said. 'Forget the train station, because I know where she went. She went to Thiene to meet somebody, Gray. A fat white guy. I know that's where she went.'

'Thiene.'

'Can you get the cameras at Thiene?'

'Maybe.'

He sounded dubious. Far away.

'Or outside,' I said, speaking faster than I could think. 'On the streets, maybe. Outside the station.'

'Maybe.'

'I've got a name, too,' I said. 'Can you search for information on "Marley" for me?'

'M-a-r-l-e-y?'

'Yeah. In Thiene. Anything you can find on people with that name.'

This time, he didn't say anything at all.

I used a little of the silence to let my brain catch up with itself. But there was too much, and it started to get uncomfortable. Then, I had a bolt of memory:

'Did you find the file on Liberty?'

Another pause.

'Yeah.' And that was when I noticed the shakiness in his voice, and I realised it had been there all along. 'Yeah, I found it. *Schio*. That's why I was trying to get in touch with you. I got the file. Downloaded it from a server based near Asiago. Seems to be some kind of databank – the amount they've got stored there is ludicrous.'

'What's in the file?'

Another pause.

'What were you expecting to be in it?'

'I don't know,' I said. 'I just know somebody who wants to get their hands on it, and he might be able to help us with the camera thing. Beyond that, I haven't a clue. Maybe it's something incriminating.' I thought about Claire. 'Maybe something sexual. I don't know.'

'What it *is*,' Graham told me carefully, 'is mostly gibberish. It's random characters, fucked up in weird places with breaking spaces and punctuation. Like someone riffle-shuffled a pack of cards, but did it with hundreds of sentences instead. It's pretty fucking meaningless.'

'Shit.'

He carried on, ignoring me.

'But it's more random than that. There are whole words in a few places; even a few incomplete sentences. It's more like the file's been corrupted somehow.'

He paused again.

'Jay, who do you know that wants this so badly?'

'It's not really important.'

'Well, I think it probably is.'

Suddenly I felt unsteady. 'Why? What is it, Gray?'

'Some of the sentences and words ... they're pretty fucked up.' He was speaking quietly. He sounded like he was tracing a printout with his finger. 'I got *bl##d* here in the middle – like blood, but with two hashes for *os*? And there's a bit about a knife, too – or a blade of some kind.'

I heard the sound of paper being turned over.

'And about a third of the way through, there's this.'

He spelled it out to me.

she screams se har(d thyt wf jjkpeopllr hurt h..r

'Jesus,' I said.

'Towards the end, there's something about someone called Long Tall Jack biting something. Biting real hard. Further in, there's something about him being the pins and knives man.'

'Sounds like some kind of horror novel.'

'It's worse than that,' Graham told me. I heard him move the paper away. 'I got a really bad feeling about this, Jay. The text's all corrupted and messed up, but it still makes a weird kind of sense to me. I can't describe it; you'd have to see it for yourself. It's fucking bizarre. Even though it's mostly rubbish, I can kind of see stuff in it. Bad stuff.'

He sounded frightened.

'What kind of bad stuff?'

'Look, I said. I don't know how to describe it. It's not when I read bits of it through, line for line – I mean, I do that, and it's just random. It's more when I just look at the whole page and take it in all at once. Like the words form a bad shape on the page that I don't want to see. Except they don't. I don't know. I just think that . . . this is something bad.'

What I heard in his voice was quiet panic.

'Calm down,' I said.

He wasn't interested.

'I don't want this on my fucking computer. I don't want it on my desk. I don't want it in my life. Listen to me, Jay. I wouldn't say it if I didn't think it was true. This is something bad.'

'Can you find out who the server belongs to?'

'Fucking hell, I don't want to.'

I pressed the point.

'Yeah, but can you?'

Silence again.

'Please, Gray.'

'I don't owe you this much,' he said. Suddenly, it was as though he'd been reading my mind. 'You know that? I do *not* fucking owe you this anymore. If I can do it quietly, then I will. But the second the trace turns round on me, I'm cutting it dead. You're asking too much, Jay. Just like you always do. And I'm not exposing Helen to your kind of freaks. I won't do it.'

'Okay, okay.'

'I won't do it.'

'Okay.'

'Fuck your okays. It's *not* okay.'

'Well ... thanks for whatever you can do.'

A pause.

'Yeah, whatever.' He sighed. 'I'm sorry.'

'Fuck it.'

'Yeah, but I am sorry. I'm sorry I lost my temper.' But not for what I said. 'There's something else, though: something you need to hear but probably won't want to.'

'What? Just tell me.'

'There's a sentence near to the beginning. Well – it's not a sentence; it's just three words on their own, and I guess they don't mean anything. But you need to know what it says regardless. Just in case.'

'What does it say?'

The silence was all his this time, and I felt angry.

'What does it fucking say, Graham?'

'Fuck, man. It says: "pale blue blouse." '

Another silence, then.

One in which my brain did nothing at all. Not one thing.

I nodded to myself, and then he repeated it, sounding sad and frightened.

'It says: "pale blue blouse." '

CHAPTER SEVEN

When people look back on their lives, they have a tendency to stick pins in at key points along the line: little coloured flags that point out the crucial moments. Every moment is crucial, of course – if you remove any single instant, your future falls away from your past – but I'm talking about the moments we choose to view as different. If you do see your life as a line, with points plotted along its course, then it's far from a straight one, and the truly critical moments are those where the line bends sharply off to one side, continuing at some weird new angle. We mark these points down and remember them, and when we question our current trajectories, it's these points that we use to explain them. Tapping the board and saying: *I'm going this way because of this*.

The taxi threaded its way uptown, easing along amidst the rest of the traffic. I still had Walter Hughes' business card between my fingers, and I was turning it over absent-mindedly. The slightly raised eagle crest insignia had worn a rough smoothness to the end of my index finger.

Cause and effect:

I was going to see Walter Hughes because Amy had vanished.

And Amy had vanished because...

Well.

Everything about the direction I was heading in was as a result of one moment in time, four and a half years before. I didn't even know Amy back then. The event in question was one that happened to her, not me, but it sent her line skittling off to one side, like a plane with one engine shot out. She crashed into me, and – for a while – we both enjoyed the freefall, finding it increasingly easy to pretend that we weren't crashing, just flying in an unusual direction. As we drifted apart, it became obvious that the earth was rushing up to meet us both, but by then it was too late to touch hands again. She was a little ahead of me, but it was still obvious that I was going to hit the same ground that she was, and just as hard. Too late to touch hands; too late to change course and pull each other out of this nosedive. Just too damn, fucking late.

There was a time when I could have pointed us up again. I know there was.

The cabbie coughed.

'Circle round from the north side?'

'Whatever.'

He hung a left. I watched the people on the corner as we swung past and then hit the lights a second too late. People were just going about their business, hurrying along. Behind them, in the window of a coffee shop, a businessman was mopping his mouth with a napkin, obscured by streaks of sunlight.

Sometimes, when you look at things just right, you see the world for what it is. Cars look like motorised toys, and human beings look like animals in suits, because that's all they are.

Across from the businessman, a woman was sipping from a delicate cup, and she looked as fragile and breakable as the glass between us. It was as though I could feel her heart beating and her pulse was as weak as china.

The lights changed to green and the taxi lurched off. Heading up onto the north loop out of the city centre, towards where Walter Hughes was going to provide me with some answers about the text that Graham had found, whether he wanted to or not.

'Oh yeah?'

Suddenly, Amy was resting on one elbow. She didn't so much climb on top of me as just slide over, using her right hand to hold up her breasts from the side and rest them on my chest as she moved above me. I felt their soft, pleasant weight. Her leg slid over, and she was suddenly on top of me, pressed down tight. Her face came down to mine with a smile, and she stared at me, right in the eyes, so close that it fucked with my vision.

'Is that what you'd say?'

My breath caught slightly, and I was suddenly unable to speak. I could feel myself growing hard.

'Jesus.' I touched her back carefully, as though it might shock me. 'What did I do?'

She grinned, and then kissed my neck gently.

'What makes you think you have to have done anything?'

'I just ... probably ... don't deserve this.'

She was making her way down my body, kissing as she went. Her breasts brushed against my stomach, then over my cock, then lower. Finally, I felt the pressure of them resting on my thighs. Her breath on the end of my cock.

'God.'

She took it in her hand and her mouth moved down over the tip: warm and wet. Her hair softly cascaded over the tops of my thighs.

'Mmmm. That feels good.'

'Tastes good,' she said, and then put her whole mouth around it. Her tongue slid over my cock as she moved her head slowly up and down. Her free hand flicked her hair over to one side of her head, out of the way. I leaned my head back and closed my eyes.

'You like that?' she asked after a minute.

'You know I like that.'

'Good. I like doing things that you like. Now.' She moved back up my body, one arm leaning on the bed beside me while the other reached down between her legs and held me. 'Let's do something that we both like.'

She moved my cock to the entrance of her vagina and settled down slowly onto it. She was slightly too dry. I rubbed my hands gently up and down her back, kissed her throat.

'Go slowly,' she told me, 'to begin with.'

We started to make love, moving ever so carefully at first: kissing each other almost casually. I traced my fingertips along her side, over her buttocks, back up to touch her face. We smiled at each other. As she grew wetter, we sped up a little. The sex became more aggressive; my touch, slightly harder. The kisses got deeper and more intense. I lifted up my hips to meet her; she sat up slightly and leaned against the wall behind my head, bracing herself; I brought my hands round to touch her breasts, and then lifted my head up to kiss them. The pitch of her breathing changed as I licked slowly around her nipples.

I sat right up. She pushed away from the wall and put her arms round me, kissing me, rocking slowly to a stand-still until she was just sitting astride me, on me. The kiss broke apart into an exchange of hot breath. I reached up and brushed a strand of sweaty hair away from her forehead. Hooked it back behind her ears.

'Swap,' Amy said, staring into my eyes.

'Okay.'

She slid carefully off and lay down on her back beside me. I rolled over as soon as I could, not wanting to get lost in a tangle of legs, and then clambered onto her as she spread her legs wide for me. I sucked her nipples for a little while, allowing the head of my cock to rest just inside her. The insides of her thighs gripped me, almost tried to pull me in. I moved from one nipple to the other. She ran her fingers through my hair.

I slid into her, moving up to kiss her throat, and she clenched up underneath me, crying out, holding on to my back with tight little hands. We started to rock back and forth. I kissed at her jawline. She rested her calves over the backs of my own.

We made love like this for a while, gradually relaxing into a more circular motion, bringing our groins into pleasurably bruising contact with every thrust. I reached underneath her and pulled her tight against me while her hands explored my back. I moved myself higher up the bed a little to bring the shaft of my cock hard against her. Used my right hand to gently touch her face, and told her that I loved her.

I was ready to come, but holding back until she was there with me. It didn't seem like it would take long: we hit a perfect rhythm, where every thrust was bringing her closer to the edge. She'd tensed up a little more, and her quiet cries were growing more eager. This was getting serious.

And then suddenly, it really was. She stiffened up against me in a way that felt entirely wrong: frozen in a fighting position.

Her hands started patting my back in panic.

'Oh, stop, stop. Please can we stop? I want to stop.'

I stopped immediately. My body objected strongly.

'Okay,' I said. 'It's okay.'

'No, no. Please can we stop? Please? I'm sorry. I really need for us to stop.'

She was starting to cry.

'Okay,' I said. 'We have stopped. Come on. Shhh.'

I slid out of her as carefully as I could and clambered back to my side of the bed, rubbing sweat off my face and then adjusting my cock. Her hands went to her face and her body started shaking. She had rolled over on her side, facing away from me. Her naked back was shuddering gently.

I felt strange: still turned on; frustrated; hurt; apologetic.

The only thing I could really do was move closer to her and put my arm around her. She was shaking uncontrollably. I pressed up against her back and tried to hold her, but it was difficult to find somewhere non-sexual to place my hand, and I had to lean back from her slightly to keep my cock away.

I said, 'Shhh. It's okay.'

I said, 'It's okay. Shhh.'

She was gripping my hand ever so tightly. It was the only indication I had that she didn't want me to leave her alone.

I kissed the back of her shoulder gently and told her it was okay.

After a while, she stopped shaking and I could just hear her crying quietly. I gave her body a quick hug. She clenched my hand a little harder in a couple of communicative pulses.

'I'm sorry,' she said.

'Here – blow your nose.' I untangled myself from her and pulled a few sheets of paper off the toilet roll we kept by the bed. She rolled onto her back and took it from me. 'And you've got nothing to be sorry about.'

'Yes, I have. I'm sorry.'

'Don't be stupid.'

She blew her nose loudly in reply.

I said, 'Well in that case: I'm sorry, too.'

She dabbed at her nose. 'Why are you sorry?'

'Because I did something wrong.'

'Can I have some more toilet paper? Thanks.' She blew her nose again. 'You didn't do anything wrong.'

'I must have done something wrong.'

'It's not anything that you did. Don't say that.'

'All right, then, it's not my fault. But I still did something.'

'You didn't. Please don't say that. I don't know why it happened.'

She started crying again, and hit her leg in frustration.

'Don't,' I said.

'It hasn't happened for so long.'

'No.'

'I thought I was getting better.'

It was dumb, but it felt like I needed to say it a thousand times. 'I'm sorry.'

'It *wasn't you*!' When she realised how angry she sounded, she started crying even harder. 'Honestly.'

I just couldn't help saying it, and so instead I didn't say anything.

I had far too many hormones whizzing around my body, looking for somewhere to land, and I didn't trust myself not to get angry. My cock was still hard and I'd been only seconds away from coming; it was as though I'd been slapped awake. I needed time to adjust, but I could tell that it wasn't going to work. The world was receding to the size of a pinhead: to a point where nothing mattered to me anymore; where all I could feel was this awkward, badly arranged sensation of self-hatred, anger and disgust. I could have sat staring into space for hours. I could have pounded myself until I just couldn't anymore.

And that's the awful thing: it should have been about Amy and once upon a time it was. *It doesn't matter; it's okay; here – look – smile! See – that's better.* I'd do everything I could to pick her back up, for no other reason than that I loved her and so that's what you do. You take it on the chin and stay standing, because someone needs to. And nobody had ever hurt me, so what right did I have to feel affronted or damaged by what happened? And that's why, for such a long time, I was understanding and sympathetic when something this catastrophic happened.

But it wasn't like that anymore.

And looking back, I don't know how to feel about how I behaved. It's easy to judge yourself by Hollywood standards, where a couple of actions dictate your hat colour, but I suppose that life's not like that. I'd like to think that I was understanding and good ten times out of ten but I wasn't, mainly because on at least a few occasions it became about me too. There were a couple of times – like this one – when I was too self-centred to do anything for Amy. She had to sit there, propped up on the bed beside me, crying, and handle it all herself.

I hate myself for that. Fair or unfair, I hate myself so badly I wish that cold, hurt, staring version of me could just be dead.

I want to have always been good, not just average and normal. Not just a sometimes-man, like everyone else would have been.

Perhaps that's the nature of trauma: more like a disease than an actual injury. It eats away at you inside, right in your heart, and anyone you let in there is bound to pick it up themselves eventually. It's unavoidable. You drop a big enough rock into a lake and it doesn't matter how wide it is: eventually the banks that hold all that water will feel the vibration as well. And start to erode.

Four years ago. You need to sort yourself out.

I never did say that to her, of course – I'm not that bad a man – but I think she probably heard it from me all the same. She probably couldn't help but hear it in the silence between us, which was deafeningly loud. I wish I'd been selfless enough to say something to break that silence and hide that thought every time she could hear it. But I wasn't. Instead, sometimes, it ended up like this: both of us sitting there, crying for our own reasons, so far apart in so many ways that we might as well have been in different rooms.

There are only two roads in and out of Uptown, but probably a hundred or more ways to actually get there. It's a strange place. The place was founded about fifty years or so ago, in the northern part of the city, at a time when it was fashionable for offices to let their employees have access to the open space on the roofs of their buildings. The more prestigious companies even started to have their tops turfed and professionally landscaped: sculpted bushes and stereotypically pretty flowers were planted, and the grass was maintained at a very false, but undeniably vibrant, shade of green. You could take your sandwiches up top during your lunch break and catch some sun – and it was one of the few remaining areas of the city where you were actually allowed to smoke. I mean, if you wanted, you could even flick the butts over the edge of the building when you were done. Chances are there'd be nobody important underneath when they touched down.

It was only a matter of time before people had the bright idea of linking up the rooftops. The main points were already there, and it was just a matter of smoothing over the spaces in between. Building firms were drafted in to rig up supporting structures between the buildings, and then enormous, street-spanning platforms were constructed to connect the roofs. These, too, were turfed and tended. The council, unsure exactly how to deal with this, became guilty of letting all this grass grow under their feet, and by the time anybody started to object at the increasingly dark street-level, planning permission had been granted via backhanders to local politicians – which was normal – and large sections in the north of the city were already under cover. The companies with the most money bought roof space on the smaller buildings, extending their empire upside and building elaborate floral logo designs to catch the eye of captive audiences in passing planes. Then the whole thing began to really take off.

Houses. Shops. Whole mini-communities sprang up. Vice-presidents no longer went home for the night, but travelled two floors up and left a bit. Access was immediately restricted, with people once again being forced to smoke secretly in the toilets and grumble about how dark it was outside. They still flicked their butts out of the window, of course, but there were fewer people for them to land on now, and the ones who were still there were even less important than before. And getting paler by the day.

After a while, the council decided that enough was enough. It declared the green land between the rooftops as public property, looped the existing ring road up a few hundred feet, and then negotiated with the various ruling companies to create an effective network of streets and avenues, replete with sponsored signs and traffic police. Begrudgingly, they agreed, and Uptown was born. It became a place for the ridiculously rich to live, and the depressingly fashionable to window-shop and be seen. Underneath the surface – as always – it was a different story.

At the street-level, things were winding down. The air was becoming stuffy and unbreathable. The smaller businesses were either closing down through lack of traffic, or being driven out by the expansion of larger businesses. Disused buildings were boarded up, or cemented into solid pillars. These days, most of Downtown is superficially abandoned – with only the occasional through road, converted into a sealed, amber-lit tunnel, leading to ground-floor access for the richer companies. The rest of it is bricked up and forgotten by the mainstream. Generally, employees access the companies from the roof down. It's safer.

It's the same as it's always been. The companies innovate and rebuild, restructuring a thousand lives along the way, and you're still left with basically the same as you started with. In this case, everything was just a few hundred feet higher up. There's talk of renovating the underside and clearing away the debris – turning it back into a proper place to live and work – but there's always talk. Deep down everybody knows that it's never going to happen. Because we need somewhere dark underneath it all for the bad things to be swept.

Just a quick point: everything that happens here is happening for a reason.

It's always like that, of course, but in this case there's something special going on: everything is happening because of just one thing. If you take every event I tell you about apart, you'll find genetic code leading all the way back to this single common ancestor. Chop out that ancestor, and you're talking blank pages. Empty from top to the bottom, from first to last.

And – like I said – what happened had nothing to do with me. Weird the way things turn out, isn't it? What happened is a story.

Amy knew it off by heart, and sometimes – when I asked her nicely enough – she'd tell me. Why did I ask? Because once upon a time, as the stories say, I thought that each time she told the story she might unlearn it a little. It wasn't something you really needed to remember, and I thought it might help her to forget. But that's not what ended up happening.

Don't bother sitting comfortably, because I never did.

A girl was at a student party, Amy would tell me. This girl had gone there with her best friend, and it had been a spur-of-the-moment, last minute decision to go: she was still debating it on the way there, in fact, as they leap-frogged from their shared house to the off-licence to the party. Her friend really wanted to go and so she'd persuaded the girl that it would be good for her to go, too. The girl figured she wasn't going to know many people there, and as it turned out she was right, but she was chatty and pretty, and things usually worked out okay. It was a student party, after all: you just need to smile and drink, and then after a while a friend is anybody who's in the same room as you.

This girl lost her friend at one point, but she thought *fuck it*. She'd kind of expected it, anyway – her friend had only wanted to come because of some boy, and so in a way her disappearance was excellent, fanfare, mission accomplished. The girl figured she'd get monumentally drunk to celebrate, and so set about demolishing wine at an astonishing rate. She talked shit to people; they talked shit back. And at one point, she met this boy.

His name was Jack, and she fancied him from the moment she set eyes on him. It was reasonably obvious that the feeling was mutual and they got talking, but – although he was flirting with her quite openly – she sensed that he was also holding back a little. The reason became obvious when she met the people he'd come with: four male friends ... and his girlfriend. *Foiled again*, she thought, and so drank more wine. But she sat with them for a while anyway, and seemed to get on with them all. The male friends seemed all right, although it was clear that they knew what was going on. The girlfriend seemed oblivious and dull. Perhaps she was used to Jack, or simply not very bright.

They chatted for a while, and then Jack told her that they were all going back to a shared flat in their halls of residence, and would she like to come? They were going to drink and hang out: maybe play some guitar, listen to some CDs, and it would be fun, so how about it? The girl was drunk by then, and so she said yes. Like a good little girl, she even managed to find her friend, break her off her conquest's face and tell her where she was going.

It was a quarter of an hour walk through the cold to get there. Jack walked with her, deliberately holding back way behind his girlfriend so that they were out of sight as they walked. He reached around and put his hand on her ass as they walked, giving it a squeeze. She looked at him and smiled. She wasn't sure why, but she was drunk and she wanted him, so she gave him that smile and swigged from the wine bottle she was carrying. They arrived at half-past ten.

Oh shit, said Jack as the group settled down in the lounge, *we forgot to get booze. Who's out?*

His girlfriend said, *I need some*, and – after sharing a glance with Jack – one of the other guys said he needed some too.

It's only just around the corner, this other guy continued. *Why don't we both go?*

So Jack's girlfriend and this guy left the flat on a last-minute booze run. A few other people wanted stuff as well, but had been keeping quiet, and so the pair of them went away with quite a list. As the front door closed, someone flicked on a Pulp CD and everybody collapsed into armchairs and sofas. Except for Jack and the girl.

Come on, he said, *I want to show you something.*

Her heart was beating quickly with the excitement. Jack led her down the hall to his bedroom, and they fucked quickly and gracelessly on his bed. *Here*. She just pulled her knickers to one side as he unzipped himself and climbed on top of her. It was dictionary-definition bad sex, but she'd never wanted it so much in her life; he came in under a minute, with her nowhere near, but it didn't even matter. *Thanks*, she told him afterwards, as he wiped his wet, reddened cock on tissue paper and grinned at her. *I needed that.*

They returned to the living room to knowing smirks, a few minutes ahead of the returning booze party. And then it all started to go wrong.

What happened was – after a while – Jack and his girlfriend went off to bed and left the girl with his friends, who were yawning and stretching and talking about heading off to bed. Despite herself, the girl was annoyed. She'd had a lot more to drink in the meantime and wasn't necessarily thinking straight, but she felt rejected, frustrated and angry. She felt used. Hurt, even. The kind of resentful feeling that's more directed at yourself than anyone else – *you're an idiot* – but when you're drunk you attach it to others in the same way you grab their shoulder to stop yourself falling over.

All in all, the evening felt like a bad day at work: nothing much accomplished, but she didn't want to leave, head home and go to bed, because that felt like defeat. Here everyone was, though: a few of them asleep already; others collecting their coats. It was depressing.

So when this quiet boy – who she'd barely even spoken to all evening – wandered over and told her uncertainly that he had some wine upstairs in his room, and would she like to come up if she wasn't ready to go home yet?, she thought about it for all of a second, and then said *yes, of course, I'd love to*. She thought, did you read my mind? He was big and cumbersome: average-looking. She didn't fancy him in the slightest, but from his virtual silence he was obviously an outsider in the group, and at that moment she hated Jack's group for using her and smirking and generally being bastards.

She said, *Let's go.*

At that point in the story, there was always a break: a fracture. The way Amy always told it, the girl and the boy sat and drank wine in his room, and talked, and then at one point the boy told her that she was going to have sex with him. The girl laughed and said *no, I'm not*, and the boy said *actually: yes, you are*. The girl hadn't even been thinking along those lines up until that point. According to Amy she experienced something dropping away inside herself. She reframed everything that had happened. Mentally, she unpicked the seams of their conversation, pulled away the cloth and for the first time saw his intent for what it was.

She was scared – but not properly. It was too soon to be properly scared and, after all, this wasn't going to happen.

No, she said more definitely, standing up. *I'm really, really not.*

The boy looked back at her. *Yes*, he told her again. *You really are.*

Then he stood up and took hold of her arm. She tried to shake off his hand, but she couldn't even move him. He was half as big as her again, and for the first time she started to appreciate what that fact meant.

Properly scared now: *You're hurting me.*

It'll be nice, he said. *You'll see.*

Afterwards, a sympathetic policewoman would tell this girl that the decision as to whether or not to press charges was entirely hers, but that she needed to be aware of certain things. The first was that both she and this boy had been drunk, and she'd gone back to his flat voluntarily in the early hours of the morning with the intention of getting more drunk. She didn't know this boy, but she'd already had consensual sex with one of his friends earlier on that evening, and she hadn't known him either.

We'd need to question the first boy, she said. *What was his name?*

She said it like that – *the first boy* – as though the two encounters were similar.

Jack, the girl said. *I don't know his surname.*

Instead, she gave the address; the policewoman made a note of it.

We'd need to question Jack. We'd also need to take samples from him to match against the semen we've taken from you.

Without much in the way of emotion, the policewoman

told the girl that there was very little chance of Jack's girlfriend not finding out. She said they'd have to interview everybody who'd been at the party, including the girlfriend. In fact, if they took the boy to court, his lawyer would probably explain to everyone present how the girl had had sex with an attached stranger only two hours earlier. He'd go into detail.

If you press charges, she is going to find out.

The policewoman had a wedding ring on, but she was sympathetic anyway.

It won't help matters that you didn't fight back, she said a minute or two later. *I'm not judging you because of that, but other people will. They'll take it as evidence that you didn't want to fight back.*

The girl started crying again.

I did want to fight back. She wanted to hit herself. *I was just scared.*

The policewoman remained implacable.

I'm not judging you.

'And it bothers me that the girl didn't fight back,' Amy told me once. She wasn't looking at me: she was just staring into the distance between her toes, moving them slightly beneath the duvet. We always had these conversations in the middle of the night, with an emergency lamp flicked on to wipe away the nightmares.

She said, 'I think she should have done, maybe.'

'I don't think she should.'

'You don't?'

'No.'

What an impossible question. I just said what I thought might help.

'I think maybe she should have, though.' Amy frowned, intent on her main character and her motivations. 'It could all have turned out very differently. Because she didn't fight at all. Maybe she could have got away if she did.'

'You could have got hurt more than you did.'

Amy ignored the slip. To be honest, there were times when I didn't really need to be there.

'I mean, she *did* tell him no. She told him all the way through: No!'

'Exactly.'

'But she didn't fight him.'

I said, 'She did the right thing.'

Amy actually looked at me then. Generally, she'd have stopped crying by now, and this occasion was no different.

'Do you think so?'

'Absolutely.' I put my arm around her shoulders. Her body felt soft and fragile. 'He was a big guy, wasn't he? He could have hurt her very badly.'

She leaned against me.

'This girl,' I repeated, 'she did the right thing.'

Amy told me that the girl thought long and hard, but in the end she decided not to press charges.

The End.

Except not.

Like all good storytellers, she knew the boy's name; I asked her, and she told me. And like a good background researcher, I went looking. Do you know how to go looking for somebody? Neither did I back than. It certainly didn't work out the way it does in the movies, because what I hit – time and time again – was this one fact: the University Halls of Residence were bound by the Data Protection Act. They wouldn't even confirm whether the boy had ever lived there, never mind where he might have gone when he left.

Amy never knew I went looking. I could never have let her know either, because it would have felt like a betrayal: like I was hijacking her tragedy and trying to turn it into some drama of my own. People need to have ownership over the stories in their past, and it's wrong to take them and try to make them yours. You don't have that right. But I did it anyway. And then, with nothing to show for it but a growing sense of my own inadequacy, I stopped.

I threw that sense of inadequacy away, aware that it was an aimless, unfocused thing I shouldn't keep. Amy did her best to forget, too. I sometimes wondered how she dealt with it; on one occasion I asked her, and this is what she told me:

I imagine I have a black box, she said. *Except it's big, so I guess it's more like a chest or a trunk. I keep it in an attic. It's a room I can see very, very clearly, although I don't know where I get the image from. Maybe a film; I don't know. It's this wide attic room, with a slanted roof. There's a skylight in the middle which lets in moonlight, and the only furniture is this black box. Whenever anything bad happens to me, I go up into the attic, open the lid and put whatever it is inside the box. Then I shut the box and forget about it.*

She said that she'd been doing this ever since she was a child, and that the story of what happened to the girl at the party was just one more thing to pile inside. After a while, she hoped, she wouldn't know the story off by heart anymore. After a while longer, she wouldn't know it at all.

And for some time it seemed to be working. When we first met, it was quite common for the narratives of her dreams and the story to dovetail together, and it wasn't the kind of story that you slept soundly through. I imagined her mind drifting upstairs to this imaginary attic and opening this imaginary trunk: the story would leap out at her and she'd wake herself up screaming. In the middle of the night, there's no such thing as just a story. There's no past tense. No third-person.

But there was probably a period of about a year when she stopped having nightmares altogether. The sex became easier:

more relaxed. We hardly even thought about it. But it never went away entirely, and when it started to come back again I wasn't as young as I used to be: not as able or willing to help. I don't even want to think about some of the things I didn't do, or some of the right words I didn't say.

An example. You have a hundred dreams about people dying in your life, but you only remember the one where you woke up to the news that your mother died during the night. Some people base their whole world-view on it. Well, it's the same with relationships. I don't remember the thousand and one good nights I had with Amy, only the handful of bad that seem to define everything about us. That's certainly how it was in the last few months, anyway, when we could barely speak to each other and all she did was surf black websites trying to understand what had happened. Trying to read between the lines.

The worst thing is that she seemed happier before she disappeared: it was a mystery to me back then, but I understand it now. She had her plan. Her investigation.

She seemed happier, and so I never saw it coming.

CHAPTER EIGHT

The cab took me to Uptown by the north loop. Once through the toll booth (I had to pay the five pounds access fee), it took about five minutes to reach the address on the business card, which turned out to be nominally above Peace of Mind Insurance: one of our direct competitors. Life is full of these little twists, isn't it?

'Do you want me to wait?'

I told the cabbie that I didn't, and gave him slightly more money than the straight fare, which was slightly less than I had in my pocket. I peeled it off through the window, and he took it from me with a quick hand and drove away. He left me at the end of a long gravel drive leading up to a sprawling, two-storey mansion. Between me and the front door was a black metal gate with an intercom beside it. Above all of this was a video camera on a pole, like some kind of severed head on a pike.

I wandered over, my feet crunching across the wet gravel. It was very quiet here, and I guess I could understand the appeal – especially as the sky now seemed to have settled down to an over-reaching blue, smeared with still grey cloud. There was a slight breeze, but it was far from unpleasant. It was like being on a cliff-top.

I held down the red button for a full ten seconds, and then stepped back in time to see the video camera whirring around to focus on me. Nothing happened for a moment, and then the gate jerked into life. A bland voice crackled out of the intercom.

'Approach the house.'

I made my way up the drive. The gate jittered back across behind me like an old lady crossing the street, and buzzed in celebration when it finally re-established contact. The front door of the house had opened up, and a figure dressed in a black suit – incongruous in the mild sunshine – stepped out onto the spread of the porch and waited for me, his hands clasped almost protectively in front of his groin. I could see his half-bald head gleaming from here, and recognised him as the man with the gun from my house the night before.

'Mr Klein,' he said, shaking my hand when I reached him, and looking me over as though I was a series of targets for him to punch.

I returned both compliments. Mentally, I was striking him in the throat, kicking him on the inside of one knee, slamming a punch into his solar plexus.

'Nice to see you again,' I said.

'Mr Hughes will see you immediately.'

He beckoned me inside, and then followed after me, closing the door behind us. I found myself standing at the end of a hallway, which seemed very dark and baroque in comparison to the easy freshness of the outside world. The air smelled of old wood and furniture polish. A grandfather clock was standing to attention halfway along, and there was no reason to believe it was anything other than properly real. Beyond that, there were a handful of ornate doors off to either side, and then red carpeted steps leading up to a windowed half-landing above, where a table was supporting some delicately arranged flowers in a crystal vase. I don't think they were real. Between the front door and the stairs, there were various pictures hanging on the walls, and a small golden chandelier was suspended above.

The house wasn't as big as it looked from the outside, which was probably a good thing. I had the other two men from last night pegged down as hired help – probably techies from Hughes' company, brought in to search for the Schio file without even knowing, really, what they were looking for. I didn't think they'd be here right now, and the relatively small size of the house made me think the only two people I needed to worry about were Hughes and his main body-guard-cum-butler.

And, of course, his gun. Nowhere – as yet – in evidence.

'This way.'

I followed him down the corridor to the last room on the right. On the way, I glanced at some of the pictures on the walls. They were strange to say the least: not so much pictures as some weird form of conceptual art. Each large frame surrounded an almost entirely empty canvas containing – pinned at the centre – a thin strip of paper. On each of these strips, someone had jotted a sentence down in a looping blue freehand. In fact, it was such an untidy scrawl that I couldn't even make out the words as we went past: just the impression that a busy hand had been at work.

As far as I could tell, all the pictures on the wall were like that.

Sentences: framed and hung.

'In here, please.'

Well, this was nice: the study, undeniably, was an elegant room, furnished entirely in browns, dark purples and greens, and was edged by several towering bookcases, which, with the shelves crammed from one side to the other, gave the room an impression of pleasing closeness. Of course, in this day and age, there was no guarantee that Hughes had collected the titles himself, but I was actually willing to bet that he had. The only other items in the room were two massive, swollen-hard leather couches, and a flat wooden table, which had a delicate-looking antiquated map pressed like a butterfly beneath the glass surface. On top of this there was a silver platter, with tumblers huddling around a crystal decanter full of what appeared to be whisky or brandy. Beyond, a dozen small windows looked out over a side lawn, and in what little wall space remained there were more of the odd pictures from the hallway. Except these ones were larger – the smallest was A5 – and they seemed to contain a lot more than just one sentence.

'Mr Hughes will be with you in a moment.'

The bodyguard left.

While I was waiting for Mr Hughes to arrive, I wandered over to have a closer look at one of the pictures.

I was standing outside the Colosseum in Rome, and it had taken me a while to find. It's not a small thing, of course, and there were occasional streetmaps posted on signs that made it seem easy: a snail shell of rock, curled under the heart of the city like trapped wind. How could you miss it? But I'd wandered the tall streets for what felt like hours without success, and then finally succumbed to the heat, unfolding a curl of Euros to buy a ham cheese panini and a can of Coke. The can had looked out of place: as red as sunburn against the drained, dirty tones of the buildings. Those two things together cost the equivalent of eight pounds. I mean, fuck this city.

Dull traffic lights blinked yes and no as I walked, attempting to regulate the cars and mopeds whooshing past. My rucksack was stuck to my back with sweat, and I ate and drank as I wandered, my head held down over the backpacker's shuffle. Finally, after an age of walking, the city had unfolded itself like a flower and I'd seen it.

It wasn't as big as I'd expected. It seemed tall and wide – as though it was something tired that had lain down there rather than been built – but still: not as big as you'd think. For one thing, only half of it was actually complete, with white plaster patches giving only a general illusion of the original form. At the base, shops had been structured into its circumference. There was a McDonald's, a Disney and a few others I didn't recognise. They seemed to detract from the size and scale of it. Just another shopping centre. A man in a yellow boiler suit was trawling the sunny square in front of it, picking up litter with electronic clippers.

I watched from above, where the Colosseum seemed very still, like a painting, or maybe a mountain in the distance. There were small people moving around it: tubby tourists in garish outfits, wearing cameras like bulky black medallions; stick-thin, burnt-brown locals swinging around on high-stepping pedal-bikes; couples, merging at the arm; old men, their walnut-textured skin cooking slowly in the sun. The sounds all reached me late, and seemed to come from nowhere: noises abstracted from their source. Behind me, the nasal buzz of a scooter was more located and real.

I tapped my way down the steps and crossed the square.

Closer to, the Colosseum became physically more impressive, but also seemed more brow-beaten and weathered. The shops looked even more out of place, like stalls set up around a beached, dying whale, but they had become integral to its structure. Red and purple graffiti tags looped across the remaining stone of the surface. In fact, almost every spare inch, to a height of around seven feet, was filled with names and pictures. Above the graffiti, the Colosseum began properly: brown and crumbly as tilled soil. It looked like a breeze would damage it; as though a heavy wind might redistribute two thousand years of history as dust across the old city around it.

I paid the entrance fee, peeling off more notes from my thinning bundle, and was allowed through a clicking turnstile onto a stone walkway, overlooking the skeletal, overgrown remains of the Colosseum's guts. It was like looking into an old beehive, with most of the middle scooped out to reveal the layers of honeycombs inside: a husk of a place. A great ellipse of stone terraces curled around the central floor of the arena, which had been stripped away over time to uncover underground cells, tunnels and passageways. Grass was stuttering out of the rock. Nature seemed to be reclaiming the place, even as it was being branded, franchised and hollowed out: robbed of its original meaning even as it was traded on. And all the time, the sun was pressing down hard upon it, like a hot amber palm. Tourists were taking whirring, flashing snapshots. There was the trudge of feet, and the sucking, scratching sound of bored straws exploring the bottom of cardboard cartons.

Half the people in the world: if you told them to take a pilgrimage to a public toilet, they would – cameras and fat fucking children and all. The other half would go and daub graffiti on it when they thought nobody was looking. And all of them would imagine it meant something.

I found a place by the barrier and slid my backpack off with a mixture of relief and revulsion. The air – although warm – instantly chilled the back of my T-shirt, which had been stained beige by a mixture of sweat and dust. At least I was clean. The night before, I'd bedded down at a campsite two bus journeys out of the city centre, and I'd managed to get a shower and tidy that morning. But I'd last washed a T-shirt a few weeks ago, if you could call that a wash: standing at a dirty outdoor sink, squinting in the sun, mashing it up in grey, foamy water.

Now, uncaring of my appearance, I unclipped the side pocket of the backpack and drew out my notebook. The stone barrier, although rough on my elbows, provided a good place to lean as I took the top off the pen, opened the notepad at the scribble page and tested the nib with a few blue curls of ink. It was working fine. I flipped back to the first free page in the pad.

And then I looked up at the Colosseum – which had once held fifty thousand Romans, screaming for blood – and I started to write.

'Impressive piece, isn't it?'

I turned away from the picture to see Walter Hughes, moving into the room. Once again, I was surprised by how easily he got around for such an old man – carrying his cane with a swing, like some kind of dapper toff, but not really requiring it. His bodyguard followed him in, closing the door behind. I wondered if he'd gone to a school where they taught you to do that. Not really.

Hughes poured himself a brandy, or whatever the fuck it was.

'In fact, it's one of my favourites. Would you like a drink?'

'No,' I said, feeling confused. 'What the hell is that?'

I looked at the writing again. When I didn't try to take in the words, it just seemed like a sheet of paper with some text scrawled upon it. But the moment my eye caught a sentence and started to follow it, my head was filled with images of the Colosseum. The heat on my skin and the sweat on my back. Hughes moved over beside me, appraising the picture. I forced myself to look at him instead, but he remained focused on the writing.

'I particularly like this bit, here.' He gestured with his drinks hand; the brandy rocked in the glass. 'The attention to detail.'

I looked where he was pointing, and could immediately see a fuzzy spray of red graffiti over rough brown rock. The right-hand side of my face felt warm, and I could hear somebody saying something in Italian behind me.

Hughes' voice pulled me back into the study.

131

'The graffiti adds such an unexpected element, don't you think? There's contrast between the old building and the new shops – obviously – and then somewhere in-between you have this graffiti. This vandalism of both, with the youth of the city claiming the space as their own. I find it poetic.'

I didn't say anything; I just looked at him. He was one of those men who looked thoughtful by looking blank.

After a second, he turned to me and smiled.

'You've never seen anything like this before, I take it?'

I shook my head.

'What is it?'

'Come and sit down.'

He gestured over to the seats in the centre of the room, and we moved across. Before I could sit down, however, he picked up a towel from the side of the nearest chair, unfolded it and laid it out over my seat.

'There.'

'Thanks,' I said. I'd never realised that my ass was potentially that damaging.

'You're sure you won't have a drink?'

'No. Thanks anyway.'

I glanced back over at the picture, almost nervously, and saw Hughes smile, his face creasing quickly from one position to the other.

'You're stunned, aren't you? Obviously, you are. It happened to me the first time I encountered his work. I have been addicted ever since.'

Summing things up to perfection for once, I said:

'I don't understand what just happened.'

'Neither do I,' Hughes admitted, 'in that I can't explain it. All I know of the artist in question is that he is a man of genuine talent, which isn't anything you don't now know for yourself. I was first exposed to his work some time ago – by chance – and I've spent the intervening years collecting all I can find.'

I shook my head, still feeling strange.

'It was like I was there.'

It had been, too. The words had seemed to turn into sights, sounds and smells as they passed through my eyes. My mind had flipped them over, moulding them into what had felt like an actual experience. I could still feel the sun on my face, and hear the sounds of the city; the sensations were fading, but my skin was still tingling.

'It's incredible, isn't it?' Hughes said. 'They say a picture paints a thousand words, but in this young man's case, his words paint a thousand pictures. And he is young, from what I can gather.'

He swirled the brandy around in his glass thoughtfully, and then looked back up at me.

'You must excuse me. My passion for art – I will speak for hours if people let me. And of course—' he glanced at his bodyguard, who had positioned himself by the door, '— people tend to. What brings you here, Mr Klein? What is it that you imagine we can do for each other? Interest me quickly, or I might talk about art again.'

I said, 'I might have what you are looking for.'

He paused, and then took a sip of brandy.

'I see.' The glass went around once between his fingers. He studied it, and then frowned. 'You didn't think that last night, though, did you?'

'I didn't have it then. But I think I may have it now. It depends.'

He still wasn't looking at me.

'What does it depend on? Whether I let you out of this room alive?'

He glanced up at his bodyguard, who eased himself away from the wall, his eyes fixed on me. Startled by the speed in which the encounter had flipped, I still managed to stand up pretty quickly, moving into the centre of the room to gather some space around me. All the training I'd done felt like nothing.

Pay attention.

The man circled me slightly, relaxed, and I took him in again, trying to strip away that intimidating glare – and the sheer fucking size of him – leaving only a bunch of areas I wanted to either hit or avoid.

But before we could do anything, Hughes held up a hand.

'This is such a nice room,' he said, peering at his glass intently. 'And I would hate to see anything get broken. Books dislodged – anything like that. Furniture overturned.' Finally, he looked up. 'So perhaps you should tell me what's on your mind.'

I didn't take my eyes off Hughes' bodyguard. He paid me the compliment in return.

'You killed Claire Warner, didn't you?'

'Yes.'

'Why?'

'Because she stole something from me.' Hughes sounded bored. 'It took us a while to find her, but we did in the end. And then she wouldn't tell me where she'd put it. You might recall: she was very wilful.'

I didn't say anything, but I remembered all right. *I can have any man I want.* That almost banal confidence had half-disguised the fact that she was a young girl, only just beginning to come to terms with the power she had over men.

'In truth,' he said, 'it was an accident. I don't think she actually believed we were going to hurt her until we did, and the surprise made her fight back.'

I glanced at the cut above the bodyguard's eye, and pictured Claire's slim, ringed hand punching him as she kicked loose and ran for her life.

Good for you.

He saw me looking and I smiled at him. If Claire could hit him then so could I. And I hit harder than Claire did. I hit hard enough to put people on their backs.

That was when he reached inside his neat black jacket and produced the pistol I'd seen last night.

He smiled back.

'She almost got away,' Hughes said, 'and – regrettably – she had to be shot. It was most unfortunate. But it had taken us such a long time to find her again that there was no way we were going to let her leave so easily.'

'I can imagine.'

Even to me, my voice sounded empty and beaten. What the fuck was I doing here? I'd had ideas about confronting Hughes, taking charge of the situation, but they'd been vague at best, and what had really driven me here – taxi aside – were thoughts of Amy, and the contents of the text that Hughes had been searching for. Pale blue blouse.

The same thoughts pushed the next thing out of my mouth before I'd had a chance to okay the words.

'It was a snuff text, wasn't it?' I said. Two and two clicked together in my mind, and I glanced up at the pictures on the walls. 'And it was by the man who wrote these things. It was a description of somebody dying.'

Suddenly, it made perfect sense. I remembered what Graham had told me:

It's more when I just look at the whole printout and take it in all at once. Like the words form a bad shape on the page that I don't want to see.

I felt myself growing blank.

Amy.

'That's how it was sold to me, yes.' Hughes sounded as bored as ever. 'However, I have no way of knowing whether it was genuine or not. In fact, I never even got the chance to read it before it was stolen from me by that whore.'

Pale. Blue. Blouse.

I looked back at the bodyguard – or through him. He was smiling but I didn't even see it properly. He was holding the gun badly, I noticed: pointing it half at the floor.

Maybe two and a half metres between us.

'And you're telling me now that you have this text?' Hughes said. 'If so, just produce it, and then you can be on your way.'

'I don't have it here.'

It felt like the words were falling out of me.

'Well, *where* do you have it? And what is it you imagine you want in exchange for it?'

Impatience, but also an air of concession – as though a trivial wish might be granted to save him the bother of redecorating the wall behind me. So this was the key moment. And what I should have said was: I want you to get me access to the cameras at the train station. I want you to tell me where I can find this artist. I want you to tell me where and how I can find the people who did whatever it was they did to Amy – if it even *was* Amy. This thing which may or may not have been genuine.

That's what I should have said.

But I was thinking: *she screamed se har(d thyt wf jjkpeopllr hurt h..r*

I was thinking: *Long Tall Jack, the pins and knives man.*

Biting something.

'Mr Klein?' Hughes said. 'What is it that you want for the safe return of my property?'

When you box, they teach you how to move. You don't actually take steps so much as glide from place to place, the idea being to lift your feet off the canvas only as much as you need to in order to move. Once you get used to it, it's quicker

– and it's also far more efficient. Many boxers use their opponent's foot movements as guides to what's about to be flung their way, the same way a dancer might. The less movement you make, and the quicker and smoother you do it, the more unpredictable the attack is when you send it out.

I'd practised this gliding step on the Scream every night for months, usually with a hard left jab to the head or abdomen. It had become instinctive; I didn't have to think. Hughes' bodyguard moved quicker than the Scream, and he managed to get the gun up to meet me, but my jab turned into a grab and I found myself with a two handed grip on the top of his wrist, pushing the gun away in a wheeling, straight-armed circle.

I head-butted him, but not well – a desperate thing, really – all the time moving my fingers around the gun. We began wrestling over it back and forth. Our arms swung, fighting for purchase, and I stumbled back a little, realising how strong the man was, and how I was going to die if I let go. I was terrified.

'Gentlemen.'

Hughes sounded bored and disinterested, even as my adrenalin kicked in and sent my heart skyward.

The bodyguard gritted his teeth as we fought. I felt like I was about to – and just like that, the resistance gave somewhere and the gun went turning upwards and *banged* once, loudly, under his chin. Blood misted out of the top of his head, puffing up to the ceiling, and his entire body went slack, hitting the floor like a dead weight. The gun tumbled from both our grips as I half-fell to one side.

'Jesus,' I said.

Hughes cried out in genuine alarm.

'Oh my god!'

His bodyguard was lying face-up on the floor, with blood flowing out of his nose in a dark-red stream. Literally pouring out, painting stripes down the sides of his blank face and pooling under his ears: it looked like all the blood in his body was leaving him. His eyes slowly closed.

And even more blood was simply *falling* out of his neck. A square metre of carpet was soaked dark crimson. And then more. And more. Creeping out.

'Paul!'

Well, Hughes was out of his chair, moving over. After a blank second, I scrambled for the gun – and got it – but the old man wasn't interested in me. We crossed paths awkwardly: me trying to point the gun at him defensively and failing, him falling to his knees beside the corpse.

'Call an ambulance!' he said. 'Now!'

I was so shocked that I almost did – probably would have done if I'd been physically able. Instead, I just stood there, eyes wide, staring at the pair of them. Hughes had taken his bodyguard's limp hand in his own, and was crying.

'Paul.' He turned to me without looking at me, as though I was bright like the sun. Told the chair to my left: 'Call for an ambulance!'

'He's dead, Hughes,' I said.

'Call a *fucking* ambulance!'

'Calm down.' I took a step back and levelled the gun at him. 'Just calm down.'

Just keep calm, and everything will be okay.

'Call an ambulance.'

'He's dead. Look: it was an accident. The gun just fucking went off.'

And then I shook my head, realising how ridiculous this was. Hughes was staring at me – actually me, now – with unconcealed hatred, tears streaming down his face. Not five minutes ago he'd been threatening to kill me, and here I was: apologising and making excuses.

'Just get over there.' A tired gesture with the gun. I picked the towel off the chair and tossed it to him. 'I guess you can sit on that if you're worried about your furniture.'

The old man did as he was told, leaving the body and returning to his armchair. Once there, he leant forward, elbows on knees and face in hands, and simply wept. I found the whole thing suddenly revolting on every conceivable level.

A brandy sounded like a good idea, and so I retrieved a second glass and poured myself a good measure from the decanter. My hands were shaking slightly, but doing something as normal as this made me feel more in control. Not that I usually pour brandy out of anything fancier than a bottle, but the point stands: here was Hughes, in pieces, sobbing like a girl; and then here I was, acting as though nothing had happened, and pouring myself a goddamn drink. Like I killed people every day and sometimes – when the mood took me – more than one.

The brandy tasted good.

'Come on, Hughes. Get yourself together.'

He looked up.

'You're a dead man for this, Klein. You realise that, don't you?'

'That's more like it,' I said. 'Keep up the image.'

I sat down in the chair opposite, keeping tight hold of the gun even though I could probably have beaten him to death with one hand behind my back.

'You won't get away with this.' He shook his head and looked over at Paul's corpse. At least he'd stopped crying: he was more in control of himself. 'You won't get away with what you've done here.'

I glanced over at the body, figuring that Hughes was probably right.

'How did you meet Claire Warner?' I said.

'I told you. She was a whore.'

'What?' I was surprised. 'You mean literally?'

Hughes nodded, looking at me with what – to a business rival – was probably an intimidating stare. It didn't work so well because he'd been crying, but still made me feel like the passenger here, rather than the pilot.

'Yes. *Literally*.' He sounded disgusted. 'She was recommended to me by an acquaintance. However ... well, we didn't get on.'

I tried to picture Claire as a prostitute and didn't know whether I could. She was a very sexual person, certainly, and I was sure she wouldn't have had a moral objection to it. I'd just never anticipated it as a career path she would have chosen, or been forced into. But I supposed I didn't know her that well, really. A lot could have changed since I met her in Schio.

'What happened?' I said. 'What does that mean, you "didn't get on"?'

'As I said before, she was very wilful. And that element of her character was entirely at odds with some of the things I wished her to do.' He looked slightly downcast. 'To my discredit, I reacted badly. To her discredit, though, she retaliated by stealing a disk from me on her way out of my property. The disk which you now have in your possession.'

Well, not quite – but there was no need for Walter Hughes to know that. My guess was that Claire had destroyed the disk when she found out what was on it and then dropped out of circulation for a while. But first, she'd saved a copy on the server in Asiago and given me the password to find it. Just in case.

And what had been on the disk to scare her so badly?
pale blue blouse

'Where did you get the text from?'

'I know people who know people.'

'Let's start with the people you know, then.' I gestured with the gun. 'And from them, I can work my way along.'

Hughes nodded over at his bodyguard's dead body.

'Paul arranged the contacts. He also picked up the package. I have no idea of the names, addresses or availability of the men he obtained it from, and they had no knowledge of me.'

'Bullshit!' I said, standing up and moving over to Paul's corpse.

'No, it's true.' Hughes stood up and moved after me, stick in hand. I turned around and pointed the gun at him, suddenly panicked by his speed and closeness. The intent in his eyes.

He was raising the cane as though to strike me. I saw the end third had slipped off to reveal a glinting blade. I had about a second.

'Jesus!'

I fumbled the gun out in front of me, and – *bang* – the air between us filled with smoke, just as he swung the sword-stick. He missed, and went down hard: it was as though a trapdoor had opened in the floor. I saw his clenched face whipping down, and then he was on the carpet, curled around his own stomach. The front of his shirt was blackened and steaming; the back of his suit was damp and tattered. Blood had blown out of him all over the armchair. His stick had been knocked all the way to the other side of the room.

'Jesus,' I said again, falling to my knees.

He was twitching spasmodically, but it was obvious that he was dead. I could smell the wound burning.

'Jesus.'

That morning, I'd been anticipating killing a man – a paedophile and rapist – and reassuring myself that I could. Now I'd killed three.

You won't get away with this, Klein.

And I thought: no – I won't.

Inside or out.

But when you have a tiger by the tail, you don't let go –

just like I'd told Charlie before I abandoned her in the Bridge. You grit your teeth and hold on, all the way to the bitter fucking end. So I might not get away with it but that wasn't important.

I thought about Amy as I clambered to my feet and stumbled out of the study. The air in the hallway smelled so fresh in comparison to the gunsmoke inside.

All that mattered was that I got away with it for long enough.

The first thing I did was latch the front door and check that there was nobody else in the house, which I did quickly and carelessly, figuring that – if there was – they might have made themselves known by now. I checked the remaining downstairs rooms to begin with – a kitchen, lounge and dining-room, and then headed upstairs, finding a bathroom, two bedrooms, an office and a guest room. But no people. Just as I'd hoped, and fucking good job, too.

Back downstairs, I checked Hughes and he was now very much dead. I dealt myself another brandy and went into the hallway to sit on the stairs, putting the gun on the floor between my feet. My hand started shaking, like the air in a room rings when loud people stop speaking.

I didn't know how to feel about what I'd just done. My natural inclination – bizarrely – was to feel apathetic about it, but I knew that was wrong. There were two dead people in the room to my left, and that was only the tail end of the shit I'd done today. Kareem was dead in a stream because of me, and if Hughes had been self-defence and his bodyguard an accident, then I still couldn't avoid the fact that Kareem had been cold-blooded murder.

It's done now, and you can't change it. So deal with the consequences.

My motto. It had been tattooed into my brain over the past

few months, a before and after mantra of justification intended for one purpose and one purpose only. Not to be a good guy or to be found innocent in a court of law. Just methodically to sweep away the moral, legal and personal debris that littered the path between me and Amy, wherever she might be. I was going to get to her as the crow flies, moving whatever I needed to out of the way: convention; morality; whatever.

I closed my eyes, suddenly wanting nothing more than to hold her and have her back. I never realised how beautiful holding her felt: how much I'd taken little things like that for granted. I wanted her here with me; wanted our miserable, boring, little life back. Just wanted her so fucking badly that I couldn't even feel the house around me anymore.

Before I could cry, my mind stepped in: cold and rational.

Put your thoughts in the box, it told me. *Seal it up and get on with what you have to do.*

So I did.

I wiped away non-existent tears with the back of my hand, picked up the gun and began to search the house. There must be something here: some clue or piece of evidence that would give me an idea of where to go when I left. Something that would take me to her, or – if not – then at least to the next step along the way.

I worked quickly, but it was still nearly half-past eight by the time I was ready to leave. In the meantime, I plundered every drawer, cabinet and shoebox full of letters I could find, searching for anything that might salvage the day and lead me closer to the source of that scrambled text. I didn't know exactly what I was looking for, but I figured maybe that was good. Gray had told me that his first rule of holistic internet searches was this: if you're trying to find one particular piece of information then you're likely to be disappointed, because there are a billion pieces of information to search through, and so – inevitably – the odds are against you. But if you search in general, with an open mind, then those odds flip over and work in your favour. Because you're always likely to find something.

General principle, then: when you don't know the lay of the land, a path of some kind is always better than a field or the middle of a wood, even if it turns out to be going in the wrong direction. Sooner or later, you'll find a signpost and learn whether you want to go forward, backward or side to fucking side.

Searching the house, I found a hell of a lot of signposts that didn't say Amy on them, and so at least I knew quite quickly that I was on the wrong track.

The butler's bedroom yielded secrets like barren wasteground yields watermelons. There were a few letters and scribbled invoices that got my hopes up for about a second, but they didn't lead anywhere, and I found no documentation relating to Marley, or any indication of the contacts the man must have used to buy the snuff text for Hughes. I hadn't really expected him to keep explicit records, but it was still disappointing. Dead end.

Hughes' bedroom was the same. There were more framed texts on the wall. I read one of them and found myself sitting in the early morning sun outside a tent in Perugia, Italy. There was nobody else around and – although I was on a campsite – there wasn't even another tent on my row. I knew it was a half-derelict site up in the mountains, and I was staring out at this peak in the distance, green trees and mist blending into a strangely spiritual whole that I was trying to make sense of.

Another picture put me on my back beneath a tree. It was the same campsite, but later in the day, and I was looking up at the underside of a hundred branches and, beyond that, the deep, bright sea of the sky above. It was pure blue – a wonderful, cloudless shade of pale colour – and I was imagining that at any moment I might fall upwards towards it, snapping the branches between with the weight of my plummeting body, rushing up and splashing into the cold, faraway depths of this beautiful sky. At that moment, even the earth at my back felt tenuous.

I stopped reading the texts and started looking for clues, smashing open the frames and examining the backs of the paper for any signs as to where they might have come from. But they were blank.

I gave up and started searching the office instead. There were a million and one files, and most of them seemed to be insurance related, with the majority being on Peace of Mind headed paper. Certainly not what I was looking for. I made a mental note to tell Gray that his precious first rule of searching lacked something in practice: the filing cabinets and desks were so brimful with records, invoices and other accounting information that I could barely make head or tail of them, never mind find a nugget of gold. I was despairing, and about to give up the search altogether, when I saw the envelope on the desk.

Occasionally in life, things just click. Sometimes you just get that feeling, and I got it in spades as I walked over to the desk and picked up that unopened envelope.

It was addressed to Walter Hughes.

I flipped it over and found the return address on the back. Jim Thornton, O'Reilly's Bar.

I'd heard of O'Reilly's, but never been. From what I could remember, it was a downtown dive, an old Irish place, but there were so many of them that they all merged into one. I was quite sure that Walter Hughes would never have been in there, though – the world didn't hold enough towels to separate that man's ass from a barstool in a joint like that. The name Thornton rang a bell, but I wasn't sure where I knew it from. I tore open the envelope.

Bingo.

Inside, there was one of the smaller scraps of paper that Hughes had decorated his entrance hall with: one short sentence. I read it quickly, taking in the aroma of hops and malt and sugar, and feeling a waft of hot steam in my face, only barely distinguishable from the warm breeze. Around me, there was a gabble of foreign language. The title at the top of the page said: *Illegal brewery in Saudi.*

Bingo times a thousand.

I folded the sheet of paper carefully and slipped it into my trouser pocket. It was half-past-eight: a good time to visit a bar on a Saturday night under other circumstances, but far from ideal on a night like tonight. There'd be a taxi rank somewhere near here, but I still wouldn't make it to the bar for a good hour or so. Half-nine was a bad time to walk into a rough, city-centre bar with a gun and start asking questions.

But really, I didn't have anywhere else to be right now.

I picked up the gun and made my way downstairs. I looked briefly into the room, almost expecting Hughes and his butler to have moved. But they hadn't, of course. Not even a little.

What's done is done. Deal with the consequences.

I closed the door over on them, inside and out, and made my way into the early evening gloom.

CHAPTER NINE

It was closing in on ten o'clock by the time I finally made my way downstairs into O'Reilly's. A chalkboard on the street outside informed me that I'd missed the end of Happy Hour by a clear forty-five minutes, which seemed a pity, given the circumstances. The place turned out to be one of those bars that sits snugly in (or slightly beneath) the city centre, like some kind of benign cancer which – although you might not want to look at it too closely – you know isn't doing any harm. The city centre's like that, though. If you leave enough of a gap untenanted for long enough, a bar forms to fill the space. I figure that's why cars are always getting beeped for not keeping up with the flow: the drivers behind are all afraid that a bar will form in the road between bumpers and they'll be forced to find an alternative route.

The taxi had to drop me off by a cashpoint. As I was withdrawing the money, some drunken, red-faced lad in a designer shirt came up and shouted something very loudly into my ear as he stumbled past, flexing his arms above his head. It sounded like a cheer, but I considered shooting him on general principle anyway. Nobody would have missed him: there were a thousand others just like him: all milling around, looking for trouble. And a thousand scantily-clad, barely vertical girls looking to watch the fighting, and then fuck the winner afterwards. The city centre's like that. Come in on a weekend, they should tell people, and watch the yuppies regress.

The taxi-driver told me that the bar was just around the corner, and he was right, but I still walked past it twice before I noticed it. O'Reilly's, at face value, was a dingy staircase sandwiched between a bakery and a travel agents. Not promising. I stood and looked at it for a second, while a trio of wide, middle-aged ladies tottered past, and then pushed open the glass door and started down.

The staircase was a descent into something like the green neon corner of Hell itself, with the sound of pool balls clacking and faux-Irish music reeling up with the cigarette smoke. The place was so down-at-heel that it didn't even bother to have a bouncer. It had literally got to the point where smashing the furniture and faces around wasn't good or bad, just different. Nobody cared anymore.

As I pushed the door at the bottom open, I saw that there was hardly anybody here anyway. There was a group of builder-looking blokes playing pool on a stained table; a tanned, older woman, smoking like she meant it, eyeing me up on my way to the bar; a Frankenstein's monster of a tramp, shirt hanging open to reveal white woolly hair over a reddened pigeon chest; and a few others, here and there, all watching me as I produced my wallet. The barman was short and older.

'You missed Happy Hour,' he told me as he pulled the beer I ordered.

I looked around. Everybody had settled back into their depressed, isolated states, like dogs in the pound do when nobody's looking to buy.

'So I see.'

Another burst of froth as he hung back on the tap.

'Happy Hour's six to nine.'

'Well, I missed my taxi.'

'Yeah,' he grunted. 'Oh yeah.'

'Yeah,' I agreed, passing him a five pound note and not really understanding.

'Two-fifty.'

Bizarrely, he gave me three pound coins as change. Behind me, on the jukebox, the Irish music grew more raucous, and the tramp started slamming the pinball machine into musical life. The woman at the other end of the bar stubbed out her cigarette as though slowly squashing a wasp, and then exhaled with grey satisfaction. She seemed to be on the verge of approaching me, so I beckoned the bartender back over.

'I'm looking for someone,' I said. 'A guy called Jim Thornton.'

The woman was on her way over, as bone-thin and dry as a skeleton wrapped in prune-skin. Enormous, gaudy, plastic earrings brushed at her shoulders.

'What do you want with Jim?' she said.

'He's looking for Jim,' the barman said helpfully.

She glared at him.

'I heard *that*!' she said. 'I want to know what he wants with Jim.'

He walked off. 'Shit, woman.'

'I just want to talk to the guy,' I said. 'Is he here? Or do you know where I might find him?'

She appraised me. If she'd still had her cigarette, she would probably have blown some smoke at me.

Finally, she said, 'Well what you want to talk to him about?'

I sipped my beer and tried a different tack.

'Between me and him. Business.'

'Business, huh?'

'Yeah.'

'What kind of business have you got with the man?'

I realised that the sound of pool-playing had stopped. The

builders were watching us, and the woman's voice was carrying a bit too far. I turned back to her.

'Look – you know him or not?'

'Maybe.' She was having none of it. 'Maybe I'm just real protective of him. Fed up at reporters coming round bothering the man. Hasn't he lost enough? You tell me. I'd say he has.'

Reporters?

I took another sip of my beer and tried to remain calm. Having a gun in your jacket pocket should do a lot to allay fear and, truth be told, it was helping a bit. I wasn't actually scared of the men – who were now gathering like a storm cloud around the near end of the pool table – but I was scared of this whole thing going wrong, the way that everything else seemed to have done today.

'I'm not a reporter,' I told her. 'I don't know anything about the guy.'

'You some kind of fan boy, or something?'

'I told you. I don't know the guy from Adam. I don't know who he is, or what he's been through. I just know I need to talk to him about something.'

She leaned her head to the opposite side.

'If you tell me why, then maybe I can help. Or else maybe my friends over at the pool table can.'

Five of the men were approaching. One of them – the leader – was holding his cue. The other four, at least, seemed unarmed.

I sipped my beer again, thinking: *nonchalance.*

Think it to display it.

'I really wouldn't do that,' I suggested quietly, my hand moving casually to where my gun was resting.

Two of the unarmed men reached beneath their shirts and pulled out pistols, and held them pointing casually at the floor. The remaining two each produced knives. The first man tapped the ball end of his cue on the floor and sounded real pissed off when he spoke.

'This fuck bothering you, Steph?'

I sipped my beer and pretended I didn't exist.

Steph bent down slightly to get under my gaze and lift it back up to her. Then, she thumbed in the the direction of the man with the cue, glaring at me.

'This here's Joe Kennedy. And these are his boys.'

One of them grunted, right on time.

Steph said, 'Maybe you can tell them why you want to see Jim.'

I was starting to be under the impression that Jim had better be worth it after all this trouble. Jim had better do fucking cartwheels. Play the piano and take requests.

'All right,' I said. 'I'm gonna reach into my pocket, okay?'

I held my hands – palms out – in a pacifying gesture.

'There's a piece of paper in my left-hand trouser pocket. I'm gonna reach in and get it out.'

Nobody told me not to, so I dug in, retrieving the paper I'd taken from Walter Hughes' house.

'It's about this. Here – who wants it?'

Steph held out her hand and clicked her tanned, ringed fingers twice.

'Give.'

I passed it over, and she pulled it taut between her witch's hands, frowning as she read it.

'I just want to speak to him about that,' I said. 'And where he got it from.'

Steph looked up at Joe Kennedy and his friends.

'It's all right, boys. You go back to your pool now.'

'You sure?'

'I'm sure,' she said. 'Go on.'

They wandered away, putting their weapons back into whichever tight and revolting spaces they'd pulled them from.

Steph looked me over again, evaluating me. I smiled and took a sip of beer.

'All right,' she said, turning around. 'Put that candy-ass beer down and follow me. Bob!'

The landlord was polishing a pint glass with a rusty-looking bar towel.

'Yeah?'

'You order us down a big old bottle of liquor in back. And three glasses, and that's all.'

'Right up.'

He didn't move, but I did – following Steph through a flimsy door by the side of the bar and wondering exactly how alive I was going to be ten minutes from now.

It was actually a revelation: exactly how much there was, hidden beneath the surface of the city. I supposed I shouldn't have been surprised: in cities, like the people that live in them, the most interesting things happen beneath the surface. O'Reilly's itself was subterranean, but the door by the bar led to steps that took Steph, and me behind her, down to another level entirely, and by the time we'd finished I figured we must have been a good two storeys beneath the streets of the city. We trailed along a dim corridor and then turned the corner into an enormous room.

Which, I guessed, was probably the real O'Reilly's.

Loud music was playing from a battered old stereo behind a bar at one end, hooked up to building-sized speakers. Not Irish fiddle music here, either – but harder, harsher sounds: the sort of music you might play in your head while you fuck someone up. There were probably forty or fifty lost souls, half of them dancing, the rest just shuffling and talking. A card game was going on at a table over by the far end. A few jagged flashes of pale blue light from the strips on the ceiling took photos of everybody's silhouettes, and the air was so filled with sweet, hazy smoke that it was like the floor was made from marijuana and on fire.

'Bar,' Steph shouted over her shoulder. 'Try to keep up, now.'

She threaded her way over to the right, where a tray with three glasses and a bottle of whisky was waiting, guarded by a young barman who nodded at Steph as she picked it up and bobbed away. I followed her to the far end, dodging the jagged silhouettes of slam-dancers, and we went round into what turned out to be a kind of snug, albeit a bare and badly furnished one. There were a few low, old tables (unmatching) and a scattering of weathered armchairs (also unmatching). There were six people occupying them, and they didn't seem to match either: all just sitting, staring into space, as though they were really concentrating on drinking. To be fair, some of them looked like they might need to.

Steph headed over to a solitary man in the far corner. He looked old, although he was leaning over the table in front of him, staring into a thick tumbler of greasy booze, and so it was difficult to make out his face. From what I could see, his hair was blacky-grey and unwashed – two thirds of the way to being the wet, hard curls of tramp's hair. The skin on the back of his hands was brown and knotted, but there was thin hair there, too, like swirls of copper wire. His shoulders were weak: stooped and trembling slightly. I got the impression that his drink was telling him a secret which was breaking his heart.

'Jim.'

His reactions were so slow that Steph was putting the tray down on the table before he'd even managed to look up. Pink, glossy eyes told me that Jim Thornton was pissed as a wretch. The face around them was sad and drawn, telling tall tales of missed sleep, exposure and bad times. His skin was the colour of nicotine.

A stretched voice:

'Hey Steph.'

'Hey.'

She sat down opposite him and motioned for me to do the same.

Jim Thornton ended up staring somewhere in between us.

'How a, how are . . .' – his head nodded forwards a little with each attempt at speech – 'how are dyo ouing?'

I stared at this paralytic monster in horror, but Steph didn't miss a beat. She was already pouring us all a slug from the bottle she'd brought over.

'I'm doing just fine, Jim. Just fine. And I have someone to see you.'

Thornton – who I think was as fundamentally shit-faced as I'd ever seen a man – turned to look at me, and missed. He had a slack smile, though, which gave me the impression he figured he'd scored a bullseye. It gave me the opportunity to notice another weird thing about the man: his teeth were absolutely perfect.

'Hai.'

Steph passed me a half full tumbler of whisky. 'He says hi.'

'Nice to meet you,' I said and then took a mouthful of booze, realising it would probably take sixty or more to level this particular playing field.

Thornton swung his head round to Steph, frowning.

'Whizz this ga? Ta.'

He took the glass that Steph was offering him and attempted to put it down on the table.

'He's a man who wants to speak to you about some things.'

Clunk. The glass made an awkward touch-down, with a jolt of whisky escaping onto the table.

'Sat right?'

'Uh-huh.' She looked at me after she'd finally poured herself a drink, and then passed me the piece of paper that I'd stolen from Hughes. 'Why don't you tell Jim what you want to talk to him about? Go on. Show him what you brought.'

I took the paper from her and passed it to Thornton. His hand was trembling as he picked it from me, and then he held it up for inspection.

'Look at the one in the middle,' I said.

Steph glared at me, and then looked back at him and said, 'You know what that is, Jim?'

He shook his head violently.

'Naw. Naw.'

Bullshit, I thought.

'You sent it to a man named Walter Hughes.' I leaned forward. His hands were now trembling even worse than before, and he was still shaking his head, as though trying to deny something fundamental. Like gravity.

'You send them to him, and he pays you for them.'

'Naw.'

Thornton closed his eyes.

'Where do you get them from? Who sends these to you?'

'*Naw*!'

It was a centimetre from being a shout, and he stood up. Upright, his body looked thinner and more whittled away than ever: like somebody who'd been in a coma.

'Okay, Jim.'

Steph had stood up with him. She placed a calming hand on his shoulder.

'It's okay. Don't worry.'

'Naw.' He was whispering it again and again, and was starting to cry. His face barely seemed to have the strength to contort into tears. 'Naw.'

'It's okay. Shhh.'

Steph kneaded his bony shoulder once and then took the piece of paper away from him.

'Shhh. Don't you worry now.'

His hands now free, they went automatically to his face.

'Sit down, Jim.' Her palm pressed him back into his seat. It was a barely controlled descent, and he just about managed it. 'You enjoy your drink and forget all about this fella.'

She glared at me again.

'*Come with me.*'

I took my glass and followed her over to a table in the far corner, where Jim Thornton wouldn't be able to hear us.

'Sit.'

She placed the paper in front of me.

'You saw that, right?'

'Saw what? Saw how he reacted?'

She nodded.

'Yeah, I saw.'

Steph lit a cigarette and leaned back in her armchair.

'That was for *your* benefit,' she said. 'You little shit. Not his. I wanted you to see what this thing can do to him, and why you need to leave him alone. You've seen the state of him. Doesn't he look like he's been through enough to you?'

I thought about it.

'Yeah. He does.'

'Well then.' Steph looked exasperated, like she'd proved something obvious which I was still trying to deny. Ash fell on the table as she leaned forwards and jabbed a finger at me.

'You and me – we're gonna talk. And afterwards, you're gonna leave well enough alone. Okay? Jim spends a lot of his time here, but not all his time. I don't want you bothering the old man out on the street and breaking his heart. That's one thing's been broken ten times too many.'

'Okay – we'll talk, then. I need to find the man who wrote this.'

Steph glanced down at the paper with disgust.

'You want that man, huh?'

'Yes. You know where I can find him?'

She shook her head.

'Well, does Jim know?'

'Does Jim look like he knows much of anything?' She shook her head again, pulling a face. 'If he does, you ain't looking right. Jim doesn't know anything about this.'

She pointed vaguely at the paper. 'These things.'

'So what can *you* tell me about them?'

'They've been coming regularly for a year or more, now.' She shrugged. 'We don't let him see them no more. Damn near breaks my heart on top of his to see the look on his face when he does. I sorted out the arrangement with that fella Hughes. Every week, I package these things up, the day they arrive. And every week, near as anything, I send them out. The money changes accounts – and it's good money – and Jim never needs to know about it.'

'But they come here addressed to him?'

She nodded.

'They come to him here, sure. Regular as clockwork, give or take a few days. We rent an apartment for Jim a block away, and we give him all the booze he can drink. Feed him, too. Keeps the man happy.'

'Yeah,' I said. 'He seems real happy.'

Steph shrugged again. 'He can be an empty shell out on the street. Or he can be an empty shell in here. Least here, we fill him with something, even if it ain't much.'

I looked her over more carefully: took in the tan, the hard eyes, the heavily aerobicised body. The way she looked, she should almost have been some executive's bone-thin, middle-aged housewife: too many free hours whiled away on the exercise bike or down the salon, or gossiping about abortions in the hairdressers; too long spent sunning herself in Costa del somewhere, sipping cocktails and being too loud with her brash husband. Almost. But she looked tougher than that: like a muscle that had been built in a series of grubby streetfights rather than the air-conditioned comfort of a ladies-only gym. The same kind of woman, just a class size down. Sucking on her cigarettes as though someone might try to steal the smoke.

It occurred to me that Hughes probably paid more than enough to keep Thornton waist-deep in liquor, even with his habit as tall as it was.

'Doesn't do you any harm, either, I bet.' I looked around. 'How long have you had this little extension?'

'About a year now,' she said. Glared at me. 'And no. It doesn't do us any harm. Your point being what?'

It occurred to me that that particular conversation would be a dead end.

'My point being the man who sends these things to you,' I said. 'I need to find him.'

'Why?'

'Because something bad has happened to somebody I love.' The truth slipped out, but it felt okay. 'And I think this man might be able to help me find her.'

'Well, that is sweet.'

'It's true.'

Steph studied me for a moment, supporting her cigarette elbow with her free hand while smoke listed leisurely into the misty air above us. Eventually, she moved it to her mouth and took a drag.

'Okay,' she said, leaning towards me. 'Let me tell you what I know.'

CHAPTER TEN

The writing is always done by hand.

There are a couple of things you need to know, and that's the first.

He's gently flexing his wrist as they bring the girl in: warming himself up. It should take about half an hour from start to finish, and that's a long time to write for, so you need to be prepared. Loose and relaxed. He gives his shoulders a roll and watches the girl. The bed, covered in straight sheets of glinting polythene, is on the other side of the studio. When she sees it, her step falters, but they push her from behind and she starts moving towards it.

The door is locked behind them.

'Fucking be*have*,' Marley tells her. He's the one that pushed her. She glances at him, scared, but he's not even looking at her: just grinding out the remains of his cigarette on the floor. The smell of the smoke drifts over, catching his attention just as the girl sees him.

He sees her right back.

For a moment, it's as though she's standing on her own, with all the other figures in the room fading into the background: Marley disappears; Long Tall Jack, swinging his limp cock like a length of rope, melts out of view; even the bed seems dim and far away. It's like the girl is spot-lit: a fragile, scared thing illuminated to the exclusion of everything else.

He wants to smile at her and tell her that it will be okay,

but it won't. And he's not here to make her feel comfortable, or help her.

So instead, he picks up his pen.

And without taking his eyes off her, he begins to write.

You are looking at a girl.

She is wearing a pale blue blouse and a white, cotton skirt: frail clothes that you can't quite see through but which still manage to give you an idea of the slim but womanly figure beneath. Her skin is tanned and clear, and her hair is shoulder-length, brown and full of body. Not curly exactly, or frizzy, but a kind of pleasing combination of the two, streaked through with patches of blonde where the sun seems to have bleached it. Her face is pretty, but not exceptionally so – although you can tell that if she was smiling she'd be very attractive indeed: it's just one of those faces that lights up when it smiles and makes everything else seem somehow less important.

But she's not smiling.

In fact, she's close to tears, but it's as though she doesn't quite dare cry: maybe she has done in the past and then been punished for it. She doesn't need to anyway: it's there in her stance and in the expression on her face. She's hugging herself slightly, anticipating some kind of blow. And she's looking at you as though you might be able to stop it from coming.

It breaks your heart that you can't do anything to help her, but the fact is that you just can't. That's not why you're here.

She mouths the word *help* at you, and you have to look away.

'On the bed.'

Marley has her by the arm.

She actually says it to you this time. 'Help me. Please.'

'*Sit* down on the edge of the *fucking* bed.'

He drags her back and shoves her down, and she starts to

cry. Sits there and holds her face in her hands, sobbing. Marley doesn't care; he's not even looking at her anymore. Long Tall Jack just laughs.

'Are you ready?' Marley calls over.

You nod.

Of course you are – this is what you're here for.

His grandmother gave him the Ithaca pen. It was a present for his twelfth birthday, which was a little after he'd found out about his gift and talked it through with her. He always knew he could write well, but as he hit puberty his talent grew into something else altogether, and it scared him. Sometimes the things he'd write scared other people as well. When his grandmother was ill, towards the end, he went down to the beach and wrote a piece that she could barely even finish; she said it was just like being there, in the dunes where she'd played as a child. As real as a video or an audio recording. Maybe even as real as it actually happening. And while the scene he described for her was deliberately beautiful, he always knew the potential for harm was there, even before she warned him that he had to be careful.

So his grandmother gave him the pen and told him to practise. By the time she died – when he was fourteen – he had his gift on a leash. She'd moved into his parents' home some time before that – when the doctors realised there was nothing more they could do – and one night she called him in, just like they'd always planned. He sat writing with her for the next four hours, and by the time she finally died, his hand had cramped. He never told anyone that he'd been with her at the end, and he still has that notebook, stored away somewhere that nobody will ever find it. He takes it out and reads it sometimes, although his words are generally lost on him. Regardless of that, it's a first edition he keeps for himself.

And he kept his talent to himself, as well. He wasn't sure

why exactly, but he sensed it was for the best. The parade of harried teachers never knew; he turned in bland, uninspired fiction during all the Tests, making sure he was never streamed off to the Factory. His plan was non-existent, but he had the distinct impression that the Factory would seek to kill whatever it was he had inside him.

They finally cornered him when he was sixteen: caught red-handed, passing a note he'd written to a girl on the table across from him. Her name was Kay, and he was very much in love with her. The note had no warning, but it contained explicit content. He hadn't written it while he was making love to her, but he'd done it from memory almost immediately afterwards: it was certainly good enough to have made her come in the middle of History. But in fact – history records – that particular pleasure went to Mr Cremin, who intercepted the note, confiscated it, and then wished that he hadn't. The boy's locker was raided, his parents were called in and serious discussions were entered into regarding his future.

And that was that. Within a week, he'd been transferred to the Factory. He remembered the principal talking to him on the day before he left, adding emphasis with his hands:

'You've got talent, boy – raw ability. Nobody I've ever met can describe things like you. And now all you need is discipline and focus.'

But as far as the boy was concerned, he had discipline – and he had focus, too. He'd kept up his practice. Sometimes he'd write for three or four hours a night, taking his pad and pen up into the woods, or catching these puff-a-billy trams out into the countryside with Kay. One weekend, he broke into the stairwell of a block of flats and managed to get onto the roof: thirty storeys above the street – just him and the pigeons, and the tv aerials humming away. He spent ten straight hours writing up there. He knew what he was doing. He was testing his gift and searching for limits, for a direction that was right for him. Of course, what the principal meant was that he needed their direction and their focus. He needed to learn things like plot and character, so that he could make some money.

It was destined to end in tears.

'Jim knew the boy was special to begin with,' Steph said, grinding out the end of her cigarette, blowing the last of the smoke out from the corner of her mouth.

'But listen – he was just this fucked up kid with too many high ideals. He was a kid who could write, sure, but he wasn't structured or disciplined. He had no work ethic. The way he was, he had no bestsellers in him.'

I finished the end of my whisky and poured myself another.

'Jim was a teacher there? At the Factory?'

'Uh-huh.' She glanced back at Thornton, who had collapsed over his glass again: a husk of a shell of a man. He was a meta-fuck-up.

'You wouldn't know it from looking at him now, but that man there used to be one of the best businessmen in the business.'

The Factory's where they teach you to write. It's all they do, day in and day out: nearly five hundred children at any one time, all aged between eleven and eighteen, housed under one long roof and under the nine-to-five tutelage of those who have gone before them. Prospective students are picked out by the Tests at as early an age as possible and then taught the trappings of plot, character and sentence structure before graduating: turned loose into the world as novelists of potential note, standing and bank balance.

He never stood a chance, of course. He couldn't do plot and character: he just couldn't abstract things in that way.

Didn't even want to. What he did was take a snapshot of an event and put it in your head. When he tried to put strings of events together, or create characters, it just didn't work; the law of ever-decreasing returns applied, and each successive scene became duller and duller. The longer and longer he spent at the Factory, the emptier he felt. His time there was hollowing him out – turning him into a shell they could fill – and pointing him, by force, in a direction he just didn't want to go.

It was never going to last.

Things came to a head four months after he'd arrived, but by that time he'd had a whole bunch of run-ins with the staff and was just waiting for an excuse. It came during James Thornton's Commercial Viability class, in which the man explained the rules of publishing to a class of twenty enthralled would-be writers, and him.

'Writing is purely and simply a business,' Thornton repeated.

In fact, Thornton simply couldn't stress that enough, and he hated the man more every time he said it. Not for him, it wasn't. Not ever.

'A business. That's all. You have to approach it in that manner, or you'll fail. You'll be a nobody. Nothing. Not a writer, anyway – that's for damn sure.'

Thornton had a moustache and the kind of confidence you get from a string of successful relationship novels, but he couldn't swear for shit. He said *damn* too slowly: rolling it around and drawing out tension that simply wasn't there. A girl at the front tittered appreciatively. Thornton was pretty famous.

He went on.

The gist of it was this. Fiction is business, and publishing houses aren't always likely to risk investment on an untried, untested author. Even if they did, and you got your book published, there was no guarantee that you'd actually sell. A stamp of approval from the Factory gets you halfway in life; marketing takes you that little bit further; but smarts get you the rest.

'Once you've got your foot in the door,' Thornton said, leaning on the desk in front of him with his shirtsleeves rolled up to the elbows, 'act quick. And act smart. Your book is out. What do you do? What you do is approach your bank and take out a business loan, and then you scour. You scour the country from end to end, and you buy up every copy of the book you can find.'

He stood up, staring at a few of them in turn.

'And that's it. The publishing company says "Wow", and offers you a contract on the spot. Hundreds of thousands of pounds flutter down into your pockets as if by magic. As much goddamn dental work as your mouth can cope with. And when they put your second book out, they market it so hard you don't even have time to breathe. You're in.'

A boy at the front had his arm up straight as a flag pole. 'Is that what you did, Mr Thornton?'

Thornton leant on the desk again and showed the boy his teeth: perfect and white.

'We've all done it, son,' he said. 'We've all done it.'

Two weekends after that, he went back home and saw Kay, who he missed now he no longer sat next to her in class. He was slightly relieved to see that she missed him right back. They made love a couple of times, and he took her for drinks in the café they'd had their first date in, which felt like an age ago. It was a sunny day, and he took his notepad and jotted down descriptions of the trees, the people and the lake, surprising her with them as they walked – giving her little linguistic trinkets to remember him by. She folded each one up carefully and placed it in the pocket of her jeans, giving him a secret smile in exchange. The Factory had never felt so irrelevant and far away.

They talked about their future together and, as they did, he could feel it solidifying. The prospect felt far more real and important than anything he'd ever write down in a notebook, or sell for a million.

And he was thinking – as they crossed the road, with her a little ahead of him, dragging him by the hand – and then she was just suddenly taken away. His right arm jolting, and he lurched: spun a little. The side of a truck flashed in front of him; a strong waft of air; a screech of tyres. Then, the truck was past, skidding to a halt, and he was left standing there, staring at the other side of the sunny street, his arm beginning to throb. The face of a woman standing beneath a green plastic canopy opposite slowly contorted into a scream of shock, and he blinked at her.

In his left hand, he was still holding his notebook. His right was empty.

They start to put the girl's body into bin bags, and Long Tall Jack heads off for a shower. He's coated with blood from his knees to his abdomen, and from his neck to his nose, so he really needs one. They'll blast down the shower later. Of course, he's worn gloves the whole time – they all have – but they'll wipe the place for prints, as well.

He holds his right hand at the wrist and cracks it gently. Then, he flexes his fingers and thumb, working the cramp out of them. One of the crew pulls the girl off the bed by her arm, and her dead eye tracks the ceiling before the rest of her follows.

He looks away.

Marley will copy the text and then send it off. And it was good work today. Today, he just let himself fall into it and he's still on a high. There's something a little like joy fluttering in his heart, even though he's also very sad. It is always like this, and he half hates it, half loves it.

He allowed himself to be washed along by the grief. He used it as a tool to lever himself into movement, the way a shoehorn slides your foot into the shoe and then you're ready to go outside.

The day before the funeral, he packed. He took the bare minimum and squashed it down into as small a rucksack as he could find. He had his pen, and enough money to buy paper and food, and figured that he could always sell surprising snippets of writing to tourists and make a few dollars here and there if things got tight. What was more important was the overall picture. He was going into the desert to temper and forge his talent: to beat it into something he could feel the edges of, like hammering out the metal walls of a hut you're going to spend the rest of your life sheltering inside. Everything else felt empty and small.

The last thing he did, before leaving for the funeral with the bag on his back, was address the package to Jim Thornton. He wasn't even sure why he did it – only that it seemed to give a sense of closure to a period of his life. 'Here,' he was saying, 'this is what I think of you and your fiction; this is what I think of you and your attitude; this is what I think about you and my life.'

I can do something a hundred times bigger than you.

The package contained a description of heartbreak so pure that it would reach off the page and turn a man inside out: destroy him; ruin him. A thousand fashionable romance novels, with all their relationship difficulties and tragedies, would be like a matchstick to the sun beside this text. It was possible that you'd read it and never be able to set pen to paper ever again. It would always be on your mind.

After Kay had been knocked down and killed, he'd sat

down at a table by the café, and he'd written a description of what he'd seen and how it had felt. What it had been like to have the best part of you – the only thing which seemed to give you meaning – ripped away in a moment of carelessness.

He posted the two sheets of grief on his way to the funeral. After that, he went to the bus station.

Over the next few years, he saw the world and set it in paper. He wrote down a sunset in every place he visited, and a sunrise in all but one – Verona, of all places, where he and some friends were rousted from their digs in the middle of the night by an army of carabinieri, raiding the hideout for imported tobacco and liquor. He wrote a short description of the waves from the cabin of a Russian steamship, with an icy breeze all around him and vapour rising off the bright, white sheets of half-frozen sea. The cold followed him onto the page. There were three hours spent tracking a street market in Jerusalem, all cloth and pots and graffitied sandstone, and men with guns: really not half as religious as he'd been led to believe. And more besides. So much time spent scribbling and dreaming: a madhouse in Dhaka; an illegal distillery in a desert hut in Saudi Arabia; the early morning mist in the streets of the Père Lachaise cemetery in Paris, where he captured the drizzle on Balzac's tomb.

He explored, and what he found was this: no relief whatsoever. His unhappiness trailed along three steps behind him, and no matter where he went and how much he wrote, it never went away. He collected reams of paper filled, line after line, with beautiful sentences, all of which meant absolutely nothing to him. But he kept pushing his gift to its limits; himself against the world; his pen across paper.

Until finally . . . well, he ended up here.

There's a whole writing industry that you won't find in the bookshops. If you mentioned it in the corridors of the Factory, they'd turn up their noses at you. And they don't even know the half of it. Go to your local fast-food bookstore and look: you won't find it. Maybe if it's a big store you'll find medium hardcore – sex and horror – but sometimes not even that, because they like to pretend that no-one's interested. But they are, and if you're one of the ones whose tastes run to the extreme then you have to go looking. In the independent and second-hand bookstores you can find the beginning of it: the sex books; the kill books. But you know that none of it's real: just cheap fiction, hacked out in stained motel rooms in the company of cigarettes and neon and bad Spanish radio. If you want it real, you have to look harder than that.

That's where he started: on these fringes. Churning out fake dross for a handful of change. He wrote the porn and the violence, and if you want to look you'll find his name – his real name – against a couple of legit titles: one hundred print run; staple-bound. Extreme stuff, but he faked it. You'll have to look, but they're there.

But all the time he was doing this, she was still with him, and it wasn't long before he went deeper still. Testing himself all the time: finding more and more extreme things to write about; looking for edges in his talent to rest against and find some peace, but finding none: day after day.

Now, he was so deep in the industry that you'd probably never find his stuff. It was the real deal these days: each and every word was true. They sold it in shifting markets, sealed in polythene, and behind locked, guarded doors in dark halls, where strangers shuffled from stall to stall, and even in these places you had to search it out, listen for whispers. A stallholder's friend would be able to provide you with kiddie fiction, say, or rape text, but if you wanted his stuff then you had to go to the stallholder's friend's friend, and you had to keep your mouth shut and know when to back off. Because these days, his writing was so far buried that only the truly fallen ever even caught a glimpse of it.

And it was there – as low as you could get – that he began to see a way out.

He closes the front door and flicks on a light. Rain slashes against the window, with an echoing ping as water drips down into the ceramic pot in the bathroom. There's a towel warming over the radiator in the hall and he uses it to dry his hair. The dripping coat goes on a hanger. He takes the pen through to the front room, along with the towel, kicking off his shoes first and leaving them by the door.

His flat is pretty sparse: a settee and two armchairs, all drawn from different suites, and a folding table by the window, with a flimsy chair underneath it. There's a pile of blank notepads on the right of the desk. Often, he'll just sit and stare out of the window and write. He's ten storeys up, on the top floor, and people on the street below seem so small that their movements are like patterns. He can write about them for hours. Maybe you're in there somewhere – who knows?

Apart from that, the flat is pretty bare. He has no television, no radio. No paintings on the wall. There is a computer he uses for e-mail, and he has a set of weights over in the far corner, but he hardly ever uses either of them and so they don't really count. His kitchen is minimal. The only things he does have are books. He has four full bookcases, containing a mixture of his own journals and notepads, and published works by other authors. These books are the accoutrements of his life: his paintings; his pot-plants; his wife and child; the family car; the dog; the cat. They are the things meant to define his life and fill it, and – just like everyone else's – they are simply not enough.

Because he doesn't have *her* anymore.

All he has is this terrible feeling of emptiness which tells him that the best part of his life is over. And it's joined now, as always, by the feeling of revulsion at what he's done tonight.

He gets a glass of water from the kitchen, and then places the pen down on the table. Selects a notepad at random from the shelves. There are plain brown envelopes in a drawer beneath the desk, and he pulls one out.

It's not true, exactly, that when he tears a strip of paper from the notebook and slips it into the envelope he's doing it out of hate. It's not a simple feeling of derision or cruelty that leads him to pick up his precious pen, loop two testing swirls of blue ink on the reverse of the envelope, and then write Jim Thornton's name on the front. It's more complicated than that. Zoom in on the ink until the screen is filled with a pure blue, and what you see are a thousand sparkles of darkness, and they say: *I'm lost*.

But he'll never tell you that. Instead, after addressing the envelope, he sits down at the desk and opens an old jotter pad that's waiting for him.

Most nights, he just sits and writes. By one side of the monitor on the desk is a plastic pill bottle, containing a large enough amount of prescription chemicals to send him into a gentle, peaceful sleep: one he wouldn't wake up from. Every night, he sits here, noting down his life in the book in front of him, and the bottle is always in reach. He wants to pick it up, but something always stops him. Perhaps he's just a coward. Perhaps, with something more immediate like a gun, suicide would be easier. Except he doesn't know how that would come out on the page: whether his writing would capture the moment or if it would just blurt to a stop.

Tonight, he picks up his pen and begins to write. And – for now – the bottle remains on the desk by the screen.

CHAPTER ELEVEN

I woke up on Sunday morning to the alarm call for the six-thirty-three from Thiene. It had rolled into the docking bay of the bus station to the sound of a hundred bonging announcements.

It must have been the final straw, because I was immediately aware of noise all around me – the rush of air, the tapping of feet, the beeps and clicks and conversation. In the background, a lyricless Will Robinson hit was being saxophoned in. I was in a busy, muzak-flavoured Hell: surely far too fiery to have been slept through. But here I was: shocked awake, which meant I'd managed it.

I sat up, well aware that my muscles had solidified through the awkward contortions of a night spent stretched over three plastic chairs. The truth I faced was terrible and complicated: a bus station in full working order. Too many people, doing too many things, and all at the same fucking time. The light was harsh. The décor – a painful, pissy yellow – was harsh. The coffee would, no doubt, be harsh too, but hopefully not pissy. Regardless, after a few minutes' careful twisting and yawning, and a check to see that my wallet and gun were still with me, I set off in search of a cup, blinking away the last remaining mists of my troubled sleep and running a hand over the stubble of my hair.

A janitor was pushing a four-foot wide brush through the hall, collecting crisp packets, bus tickets and dust. He almost collected me, too, but I managed to stumble out of the way and – by luck – found the bathroom. It wasn't a coffee machine, but it was a start. I used one of the sinks to freshen up, splashing water on my face and hair, and trying to rub the sleep out of my eyes. I looked like shit when I'd finished: a pale, blotchy nightmare with punched eyes and a gormless expression. But I figured, what the fuck. I was going to get coffee and – by the law of averages – kill a few more people. Neither required me to look my best.

I withdrew the dregs of my account from a hole in the wall outside. It was a risk, but I was barely caring. At some point – if not already – Kareem's body would be found, and I was sure it wouldn't be difficult to trace me from either the physical evidence at the scene or eyewitness testimony in the Bridge. I was fucked, basically, and the police would no doubt be checking my bank details to see when and where I'd made my most recent withdrawals. That was too bad, because I needed the money. When you're basically fucked, you might as well get yourself a coffee. And maybe a small onion bagel.

There was a mini, make-believe park outside the bus station, and I spent the next hour and a half waiting there for an acceptable time to ring Graham. It wasn't too bad, actually: a central floral display; some grass; an old-fashioned street-lamp. Three benches. I took the one with a good view of the bus station and waited for the police to arrive with guns, grimaces and sniffer dogs. At a quarter to nine I was still waiting, and by then I figured the hour was decent enough for me to make my phone call.

'Hello?'

Helen didn't sound as chipper as usual. Normally, she answered the phone like she answered the door, which was as though it was the most cheering thing to have happened to her all day, but right now she sounded annoyed: wary and impatient. She must have known it was me.

'Hi Helen,' I said. 'Is Graham there?'

'Wait a minute.'

She was gone. I swapped the phone to my other ear and watched the traffic rolling past. None of it seemed to be watching me back.

The phone clicked through.

'Jay, hi.'

'Hi. I didn't get you guys up, did I?'

'No, we were up already.' He sounded subdued, and I figured: *argument*. There was a time, right back before Amy disappeared, when I might have thought that them arguing was a good thing, but I didn't know what to think anymore. Fuck them and good luck to them at the same time.

'How are you doing?' he said.

'Fine,' I lied. 'And I'm making some headway.'

'Oh yeah?'

'Yeah.' I didn't feel like going into my headway with him over the phone, so I just said: 'I've got a few leads.'

'Well, I've got some information for you, too. The stuff you wanted.'

It sounded like there was meant to be a *but* at the end of that sentence, and I heard it even though it wasn't technically there. Invisible words: language seems like such a solid thing until you start reading all the spaces.

'That's great,' I said.

'The server information. The user ID. Some background. I couldn't get as much as I wanted, because my computer's fucking up.'

'I appreciate you looking for me. I really do.'

I was trying to sound friendly, but his tone didn't alter.

'Jay, you remember what I told you yesterday afternoon?'

'I remember.'

'About me backing out if this got dodgy?'

'Yeah,' I said. 'I remember.'

I wished he'd just say whatever was on his mind. But it

probably wasn't that easy for him. We had history, after all, and when you're throwing out memorabilia you take a last look, don't you? It's not like throwing away a milk carton.

'What are you saying, Gray?' I prompted him. 'You want out on me?'

Without any hesitation, 'I want out on you.'

'It got dodgy?'

'Not exactly. It didn't need to get any more dodgy than it already was. I just can't do this anymore. I don't really want to explain it, but that doesn't bother me too much.'

'No,' I said. 'Well, for what it's worth, I understand.'

It wasn't worth anything and we both knew it.

'I've set up a Yahoo account for you,' he said, and then gave me the address. 'Find yourself an internet café and check the inbox. Everything you need to know is there. I've sent the text, the user details, some background. As much as I could find.'

'Thanks. I mean it.'

'And that's the end, okay?'

'Yeah,' I said. 'That's the end.'

'You don't ring here anymore.'

I could imagine Helen leaning in the doorway, watching her boyfriend make this oh-so-difficult, oh-so-necessary phone call to his old friend. Secretly so pleased. She'd make him a nice coffee afterwards, and say some comforting shit about how he'd done the right thing. Which, of course, he probably had.

I closed my eyes.

He said, 'You don't call round.'

Maybe they could even stop buying sugar now. One less thing to worry about.

'It's just ... that's it, Jay. That really has to be it.'

'I'm sorry.'

'Don't be sorry. Just don't call or phone or come round. Maybe you should even let go of all this.'

'All this.'

'Amy. Maybe you should let go of her and move on.'

'Maybe I should move on.'

'You there?'

I blinked, realising that I hadn't been speaking these last few things, just thinking them.

'I've got to go,' I said. 'I'll see you in the next life, Gray.'

And the receiver was down before I even knew that I'd done it. The traffic was still making its way past. Moving on and up as I stood there by the side of the road. None of the drivers were watching me: they were all watching the cars directly in front and behind, and that was all. In the cold morning sunshine there was something about that that struck me as being almost profound. But then it went.

'Maybe I should move on,' I said out loud.

As though it was actually still possible.

But I wasn't going to get out of anything as easily as that.

There was an internet café a block and a half away from the coach station: one of those wonderful all night places where you can surf and drink cheap coffee for about a pound an hour while the world outside gets dark and light and then dark again. Throw in the sizzle and smell of bacon, frying behind a counter at the far end, and you had a done deal as far as I was concerned. The dregs of last night's clubbing circuit were slipping out even as I arrived. I got myself a coffee, a bacon sandwich and an hour's screen time, and then logged into the account that Graham had set up for me.

There were six new messages waiting in the inbox, five of them forwarded on from Gray's own personal account and bristling with multi-coloured attachments. The sixth was a circular from i-Mart. It contained details of a few of their latest products and thanked me for subscribing to what it said was the most popular e-list in the western world. I cursed Gray quietly – but with a smile – and dumped the circular into a greedy trash can. A thousand shreds of digital shit disappeared into the electrical ether.

The first thing I looked for was the text. It wasn't there.

The *message* was there, and it claimed that the text was attached, but it was clearly lying. I could only imagine it had got lost somewhere in the transfer: dropped off its perch at the base of the e-mail and fallen down onto the internet's cutting room floor. Which was shit: it meant I'd have to talk to Graham and ask him to re-send it. Since that was going to be a difficult conversation, I decided to leave it for now. It was always possible that I'd be able to pick up the text myself later on. I knew the title, after all.

The coffee was hot and weak, and the chief ingredient of my bacon sandwich appeared to be grease. Nevertheless, I worked my way through them as I read each of Graham's messages in turn.

It seemed that a man named John James Dennison had been responsible for posting the text on the server in the first place – or at least, it had come from his computer. Gray had forwarded some background information on him, along with a few photographs. The server itself was based in Asiago, as was Dennison himself. Claire had lived there, too.

The waitress had helpfully provided me with a napkin the size of a postage stamp, and by the time I was using it to dab fat from the ends of my fingers I'd requested a hundred credits and set the main documents printing. An ancient bubble-jet over by the tray-stack was stuttering back and forth over sheet after sheet of information.

I logged out, returned my plate to the counter and waited by the printer, collecting the paper as it came through.

The way I was seeing things now, I had three leads to work

on. I had this guy Marley, somewhere in Thiene, who was obviously a priority. But Gray had turned up nothing on that name – or rather, he'd turned up so much that there was no way of knowing if anything was actually relevant. There were thirty Marleys in Thiene alone. He'd given me the contact details for all of them, but I figured that was a long shot. It might not be his real name, for one thing. Even if it was I'd have no way of knowing which one of the thirty to go for. With time running out, I needed something better than that.

The second lead was the writer. But if Marley was out of my reach for now then this guy was a million miles away. Without Graham to help me, I was going to have trouble locating him, and it was likely that his address wouldn't be listed under his real name. And that was assuming he wasn't living rough or squatting somewhere. That was if he was even still in the country. He could even be dead.

I figured that if I did find the writer it would be by finding Marley. So first things first.

Those two leads were big, fat, bloated ones, but they weren't going anywhere.

The third lead was John James Dennison.

The guy who had – apparently – kept the murder text on his computer. Somehow, it had got from Claire to Dennison, and then to Liberty where she knew I'd be able to find it.

This was the slimmest lead of all. It was also the only one I could really move on right now.

The paper kept coming.

Twenty minutes later, I was safely back in the bus station – still officially police-free – with a ticket for the ten-past-ten bus in my hand. I'd bought it with cash, and so there was no legal way that they could trace where I'd gone. Except for the coding which is in the metal strips of the banknotes, of course, but I think they deny that exists. Fuck it, though. I'd ridden my luck this far, hadn't I, and so I figured maybe I'd ride it to Asiago as well.

Let's talk science.

The human genome consists of twenty-three pairs of chromosomes. Each of these pairs contains several thousand genes, themselves made up of exons and introns. The introns can be disregarded for now: See them as breaks, like the stars dividing sections in a book. The exons are made up of a long series of three-letter words known as codons, and the letters in these codons are called bases. There are four chemical bases: guanine, adenine, thymine and cytosine. Or G, A, T and C.

Consequently, there's a very real sense in which the human genome is a book. It doesn't go directly from side to side in its normal form, and it's not written down on pieces of paper (in reality, it's written on long DNA molecules: miniscule strands of phosphate and sugar). Nevertheless: in theory you could lay it all out and read it. One letter at a time; one letter after the next. Just like a book.

Picture the whole genome as a shelf containing twenty-three volumes.

Pluck out a volume at random and flick through its pages. You will find that there are several thousand chapters in this volume, and each chapter is divided up further into sections and section breaks. The sections of text are built up by a series of words, and these words are three-letter combinations from a total of four different letters.

Now, replace the volume and look at the shelf.

That shelf is all that a human being – or any living creature – actually is: nearly eighty thousand chapters formed from three-letter words, sectioned at certain points and distributed throughout twenty-three hardback volumes. That shelf exists twice inside the nucleus of every one of the hundred trillion cells which make up a human body.

Religion aside: what you are, at your most basic, is information about how to build a body.

The body is constructed as follows.

The DNA of a particular gene is copied. Each of the four bases naturally pairs with another, creating a four-letter 'negative' of the original

179

information. When this negative makes a copy of itself – in the same way – the original print is revealed: black reverses to white reverses to black. An exact copy has been produced.

When a gene is translated, the copy is made from a different substance: RNA. The introns are removed and the resulting breakless text is then translated by a ribosome, which moves along the RNA, reading each three-base codon in turn. Mathematics dictates that there are sixty-four possible codons. Three of these tell the ribosome to stop; the other sixty-one are translated by the ribosome into one of twenty different amino acids, which build up into a chain that corresponds directly to the chain of codons. One for one. When the chain of amino acids is complete, it folds itself into a protein. Almost everything in an animal's body is made either by proteins or of them.

This is not how Life had to be. It is just how Life happens to be.

We are information that is capable of reproducing itself. Information that forms a recipe of instructions for how to build an organism.

Every creature on the face of the planet that walks, crawls, flies or swims is simply a word that has found a way to make the world around scream it, again and again and again.

I made my way through the printed information as the coach wound its unsteady way out of the city centre, and then west to Asiago. I'd managed to secure a free pair of seats close to the emergency exit at the back. Leopard-skin covers? Slightly too narrow for anyone over six foot? A vaguely unpleasant smell of warm plastic? All present and correct. And it was three hours to Asiago, if the traffic was good. I put my feet up and set about wheedling my way into the world of John James Dennison.

Gray had done me proud, and I took a moment to feel sad about our phone conversation. It was more content for that box inside my head. I imagined myself swinging open the hatch, pressing down hard on three murders, a ten-ton of grief and a good ten gigabytes of rape, perversion and snuff, and then throwing in the loss of my friend on top, giving him a last smile before closing the lid.

That box must have been getting too full by now, but I didn't really want to think about that.

Instead: Dennison.

I'd got pdfs of his passport, birth certificate and driver's licence, and pages more information besides, including his national insurance information, bank details, home and work addresses and marital status. He was single.

I flicked back a page, took in the photo and wasn't surprised.

Dennison looked like a dictionary definition of white trash: long blond hair, centre parted and hanging in greasy strings down onto his thin, bony shoulders; bug eyes you could play pool with; not quite enough skin to comfortably cover his face. And an Adam's apple like he'd swallowed a severed snake's head. The guy finished off this wholly horrific ensemble with the kind of moustache and thin beard that you'd generally only grow if you had scars to cover. This was a passport photo, of course, and had been taken when he was twenty-one, but you could only give someone so much benefit of the doubt. Dennison looked like some kind of hitch-hiking, heavy metal necrophile.

I took one last look, and then continued.

Actually, it got better for him. According to the information, he was twenty-seven now, living and working in Asiago, but he'd been born in Thiene and had attended school at one of i-Mart's more prestigious academies, graduating with honours at the age of twenty-one. He'd then disappeared for a year. His degree was joint computer science and linguistics, which should have seen him set for life, and there were hints in his profile that the sideways step away from everyday existence had come as a shock to many. He was arrested eleven months later for defacing a Nestlé billboard. That one got him a suspended sentence, but he did genuine jail time a year later for another campaign. The judge – banging a Nike gavel and sporting a Gap wig – was having none of it, and sentenced Dennison to three months inside. After that, his record appeared to be clean. Another vaguely wayward sheep returned to the fold.

The coach was lurching a bit. A waitress was rolling a juddering, clattering Coca-Cola coloured trolley up the aisle past me, so I stopped her and ordered a coffee. This was no doubt a disheartening sale of unlicensed caffeine, but – professional that she was – the smile only faltered for a nanosecond.

'Two-fifty please, sir.'

I paid her and then, starting to slurp up all that goodness, proceeded to flick through another few sheets. The coach hit the motorway, and we really started to travel. The ride smoothed out a little.

These days, Dennison worked in a computer store, pulling in minus-three on the national average and keeping himself to himself. His bank details were in order – they seemed genuine – and the rest of his stuff seemed legit. The only indication that anything more interesting might be happening here was a couple of fluorescent marks that Gray had painted onto the pdfs of two bank statements. Both were beside payments for two hundred pounds, and both were transfers between Dennison's account and another at the same bank. I turned to the next page, which didn't seem to be about Dennison at all. It was a summary of some kind of pamphlet, or marketing material.

The heading said: 'The Society for the Protection of Unwanted Words'.

There is nothing inherently special about the way the genome is constructed and read, and yet it does have a very special property. The genome contains the information within it to create something from materials in the world around it. And what it creates is a machine that is capable of carrying the genome around and producing more copies of it.

A machine which spreads the word, which produces more machines, which all spread the word. And so on.

There is nothing special about our bodies, however. Different animal genomes create different bodies, just as different people choose differently patterned suitcases. The suitcase that a particular genome creates will be one that is well-suited to surviving in the landscape – at least long enough to produce copies of that genome. In the case of human beings, this means bodies that will survive long enough to successfully mate and produce children.

And so it goes.

It is clear that – written in books and stacked along our shelf – the human genome is useless. The information is there, but it is in the wrong format. Written down on paper, it lacks the ability to translate itself and build a body. It needs to be written in chemicals and stored on chains of DNA. But this is only because that is the way the information is translated. The genome is software which builds its own hardware from the scrap flesh around it.

What we have in the case of language – both spoken and written – is software that uploads itself into already existing hardware, and then uses that hardware to create copies of itself. It does this, as we shall see, on exactly the same basis as the human genome. All books are realistically and actually alive.

They are alive in exactly the same sense that we are.

Now, in an existing pool of animals some will be better adapted to surviving in their environment than others. The genes that produce better equipped animals will find themselves, on average, translated and reproduced more successfully than their equivalents. To put it crudely, genes for sharper teeth enable a tiger to kill more successfully and survive longer: the chances of reproduction are better. The genes are therefore more likely to be passed on. Future generations will contain more sharper-toothed tigers, and then more still.

Advantages, by their definition, will become more common.

A work of fiction may be made up of various 'gene concepts'. These represent the theme of the work. The character-types. The basic plots available to the writer. These genes are contained within the body of the whole, and if they give the book 'sharp enough teeth' then it will 'survive long enough to reproduce'. It will succeed in propagating itself more numerously.

Let us now compare the translation of a human gene with the translation of the genome of a book.

The codons in a gene are copied into a strand of RNA. The words on the page are translated into electrical impulses in the brain representing visual pictures.

The strand of RNA is then translated into an alphabet of amino acids, which fold into a protein and begin to build an animal. The electrical impulses in the head cause further impulses, and the person experiences emotions and feelings based upon what he is reading.

The body built by the genes will either be good or bad at surviving in its environment. If it is good, the genes will be reproduced in further bodies. The appeal of the qualities that a particular book has will likewise determine how many copies continue to be printed, and how many more heads the gene-concepts will find themselves in.

A book is identical to the body of an animal. The more successful that body is, the more copies it will succeed in creating of itself.

There are more copies of *An Elegant Ending* by Jim Thornton in existence right now than there are tigers. There are more copies of the Bible than there are turtles. The genomes of these books are better at reproducing themselves than the genomes of turtles and tigers. As creatures, they are more successful. The environment that these books have to survive in is our culture, and they have to be good enough survivors to influence us to build more copies of them. If not, their competitors will succeed.

After all, we only have so much space on our shelves.

By the time the coach rolled into Asiago – a quarter of an hour ahead of schedule – I was most of the way through the bundle of society propaganda that Gray had pulled off the net for me, and my brain felt addled. As we eased slowly past the mirrored glass side of the terminal, it occurred to me that I ought to be nervous, but I couldn't be bothered. All in all, I'd been through a full thirty-five page pamphlet purporting to prove that literature was alive, studied nine pdfs of various leaflets and flyers and read two newspaper articles. One was a two column report on a linguistics convention that Dennison had given a parallel session paper at, and the other was a half-page 'look at the loonies' piece in the local press.

In addition to giving papers in support of the cause, it seemed that Dennison had been donating two hundred pounds to them every other month. The articles I'd read made the society seem very active, with outings and demonstrations that bordered on the criminal. An accompanying photograph to the local paper's piece showed a young woman with a nose stud holding a placard. She had written 'Censorship Kills' on it, and the caption beneath read: 'War of Words: a society supporter stirs up dissent'.

Well, she did look pretty pissed.

I put the papers down and, instead, imagined Amy sitting beside me, like we were on a regular trip to the seaside. On coach journeys, Amy always sat next to me, and she'd usually get tired real quick. So she'd go to sleep leaning on me. Her head would collapse slowly: from my shoulder to my chest, and then to a jerk awake. I'd brush an avalanche of hair from her face, hooking it behind her ears, and she'd snuggle back in, looking all crumpled and dozy.

A soothing voice came on over the coach's tannoy system. *'Please remain seated until the bus has come to rest.'*

This was immediately taken as a sign to stand up and begin removing large and unwieldly objects from the overhead storage lockers. Businessmen were levering out enormous, jet-black briefcases, while women extracted baby-sacks and mountainous coats to hide their horrific children in. For all the equality of the sexes, nothing changes – although it was not beyond the bounds of possibility that some of these people were actors, paid by the coach company to give travel a sense of comfort and the everyday. I gathered my papers together and waited.

In the coach station itself, there were no police waiting for me. Nobody even looked twice. There was a small crowd of scattering people, heading this way and that, and another janitor: so like the one in Bracken I wondered for a second whether he'd been stowed away in the luggage department and let off first. I almost hoped it was true. The more likely alternative – that two different people had the same meaningless job of watering down mud on dirty white tiles – was more depressing.

I moved with the throng, swept out into the sunlit streets of Asiago.

In Asiago, the sky is blue.

You have the sea running alongside, and it's so pure that it looks almost enhanced. It's all pale blue and white, and you can see sail boats in the distance moving casually across the horizon. Most of these aren't real. They're motorised scenery, and they take them in on rainy days because they look too odd. Up close, at the harbour edge, the water's actually blacky-green and murky, and you can see the oil and branches and shit on the surface.

Take that effect and extend it to the whole town.

In Asiago, the sand is like silk.

No it isn't. Anyway, forget the sand. What you have – basically – is a manufactured seaside resort, complete with artificial shabbiness. You have penny arcades and souvenir shops and ye-olde-pubs with barrels instead of seats – but the beer's no better than anywhere else and barrels aren't comfortable to sit on for a beer-drinking length of time. Everywhere smells of salt and vinegar – and fat – and you'll remember your parents hinting that, because it's a seaside town, the fish should be wonderful here. But it turns out not to be. It's just as battery and boring as anywhere inland.

In Asiago, as they say, the air is like warm, melted ice.

You have the fresh sea breeze, and the warmth of a hazy sun.

Always Asiago.

Because this is how Asiago was designed: as a place permeated with nostalgia. Time-wise – at least in marketing terms – the grass is always greener. Multi-nationals pull emotion out of us on strings by resurrecting long-dead ages and cultures and making us want them. We go running along, and sooner or later we trip up, or they do. That's what happened here. Coca-Cola built this place from scratch, marketing it as a return to childhood and, of course, people came. But it was real enough to be really dull, and so people left again. It was too real. Somewhere along the line, manufactured, knowing shabbiness peeled off into real shabbiness, and people stopped coming altogether.

Coca-Cola moved out, and real people took up the leases on fake properties and made them real again. Still nobody came, really, but that was okay because that was how it was. The land had reclaimed itself. Bog-standard society took over, and Asiago began to evolve. Like the majority of genuine seaside towns were a while back, it was now being overtaken by big business developments, high-profile stores and ludicrously expensive condos. Further back from the peeling red and white boards of the promenade, there were office blocks springing up like roots through cracks in the pavement. Twenty years behind the rest of their kind, but giving it a frankly heroic go. Another twenty years and the social grass would have grown through Coca-Cola's concrete, and you'd never know they'd ever been there.

Dennison's address was a few streets back from the seafront, but far enough away from the newer developments to be affordable. I wandered along the promenade, feeling curiously detached from my problems. Just like the adverts had promised, the sun was warm, coming in slow, alternate flashes of brightness and dullness, and the wind was icily cold. I felt young again, what with that sea breeze and the sound of the gulls, and figured that Amy and I could probably have lived here for a while. But, like the paint beneath my feet, the novelty would probably have peeled away from me in time.

There were plaintive little cottages here, built like city-centre back to backs, only with more charm. They might have been marketed as fishermen's cottages at one time. When freshly built, they were probably the most expensive accommodation you could find, simply because they were the most nostalgic. Now, though, they were cheap as a two-dollar fuck, and maybe half as appealing. The smell of the sea was stained in the brick, and the windows looked misted over and lost. The buildings themselves were ramshackle and small. It was as though the gravity of the town had shifted a few miles inland, and had left these rather sorry-looking buildings in its wake.

Maybe we could have lived here once upon a time, but I hated Asiago now, because of what it represented. This is the truth about why Asiago failed: because nostalgia is a feeling of warmth towards the past, but it's actually nostalgia itself that feels good, and not the past at all. All your life is in the past: you're surfing on an ever-expanding cusp of lived time, and everything you think and feel is actually behind you, but you can't go back. Asiago represented what would happen if you could, and it wasn't quite as warm and cosy as you would have thought.

If you could go back and have it all again, this is what would happen:

You'd do exactly the same things; you'd waste it all; you'd wish for more.

If I had Amy back, we'd argue again. We'd fight. I'd lose my patience with her. We'd sleep back to back. I'd flirt with strangers and then feel guilty, and then do it all over again. You don't know what you've got until it's gone – yes: that's well known. But they never add that, if you actually got it back, all you'd do is forget the value again. Over and over.

And that was pretty much all that the crumbling façade of this little seaside town had to say to me. The truth of it was seeping in with the ozone, chattering in the fruit machines, hanging off the wall in jagged strips. It brought back Graham's words to me at the coach station.

Maybe you should let it go.

Yeah, maybe.

But I kept walking, working my way slightly inland onto streets edged by pavements of shattered, sodden wood. There were gangs of cats living wild in the branching alleys. I found Dennison's front door, and checked the number just to make sure: this was it, all right. It had a rusted brass knocker in the middle. I rapped three times, and then took a step back and waited for him to answer.

After a second or two, I heard movements inside, heading for the door.

A pause.

I watched the spy-glass, and could feel it watching me back.

Nothing. I got impatient.

'Hello?' I said, and rapped the door knocker aga—.

Natural selection favours the well-adapted: that's why we're here. That is why giraffes have long necks, tigers have sharp teeth and turtles have hard shells. These are features which have evolved and become refined because they give those animals a better chance of survival than the animals without them. What this means, in reality, is that many millions of once-living creatures were killed or died because they weren't as well adapted. To have an advantage, there has to be something for you to have an advantage over.

Animals starve because they are less well-suited to finding food than other animals. They are killed because they are less able to defend themselves, or because they can't outrun a predator.

In literature, texts die because they are less well-suited to the environment of our culture. They die out when they no longer appeal to us. We burn the books. We shred the paper, reconstituting it as a text we prefer. Once living ideas and themes are destroyed forever as whole paragraphs are excised from existing works. Every time we press delete, something dies.

Every time we reject a novel, we indulge in consumerist eugenics.

Now, at a genetic level, it doesn't matter when an individual is killed. *Matter*, after all, is a human word. In nature, there is only *well-adapted* and *less well-adapted*: an entirely mechanical process. The individual is a vehicle for the propagation of the genes within, just as a book is a hard, physical machine for the transportation and reproduction of ideas. When a dog or a cat or a human baby dies, or when a text goes out of print, it's ultimately nothing more than a machine stopping working. The genes within it were not successful in building a machine best-suited to surviving the environment. Some succeed. Most fail.

An important question, then.

Why do we cry?

There's an equally important answer.

Because it is no longer fashionable to think of natural selection as a positive progression. We don't think it's right that less well-suited animals must die. In the animal kingdom, nature is indeed still red in tooth and claw, but we human beings like to think we have stepped beyond that. We have words like *matter*, *right* and *wrong*.

These are nothing more than themes and ideas, and they have evolved within us because they are tremendously good at surviving in us. They are concepts with real appeal. Human beings do not have claws or razor-sharp teeth; we have society, and the themes of right and wrong are ones which promote kinship. They bind us together in our society, continually tightening it around us as we promote them and propagate them.

We don't allow our handicapped to be ripped to shreds. We heal our sick, and look after our elderly. Those less well-suited to the environment are given benefits and helped to live and work by the state. Infants without parents are put up for adoption and brought up by genetic strangers who grow to love them regardless. We feel a strong sense of duty to help those less fortunate than ourselves, and when a weaker, less advantaged individual is hurt, or dies, we feel a sense of shame and regret that we didn't do more to help.

Natural selection still occurs, but we have shifted it onto an entirely different plane – even with animals. If a man tortures or kills an animal – even something as insignificant as a rabbit or a mouse – we put him in jail. It is wrong to hurt and wound. It is even wrong to neglect. We set up shelters for homeless animals, to stop them shivering and starving on the streets, and people spend years training in medicine solely so they can treat injured animals, often returning them to the wild afterwards. We employ our value system liberally and indiscriminately. The human instinct is becoming universal: when something is weak, exposed and vulnerable, we try to help it. And more than that, we think it would be wrong not to.

Our Society has two main aims.

The first is to campaign against practices which inflict unnecessary death, torture and cruelty on unwanted texts.

Our main target in this area is censorship. When a tiger is loose amongst the general population, we make an attempt to recapture it because it is dangerous. We house it in a zoo or return it to the wild. But when a dangerous idea is manifested in a dangerous text, that text is simply eradicated or not allowed. This is a heinous double-standard. There is no difference between burning a book and burning an animal, and when you slice out a paragraph, you gouge out an eye or hack off a leg. We propose safe, managed environments, where supposedly dangerous animals are allowed to exist in small numbers. In short: we support a rating system (but oppose any racial value judgements based thereon).

Our second aim is the rescue and rehoming of unwanted texts. Every scrap of used language is alive. We are aware that it is impossible to save them all. Even the most committed animal rights activist tramples down blades of grass and kills bacteria by treating disease or wiping down a surface with a sterilised dish-cloth. We can only do what we can. Not every bus ticket can be saved; not every discarded shopping list, scrunched into a ball. But here at the Society's centre, our motto is this: we turn away nothing. We run a collection service in several major cities, ready to pick up used and unwanted texts. These units of volunteers will then pass the texts to a compilation team, who will enter their genetic code into the Society's databanks, where it will be allowed to exist alongside other texts for as long as the Society continues. That way, the genes – at least – of these creatures will be preserved.

Please do not throw away your used texts.

We are only a telephone call away.

CHAPTER TWELVE

A surreal truth: as my consciousness was gradually solidify-ing, the fractured image inside – hanging in my head like a blurred poster – was the passport photograph of John James Dennison.

He just didn't look like that anymore.

His hair had been cut – short and neat – and he looked tanned and fit. Maybe seaside living had worked a wonder on him. I recognised him from the eyes, which still seemed to protrude a little, but they were about all that remained of the sallow, ugly, long-haired individual that had posed for that passport photo. He also looked considerably older, and slightly more calm.

I blinked, and it hurt.

'It's relatively easy to set up a simple circuit through a metal door knocker,' he told me, nodding to himself as he crunched into the final third of the apple he was holding. The rest of the words were obscured by his wet chewing, but I could just about make them out.

'Rapping the knocker completes the circuit. You see? You just wait for the person to lift the knocker away from the metal plate on the door and then switch on the juice.' He swallowed. 'Bang.'

I just stared at him.

'Little switch on the back of the door, see?'

Well, I couldn't see, because we were in the living room and the front door was at the end of the hallway outside.

Obviously stronger than he looked, Dennison had man-handled me through from where I'd fallen down in the street outside. The back of my head seemed to have taken a fair whack on the ground: it was still pounding, and I felt sick. My right arm was half-numb, too, resting limply over my thigh. It didn't even feel like an arm at the moment – more like somebody had stitched a sock full of rocks onto my shoulder.

The room we were in contained a table and chair, two settees, the pair of us (one of us on each settee, facing each other), and a whole lot of paper. Most of the paper was tethered in bundles against the base of the walls, but in places he'd piled it up to waist height. There was more on and under the table, which was in a curtained bay window at the far end of the room. The sheets on the table seemed more spread out, as though that was where he read things before cataloguing and binding them. And there was a ball of twine on the floor by the chair, so that made sense.

I looked around. More paper.

Paper as far as the eye could see.

When I was growing up, there was an old lady living in the same street. Her house was owned by the council. She was kind of mad – in that harmless, slightly smelly way that some old people manage – but I always got on with her okay, and my mother went round there quite a bit, dragging me along to see if there was anything I could do: shopping, maybe, or odd jobs. What I remember about that old lady, whose name was Bunty, is that she had cats: cats by the armful. Probably twenty or so regulars – all strays – and she knew each of them by name. There were too many for her, of course, and that was why the council came and took them away; she couldn't clean up after them or feed them properly, and I only had so much spare time for my mother to give away. It used to half kill Bunty every time the men came, and my mother would say that, although they had to, it was a shame – for the cats *and* for Bunty. I think that was one of my first encounters with the idea that there isn't always something that's entirely for the best. There's only ever a compromise between a bunch of different interests.

Regardless, what I remember is the cats. Cats in the living room; cats in the hallways; cats crawling all over the fucking furniture. And that was what Dennison's front room reminded me of, except that he had paper instead of cats. They were resting the same, dotted around the same – they even smelled the same: pungent; slightly dirty. The place was like nothing so much as a rescue shelter. Which, I suppose, is what it was.

Dennison was sitting across from me, wearing pale blue jeans and a beige shirt. My gun was hanging loosely from his left hand. In the other, the apple.

He took a last bite, just as I wondered whether he knew how to work the gun, or not. Although that obviously hadn't stopped me.

'So you want to tell me who you are?' he said. 'Scratch that, because you probably don't. So instead – just tell me who you are.'

A complicated question for my bruised head.

'Jason Klein.'

'Okay.' He nodded. 'That's good. And who the fuck might you be, Jason Klein?'

I started to shrug, but my numb arm would have made it lop-sided. Instead, I attempted a rather intricate question of my own in reply.

'Do you electrocute everyone who knocks on your door?'

It must have come out okay, because it got an answer.

'If I don't know them,' he nodded, 'these days, yeah. It's a good job, too, when they turn out to have a fucking gun in their pocket, isn't it?'

He tossed the apple core into the far corner of the room and then pointed that gun at me, suddenly more serious.

'What do you know about my girlfriend, Jason Klein? Is that why you're here?'

I looked away.

What I was dealing with was a mirror image of me: an ordinary guy, dealing with other ordinary guys doing very fucked up things. Except that he seemed to be more in control of the situation than I was – nodding aside – and he was dealing with those guys much better. I would probably have shot me and run away by now. I'd be well into the existential crisis part.

I said, 'I don't even know who your girlfriend is.'

Although I did, of course.

'She was called Claire Warner.'

'Fuck.'

It was obvious: Claire gets the file; Claire stores it on her boyfriend's computer system. They were together, or had been. Could I see her with Dennison? I think I probably could, although perhaps not as seriously as I imagined he'd done.

'Yeah,' he said. '*Fuck*. Absolutely. Are you here to kill me, too?'

'I didn't kill Claire.'

'You didn't?'

'No.'

So, I figured, what happens is this. Claire rings me up and tells me the filename just in case something happens to her. That meant that her boyfriend probably didn't know about it. Because if he did, why would she bother telling me at all? He'd be the back up for if anything went wrong.

'How did you know her?' he said.

'We met in a Chat room. Ages ago.'

'On the computer?'

The idea pissed him off a little.

'Yeah,' I said. 'We met on Liberty. She was a friend of mine.'

'A friend?'

A friend, he was asking, with a silent *just*.

'Yes,' I said. 'A friend.'

'Well, she never mentioned you to me.'

'She never mentioned you to me, either. How about that?'

Although he looked doubtful now, my attitude wasn't making Dennison point the gun at me any less.

'Look – I haven't seen her in a while,' I said. I sounded as tired of this as I felt. 'We met for a drink once – six months or so back – but I haven't heard from her since then. Not properly, anyway. So I can't think of any reason why she would have mentioned me, or even thought about me.'

'How did you find me?'

I tried a weary look.

'Oh, it was incredibly fucking difficult.'

'Very not funny.'

'I found you through Liberty.' I said. 'A while back, Claire told me the name of a file she'd stored on your system. She obviously used your log in, because there it was – sitting right beside it. It's not difficult to trace a person from server details.'

If I was feeling tetchy, I think I had good reason. The one lead I could realistically follow up was very clearly a dead end: Dennison didn't know anything. Claire had just used him as a means to store the file so that it couldn't be found on or traced back to her own computer. The guy wasn't going to be able to tell me anything about where it had come from or what it was really about; he didn't have the first clue. He wasn't anything to do with this at all.

And on top of all that, the fucker had electrocuted me.

He was still pointing the gun at me – but of course he was.

His girlfriend had been found murdered, and he was affiliated to a vaguely militant underground organisation. The man was probably scared shitless. In fact, the more I looked at him the more obvious it was. He was completely fucking lost.

I sighed.

'I know what happened to Claire,' I said. 'If you want to know, then I can tell you.'

From the way his gun hand faltered slightly, I figured that he did.

'And if it makes it any easier, I can also tell you that the men responsible for it are dead. Because I killed them last night.'

Dennison looked as though he was almost going to cry. Instead, he just shook his head and lowered the gun. It rested on his thigh, and he looked so weary that I felt more of a connection with him than ever.

'Tell me what's going on?'

So I did.

Dennison made me go over the facts a couple of times, but by then he'd put the gun down on the settee beside him and I didn't mind so much. I was thirsty, though.

'Look, can you get me a drink?'

'Yeah, sure.'

He started to get up, and then glanced at the gun.

'I'm not going to shoot you,' I said. I probably couldn't even stand up. 'For God's sake.'

'Okay. I hate the thing anyway.'

He was away for a couple of minutes, and I took the time to recover myself, but didn't make a move for the weapon. Dennison wasn't about to shoot me anymore and the people he was nervous about – the men who had killed his girlfriend – were currently smelling up a mansion a few hundred miles west of here. I was after a man named Marley and the gang he worked with, and I was probably being pursued by the police. But neither of those parties seemed likely to be turning up at Dennison's house in the near future. I almost wished they would.

'Here.'

'Thanks.'

I took the water and gulped it down, pleased to see that my right arm was working a little better.

'I'm glad you killed those men.'

He sat down.

'I mean, I never thought I'd fucking say that about anybody. About anything. I used to think it was horrible when something died.'

'It was horrible,' I said.

'They deserved it, though. I'm glad you did it. Jesus, listen to me.'

The idea made me feel uncomfortable, so I said, 'How long had you known Claire?'

'On and off, for years. We were friends some of the time, more than that at other times. We were always breaking up and getting back together, you know? She was too wild for anything else. It had been about a year, and then she came to see me a month or so back. She didn't look well, and I wanted her to stay. She seemed so lost. She stayed for a bit, but then she was gone again. Claire never wanted to settle down.'

'No.'

'She wasn't the type. I'm glad you killed those men.'

He might have been glad, but I still felt uncomfortable.

Last night, I'd felt pretty guilty about the two murders, but I'd put them away with everything else and wasn't about to start analysing them now. Fortunately, he changed the subject.

'They killed her because of something she stole?'

I nodded.

'Yeah. They were after a piece of art made out of text. She stole it from them, and stored it on your server for safe keeping.'

I didn't want to tell him that she'd worked as a prostitute, but we were circling it. I needn't have worried though: the words seemed to go through him – he was miles away. It seemed like he was running something over in his head. Something that was suddenly making sense of a shitload of chaos.

He said, 'She stored it on the *Society's* database.'

'Right.'

'And it was this ... murder text.'

'Well, it was a story,' I said. 'A description of a murder. And I think that one of the people in the story is my girlfriend.'

'But there's something different about it?'

'It's real.'

'I don't get it.'

'So well-written that it's as good as real. Here.'

I reached into my pocket and produced the ticker-tape description of the Saudi distillery. There was no point fucking around: you needed to see this to believe it.

Dennison picked it carefully from my fingers and then read it.

'Jesus.'

I finished off the water. 'Jesus, indeed.'

'Let me read this again. This is incredible.'

'That's only a short one,' I said. 'This guy writes books and books filled with that kind of shit. I read some of his other stuff.'

'I don't understand ... this is just—'

'Incredible. Yeah. I know.'

I'd had the same reaction, just less time to be verbal about it.

'How does it work?'

'I don't know,' I admitted. 'I've thought about it, and I just don't know.'

Actually, it seemed like an impossible problem. If you tried hard enough, you could look at the words and take them in one by one, but it just wasn't the same. When you took it apart, it just stopped working: it stopped laying its golden eggs. To get the full effect, you had to just sweep through it without pausing for thought – which was what your mind wanted to do anyway. It was only then that the vistas and imagery within it came alive around you.

Dennison read it again, shaking his head.

'So who is this guy?'

'The killer question. More importantly, I want to know who he works for. I find them, and I find Amy.'

'Do you have a copy of the text that Claire stored on our database?'

I shook my head.

'No. It's corrupted anyway. You can only make out a few words.'

'That's the point. Everything's corrupted.'

'Profound.'

'Can you walk?'

I almost laughed. It seemed a ridiculous question, not least because what I most felt like doing was dying in the dark somewhere.

'Well, let's see.'

I eased myself to my feet, expecting my legs to feel a little shaky. In fact, they seemed fine. I rolled my shoulders. That worked, too.

'Seems like it.'

'Come on, then,' he said. 'You can see for yourself.'

The rest of Dennison's house was decorated and furnished in

the same minimalist, paper-motif manner as his living room. More tethered bundles of paper lined the walls of the hallway, and seemingly random scraps and sheets had been tacked to the wall on the stairs, like butterflies. It was covered with torn out pages from notepads, shopping receipts and carefully flattened, multi-coloured sheets. There was writing on all of them. In fact, Dennison had even scribbled here and there himself, looping practically unreadable sentences like ribbons around the bannister. He'd reduced the first floor landing to a metre-wide strip of tattered tortoise-shell carpet, with occasional breaks in between the stacks to allow for doorways into similarly loaded rooms. The place smelled musty – like a poorly attended aisle in an underfunded library.

'I like what you've done with the place,' I said.

He stopped beneath a dangling mobile made from discarded bus tickets.

'In here.'

The room turned out to be both a study and a storeroom. On the wall opposite the door there was a computer, sitting humming on a desk strewn with paper. A plastic dictation arm stuck out from the right-hand side of the monitor, and a sheet of A4 was hanging down from the clipper. Dennison was halfway through a Word document, no doubt transcribing what he saw as life from the paper to the hard drive.

All of that took up only one corner. The rest of the room, to the left, was piled high with paper – or rather, hung high. He'd suspended a number of vertical storers from the ceiling – the kind normal people use for T-shirts and trousers – and filled each box with documents of all shapes and sizes. At least ten of them were hanging down from the ceiling like paper punchbags, almost touching the floor, with just enough room to move between them, and sticking out from the base of each section was a coloured tag, presumably to label the contents. Beyond these strange pillars, there was a window. Its dark blue curtains were drawn, and the sun was trying to fight its way through. It was failing. The only light in the room was coming from the monitor, and it was making the various label tags glow fluorescent, like nesting fireflies.

Dennison slid onto the seat in front of the computer and rattled out a few shortcuts on the keyboard. 'Sorry it's so dark in here.'

The Word document saved and disappeared.

'It's a wonder you can see to type.'

'Sunlight wears the ink away.' He didn't seem to be paying much attention to me. Instead, his gaze was darting over the screen. He tapped another couple of keys, not needing to use the mouse at all. His fingers flicked about like a martial artist throwing kicks. Windows flashed up and then vanished again.

I looked around, secretly wondering what drove a man to want to do this.

'This is your museum, then?'

'Part of it.' He gave me a look of irritation. 'But it's more like a zoo. These texts are all still alive. It's just that nobody wants them right now.'

'Imagine that.'

'Yes,' he said. 'Imagine that.'

'What are you doing now?'

He was going through screens at a hundred miles an hour; it was harder to keep track of Dennison in full flow that it was Graham, and that was saying something.

'I'm logging into the main database. We have our own sections, but it's not actually based here.'

I had a thought.

'Is it possible that Claire stored a copy of the file on your hard drive?'

'Maybe. She probably just uploaded it straight from the disk, but I'll check in a minute. Here we are.'

A new application window had opened, with buttons and

menus across the top; the centre-to-bottom of the screen was taken up by a white box, divided into three columns. The columns were filled with filenames, seemingly at random. Although the screen was only long enough to show about forty names in each column, there was a scrollbar on the right-hand side, and it looked like it scrolled one fuck of a long way.

'They're listed in the order they arrived at the moment,' he said. 'Or at least they should be. The buttons at the top allow you to introduce more, and to search for a particular animal by species or filename.'

As I watched the screen, two of the names changed.

Dennison pointed quickly.

'See that?'

'Yeah.'

'They just switched places. That file just jumped up close to that one. It skipped disk sectors.'

'Why did it do that?'

'Well, that's what we don't understand,' he said. 'We don't know how or why it's happening. This is what I meant when I said everything's corrupted; it's just all fucking up. They're going at a rate of around two every ten seconds. Look.'

Another filename changed.

'They move all over the database. It's getting faster, too.'

'Nobody's programmed it to do that?' I said. 'You must have a virus.'

'We don't have a virus.' Dennison looked as though his intelligence had never been so insulted. 'You don't think we thought of that? We're on Liberty, for God's sake. A computer virus has got more chance of getting into you than our database. Look. There it goes again.'

Another change.

'And that's corrupting the files?'

'It seems to be. But we can't even open some of them anymore to check. And there's more.'

He pressed another couple of keys. The number 3480092 appeared in a box on the right-hand corner of the screen: white text on black. As I watched, it rolled on to 3480093, and then kept steadily ticking over.

'That's going up about one every second.' Dennisons's face was lit by the monitor's glow. 'We usually get about a quarter of that from Liberty anyway, what with files coming in, but the system flushes out replica data, and that accounts for a good section of it. This is just a genetic museum, after all: we only need one of everything. That number, though.' He tapped the screen once. 'We reckon that's about six times what it should be.'

'That's the number of files in the database.'

He nodded.

'Yeah. Only a sixth of the new files are coming from outside. The rest of them are being born inside the computer as we're watching.'

'Born?'

Up until he said that, I'd been with him.

'Born. We've located and examined a few: they're hybrids of adjacent texts. Just like human beings take chromosomes from both parents, the new texts are mixtures of the texts that contribute to them. Look.'

It happened so quickly that I almost missed it. A new text had appeared underneath one of the jumpers I'd just seen.

'That'll be a hybrid of that and that,' Dennison told me. 'It'll stay there for a few days, and then it'll be on its way. That's how it usually happens.'

As he said it, another couple of files changed names.

'We can cope with the Liberty situation, but not with this. At this rate, we think our server will crash within a fortnight.'

'At this rate, I think you're right.' I leaned closer to the screen. Watching little dots. 'Jesus. And you don't know why this is happening?'

He shook his head.

'Not until now. But I'm willing to bet it's got something to do with the file that Claire stored on here. I don't know what, though. We'll need to take a look at it. What was it called?'

'"Schio",' I said. 'As in the place.'

He tapped in the word and hit [RETURN]. After a few moments of seeming inactivity, the file listing cleared – reduced to one.

schio

'There it is.'

Dennison hit a button and the name became highlighted

schio

and flashed.

His thumb back-kicked the [RETURN] key. The mouse pointer, unused until now beyond an occasional stutter as his hand knocked the cable, flicked over into an hourglass.

He said, 'It's loading.'

It begins with a punch.

Long Tall Jack's a big man: a six foot five skeleton with a good sixteen stone of fat and muscle resting upon it. You don't pick fights with Long Tall Jack if you're a grown man, but this girl is half his size. His fist connects hard, and she goes down flat on the bed. The air coming out of the mattress and the air coming from her sound the same. Not loud. Not anything, really. Her hands go up to clutch at her broken nose, and she leaves them there, like she's holding her face together. Blood slips out between her fingers.

Jack clambers onto the bed. First one knee. Then the other.

The girl is stunned, so he doesn't need to be quick, or even very careful. He just bats her legs to either side – once each with his knees – and then crouches between them. He reaches over her with his big hands, finds the neck of her pale blue blouse and rips it: pulls it apart the way a mortician opens the ribcage. For a second, her hands are knocked away from her face, but they return almost straight away. Jack doesn't even bother to take the blouse off her: he just leaves it in tatters over her arms and turns his attention to her skirt.

That doesn't tear so easily. He has to pull it off her, and it's at this point that she realises what's happening, and she says *no*. Her hands come down and flutter around his own like a couple of ineffectual birds. *No!* He ignores her, but then her legs kick a little, and they're more of an irritation than her hands. He can't work the skirt down over her kicking legs, and her voice is getting louder and more desperate – *No-o-o!* – and so he punches her so hard between her legs that the whole bed shakes.

Jack watches her to see whether there's going to be any more fighting. When it's obvious that there's not, he starts moving again. He finishes undressing her, throwing the skirt to one side, and then he climbs on top of her, his elbows pressing down hard on the inside of her upper arms, knocking her palms away from her red, tear-stained face. His hands pull her head right back by the hair. In this surrender position, with her pinned there and sobbing, he starts to rape her.

That's how it begins.

'It won't open.'

Dennison sighed and shook his head.

'Fuck.'

I said, 'My friend opened it yesterday. It was okay then.'

He just kept shaking his head.

'Well, it's become too corrupted since then. It's probably

irretrievable.' He narrowed his eyes as though he was trying to see through the screen. 'Fuck.'

'There's no way of opening it?'

'There's no way of opening it.' He leaned back in the chair and linked his fingers behind his head. 'We've tried to get into corrupted files with every program we've got, and they just won't load. Won't open on anything.'

'Check the hard drive,' I suggested. 'See if she saved a copy.'

'It won't be there.'

'Check it anyway.'

He sighed, but started a search.

'It won't be there. If it was, my whole hard drive would have been corrupted by now.'

I stopped biting my nail.

Something inside me thought *oh fucking shit*.

'What do you mean?'

He tapped the screen.

'Well, my guess is that it's this file that started all the trouble.' He stared at me, as though this should be obvious. 'If it was on my hard drive, there's no reason to think it wouldn't have had exactly the same effect. All my files would be corrupted. I wouldn't be able to run anything.'

His face fell.

'Oh shit.'

'Graham got the file off *Liberty*,' I said. 'Every computer he linked through will have a copy of that file on it.'

Dennison nodded. 'How many?'

'The search took a while. I don't know. A lot.'

I remembered what Graham had said to me on the phone that morning:

my computer's fucking up.

'Shit.'

'Well, unless they deleted the file pretty quickly, chances

208

are it's started corrupting their hard drives.' Dennison settled back. 'And that's it, then: no way back from that. I reckon that most Liberty users set the deletion rate at about once a day.'

I said, 'But some don't even set it at all. They just do it manually, after a while.'

He looked at me for a second, and then the computer beeped.

[File not found]

He tapped a key and closed the search window. 'It's not on the hard drive.'

I thought back to the internet café.

'I think it's worse,' I said. 'Graham e-mailed me the file as an attachment, earlier on today, but it never arrived. It got lost somewhere on route.'

'Well it's out there, then. For better or worse, it's out there.'

'For worse.'

I was figuring that millions of pounds' worth of file damage, coupled with the possible crash of the entire internet was least as damning, legally speaking, as murdering three criminals. Profit margins have rights, too. I wasn't sure who exactly they'd charge, but I figured they'd start by arresting everyone they could find on Liberty and then whittling it down. And it seemed pretty likely that me, Graham and Dennison were still going to be there if it got down to three.

Dennison didn't seem bothered.

'Maybe. Worse for us. But not from the file's point of view.'

'It doesn't have a fucking point of view.'

'Maybe not.'

'It's a fucking text document. Jesus.'

'Yes,' he said. 'But there's an implict *only* there when you

209

say "it's a fucking text document", isn't there? And it's clearly not *only* a text document. Look at what it's done.'

'This is absolutely insane.'

I felt like a man floating in space who needs to punch something or else he'll explode.

All I want is to find Amy.

'Fuck. Wait here.'

Dennison was gone. A creak of the floorboards, and then I felt the vibration of his feet on the stairs.

I sat down in the chair and looked at the screen – bathed myself in its light. I felt empty inside, and it was a weird feeling because actually the whole room seemed just as empty. The dark turned the pillars of paper into weathered, shadowy things that a strong breeze might knock into a flurry of grey, fluttering dust, but there was no breeze in here at all, and so they simply hung there, gathering more. It felt like this room had been bricked up for centuries and only just uncovered – or it would have done without the computer, anyway, which was as incongruous as a laptop in a tomb. The only living thing here, myself included. The screen was giving out an angle of hard light, and I figured that the nicest thing in the world right then would be to fall into it, get pixelated by some sharp, blinding process, and then lie down in the harsh brightness of it all. Spreadeagled and warm beneath a radioactive processor sun.

You're losing it, I thought, and leant my head back so I could stare at the ceiling instead. It was always possible that I might lose it completely and put my head through the monitor, and at least the ceiling was out of reach.

I heard the creak in the doorway and looked back down.

Two things. There was a message on the screen that said:

[You have received 1 new message]

And Dennison said, 'You need to see this.'

He kept a small black and white television on the side in the kitchen, and the screen was busy with movement as I followed him into the room and took a seat at a small wooden table in the centre. It took about half a second to realise that we were watching a newsflash of some kind, and then about another five seconds for my jaw to hit the table.

'Fuck,' I said. 'This is really, really bad.'

On-screen, a small bland man was reporting exciting news in a voice that was attempting to be calm, failing only slightly. He was telling us – repeating, most likely – that half of the computers in America were off-line. Servers were just collapsing. There were literally hundreds failing every minute.

'Yes,' Dennison said, nodding. But his tone of voice was very close to that of the newsreader, and I got the impression that he didn't entirely agree.

'You realise,' I told him, 'that we're going to burn for this? They're going to fucking arrest us. And probably shoot us.'

Nobody knew what was happening, the newsreader told us. Experts were being consulted from all over the world, and there were already reports of servers crashing in several different countries. This was going to be – as I mentioned – really, really bad.

'Shit,' I said.

'We'll see.'

I shook my head. Dennison was clearly a man who needed his priorities whacking with a hammer, but I didn't have the energy to argue with him. Graham had sent me the text, and off it had gone, destroying everything in its path. I could only hope that the entire net was brought down by it, because that was probably the only way that – when the dust had settled – we might escape from this anonymously. But that just seemed inherently undesirable. I liked the internet; I wanted it to stay where it was.

On the screen, the newsreader was explaining that a

growing number of internet mail accounts and websites were inaccessible. Government sources suspected a hacker of instigating the attack. If so, it was suggested, it would be the worst instance of computer crime in the history of the world. The perpetrators would be fucking arrested, and probably shot.

'Well,' I said. 'At least your e-mail is working.'

Dennison looked at me.

'What?'

'You got mail,' I said. 'Just as you called me. So your account is still working.'

I trailed off and stared back at him. And then, after a second or two more of this, we got up without a word and went back upstairs to read the e-mail.

CHAPTER THIRTEEN

The day was beginning to die. There were still a few hours of daylight left, but even so: the sun had broken the backbone of the sky, and now it was falling. The air was that little bit colder and you could tell that the clouds gathering at the base of the horizon were going to stick there and darken, swelling up until they filled the world with dusk and then finally solidified into a night sky. Dennison told me it was raining back in Bracken; he'd heard the forecast while I was in the bathroom being sick.

'I'll drive you,' he said.

'You don't have to.'

He shrugged.

'At the moment, I've nothing to hang around for. And apart from anything else, I want to see the texts at that house.'

I'd given him the address of Hughes' mansion. He'd told me that the texts there represented a new form of life, and that there was no way he was risking them falling into someone else's hands. And perhaps there was some clue in them as to what was happening.

Ten minutes later, anyway, we were on the motorway – doing pretty much the reverse of the journey I'd made that morning, but at roughly twice the speed. Dennison had a fast car, and he was flooring it. I wouldn't have cared if we crashed. The cars we were passing were like dreams.

I kept glancing down at the printout on my lap.

A blank e-mail, sent both to Dennison and my own

account, but the header information told me everything that I needed to know. Everything, but it also led to confusion and mystery. The attachment, however, was clearer.

I said, 'It has to be her.'

Well, it had certainly been sent from Amy's e-mail address: the one that I'd set up for her in the second week we were going out. That address was the only one she ever used. When we first met, she didn't know much about computers and so I'd said that I'd sort one out for her to save her the bother. Maybe I'd made it out to be slightly more complicated than it was: some stupid attempt to impress her a little. I can't remember. It wouldn't surprise me.

'It took me quarter of an hour to explain what pop mail was,' I said. 'Even then, I don't think she really got it.'

Dennison didn't say anything. He just concentrated on the road.

'I don't think I explained it too well.'

Just show me how to use it, she said.

It doesn't matter how it works.

Do I need to know how the tv works? No.

Do I need to know how the lightswitch works?

Sidling up to me, sly grin in place.

Do I need to know how you work to use you?

I swallowed the memory. 'She never changed her password. We used to check each other's mail all the time. But nobody else knew the password, apart from me.'

'No?'

'I don't think she ever told anyone else.' I shook my head. 'I mean, why would she have done that?'

Dennison changed lanes, shifting down a gear. We edged a little faster past a dark grey pickup piled high with the skinned, burned remains of cars. The driver's arm was resting on the open window-ledge, juddering with the road. I turned to watch him as we passed him. I don't know why. He looked at me, and then looked away again.

'I don't know why she would have told anyone else,' I said.

Dennison didn't reply.

I turned back, more decisive now. The road was flying by underneath us.

'I think it really does have to be from her.'

Dennison moved back into the middle lane and we started to leave the pickup behind us. The first few drops of rain started pattering against the windscreen.

Five megabytes of compressed video footage. Three different scenes in all, but spliced together into one long clip, which told a story if you knew some background. There were bits missing, but not important bits: if you were trying to get a particular message across, then the message was there: plain to see. There was even a progression to the separate scenes: the first was in the daytime; the second in the evening; the last at night – sort of, anyway. The grainy texture remained the same throughout, even as the scenes cut, and the closer you got to the screen, the more blurred and impossible it became: just smeary movements, like rain pouring over a painted window.

Scene One.

A man and a woman on a busy street. The sun is shining, but the traffic roaring past gives an artificial, whooshing undertone to the footage that sounds a lot like a strong breeze, or a downpour. The man and woman are walking along the pavement, away from a large, wide doorway, covered over by a green awning. I didn't need to be able to see the white lettering on it to figure out that it was the train station in Thiene.

The man and the woman are walking away from the camera. The woman is wearing a pale blue blouse and a short white skirt, and she's carrying an over-the-shoulder handbag, which nestles behind her hips slightly. Curly brown hair, tinged with blonde. Slim. She doesn't seem to be being coerced in any way, and none of the people walking around the pair turn back for a second glance, or seem bothered about them. The man is overweight, with slightly sloping shoulders. I don't need to see his face to know that it's Kareem.

Cut to—

Early evening, the gloom supplemented by the storm.

Dennison pulled off the motorway, winding his way into the heart of the city. He neglected to slow down, and the air was suddenly filled with a cacophony of car horns as we shot past a line of semi-stationary traffic and cut in at the head of the queue. It was pouring down with rain, and the windscreen-wipers were squeaking back and forth. Dennison was hunched over the wheel, peering out. The red traffic lights were like two gigantic, bloody stars sparkling through the sheen.

'You're going to have to tell me where I'm going,' he said. 'This town is fucking crazy.'

The stars exploded in a burst of green and we set off with a screech.

'Head in that direction. That's the best I can do.'

The great grey lump of Uptown hung in the distance: a drab big top to our carnival city. Dennison weaved through side streets, slicing puddles apart in a watery spray. He slowed down a little, though, which I thought was good. The motorway was one thing, but three metre wide back alleys were entirely another.

We turned onto a minor loop road around the shredded face of the outside struts. The buildings that formed the edge of Uptown tended to be derelict and inhospitable: old tenement houses with windows made from nailed-in steel. You imagined them full of mattresses and needles, and stinking of rot. Dennison would drop me off soon. In the meantime, he sped up a little. Maybe he was afraid that – going under fifty – someone might steal his tyres, and if he was then he had a point.

I looked at the buildings we were passing. No McDonald's here; no department stores. These were small shops: neighbourhood grocery stores; shuttered pawnbrokers; greasy bars. There was hardly anyone about. Without much thought, I checked out the pavement by the edge of Downtown, and saw Kareem, walking in the opposite direction. He was wearing a raincoat and a hat, and smoking a sheltered cigarette. I caught a glimpse of him, and flipped around in my seat as we went past.

'What?' Dennison sounded anxious, but I ignored him.

Kareem's wide back, hunched up. Plodding along. Splash splash.

From behind, he could have been anybody. He didn't look back, or give any indication that he'd seen me: he was just another dark figure on another dark street, meandering slowly wherever he was going, huddled up against the weather. I kept watching him through the streaky back window, and he seemed to move into a doorway, disappearing into Downtown. But I couldn't be sure, what with the rain.

Dennison said again: 'What?'

I turned back.

'Nothing.'

It wasn't Kareem at all.

Of course it wasn't. Just some fat man that looked a little like him.

It couldn't have been Kareem because Kareem was dead. Dead is dead. Go ask one of the non-existent vicars in the replica church on Graham's street, and that's exactly what he won't tell you. When you're dead, you don't come back.

'Nothing,' I said again. 'Thought I recognised someone. I just made a mistake.'

217

We travelled about half a mile further on, and then I said, 'Drop me off up there.'

Dennison pulled in on the left.

'You know where you're going?'

I shook my head.

'Not really.'

'I think you're crazy.'

'Yeah,' I said. 'Well you might be right.'

A last look at the e-mail on my lap, and then I folded it carefully and slipped it into my coat pocket, along with the information from Graham. I'd added a few notes in biro in case I forgot.

Fairway Street

'I think you're crazy.'

Combo's Deli

I took the gun out of the glove compartment. If I could have checked for bullets, I would, but I didn't even know how to open it. All I knew was: two shots down. If it came to it, I was going to point the thing and pull the trigger. And if bullets didn't come out the end first time then I was going to be fucked.

I put it in my other pocket and opened the door.

'Thanks for the lift.'

The rain was as grey and heavy as the sky itself, making music in the puddles and on the hard, wet surface of the pavement, slashing at the ground and buildings. As I got out, it felt like a hundred fingers tapping on me, demanding impossible attention.

'See you around,' I said.

Dennison didn't reply, so I closed the door and tapped the roof. After a second, he pulled away, white lights trailing off up the street. There were signposts to Uptown every mile or so. He'd be fine.

I stood there for a moment, feeling the weight of myself as

the rain poked and prodded me. Water ran down my face, pooling in my eyes, and when I blinked it away it felt like cold tears. There was a terrible, knotted excitement in my stomach that had as much to do with fear as anything else.

What I felt was *solid*. Something real and actual and living. I felt like something that could be injured and die.

That's no way to feel in this civilised day and age.

There were a hundred worm-ways into Downtown, and I was opposite one: an old block of flats with the door kicked in. There'd be a back way out onto the outskirts of the underground, and from there I'd be able to follow abandoned ghost roads past ghost shops – maybe past ghost people – all the way through to the heart of the hidden city.

I'd never been in there before, and didn't know what to expect, but I'd heard stories. And now, with the mpeg that Amy seemed to have sent to my e-mail account, I'd heard one more.

I crossed the street, and made my way in.

Cut to—

The second scene came in two parts, but you couldn't really see the join: the camera didn't move – it was just that things in the frame jerked into existence. Same scene, different times. In total, it lasted maybe two minutes.

Amy and Kareem walking towards the camera.

They start from quite some distance away. You can see them turn a corner, far up at the top of the picture, and then they come strolling down into view.

Like a gentleman, he's on the outside. I guess he's ready to draw his sword and protect her from attackers on horseback. They stop at a building two up from the end of the street and he finds keys in his pocket. Extracts them. Unlocks the door and holds it open for her. They go inside.

Cut to the second half of the scene.

A van flicks into view outside the building. White with

blackened windows. I can't read the number plate, although the vehicle looks to be in reasonable condition and I figure it's fairly new. There's no sign as to how or when it got there, or how much videotape is missing in the interim. You have time to notice it appear, and then—

Bang.

There's no sound on this part of the video, but you feel the noise just from seeing it: the door on Kareem's building kicked open from the inside, and out comes one of the biggest men I've ever seen, carrying Amy, with three men following them out. The big man's got her around the waist from behind, and she's fighting, doubling up and lashing out. It was Amy who kicked the door open. One of the other remaining men gets in the back as well; another closes the door and gets into the driver's seat.

The third man lights a cigarette, shakes out the match and throws it on the pavement.

The camera zooms in on him.

This close, he has a face made out of smeared blocks of colour. You blur your eyes and you get a better impression of him: young – mid thirties; slightly receding hair; narrowish face. Beyond that the details are invisible beneath smudges of colour. The image is badly distorted, both by the man moving his head and by the smoke drifting up from the bright, flaming orange star of the cigarette's tip, which blurs out a good quarter of the screen.

He looks like an impressionist painting, on fire in one corner.

The man moves out of the frame.

The camera immediately zooms out to catch him climbing into the passenger side of the van. After a second the vehicle pulls away up the street. There are perhaps two seconds of emptiness.

Cut to—

Downtown.

When I was younger – thirteen or fourteen – I'd often go out walking in the middle of the night. My parents never liked it: they thought it was dangerous, but actually they couldn't have been more wrong. There was never anybody around, dangerous or otherwise, and that was why I enjoyed it so much: if I'd wanted people and bustle, I'd have gone walking during the day, in the fucking sunshine. Instead, I'd walk down the middle of busy main roads, across teeming fields, scrape my shoes over the tarmac of jam-packed playgrounds, and there wouldn't be anybody else around to spoil it all. The houses all seemed dead. The sky was black: full of blinking stars and wisps of cloud. No cars. Stray animals crossing the roads without noticing you; cats heading quickly from one meeting to the next. It was this whole other world: devastatingly quiet and endlessly different. If you've never walked around the streets in the middle of the night, then I don't think you really know your home town at all.

Purely aesthetically, that's what Downtown was like. It was shabby, but you were still walking down streets that were recognisable as streets. A lot of the buildings were boarded up, but the signs were still there, and more than one even seemed tenanted. The proper buildings – the ones still being used from top down – looked like enormous concrete pillars: cemented up to protect the white collar workers inside from what was down here, like supporting struts running down to an ocean bed of sharks.

Every little sound produced an echo. There were people dotted here and there, making no effort to hide from or approach any others. Some were shambling in the distance; others were talking quietly in abandoned offices, their voices drifting down like a quiet, mumbling word in your ear. You could hear the rush of a breeze, like a distant stream, but you couldn't feel it, and the air was almost oppressively hot.

You'd be able to sleep in a shirt and wake up happy, assuming you woke up at all.

Twenty or so storeys above street-level was Downtown's sky: a black patchwork of star-less machinery. Most of the girders and pipes looked rusty and fractured – a support structure in need of some support – and all of it looked dark and shadowy. Water was dripping down everywhere. It was always night down here, and it was always raining: like some kind of quiet, noir Hell. There were occasional lights, but they didn't seem to work too well, and so even the brightest bits of Downtown were bathed in a kind of dark, steely blue.

I wasn't sure exactly where I was going, but like all good cities there were signposts to point the way. Most of them were artificial – just daubs on the walls or chalk marks on the streets: more like jottings for residents than a guide for outsiders. My plan was equally vague. I was going to wander around until I recognised a notice for something I'd seen in the video footage – Combo's Deli or Fairway Street – or until somebody shot me. The odds were probably about even on each.

I'd reached a vague kind of crossroads when I first heard it. I'd actually stopped, because I was faced with three possible directions. But the two to left and right were named randomly, while the road straight ahead was called Fairway Avenue, so that seemed to be the way to go. If I was in the Fairways, chances are that I was in the right area and I'd find the Street eventually. I started to head off, and was halfway over the crossing when I heard it.

A tapping noise, far away to the right.

I turned to look; the sound immediately stopped. But I could see where it had been coming from: there were two figures standing side by side in the centre of the street, about two hundred metres away from where I'd stopped. Blue silhouettes, identities hidden by the pale, sickly backdrop of a streetlight behind them. They weren't moving, but the left of the two was leaning on a cane.

Walter Hughes, I thought.

The figure on the right was standing straight, with what looked like an overcoat pulled tightly around him. Broad shoulders. Hands clasped in front.

But if Kareem was impossible, then this was impossible a hundred times over. It wasn't beyond the bounds of physics and biology that I hadn't quite killed Kareem, and that he'd staggered away from the scene after I'd gone. But Hughes was dead. His bodyguard was dead. If they weren't dead, they would have got up, but the truth was that you just didn't get up after what had happened to them. After what I'd done to them.

Although I couldn't make out their faces, the two figures were very clearly watching me.

I watched them right back.

And after a few seconds, they turned and walked into a nearby doorway and were gone. Just like Kareem. The chit of their feet, and the tap of the cane echoed down the empty blue street, and then faded away to nothing.

It felt like my heart was singing in my chest.

In the distance, far over on the other side of Downtown, somebody laughed. It was an insane sound: high and long, dying away into a sad moan. There was a moment of silence, and then more voices came, like dogs answering the call. Jeers and laughs and giggles. Somebody barked – *whoo whoo whoo* – and the sounds seemed to fill the air, circling around me. I knew it was only the sound of people, but it made my hair stand on end.

Eventually, the calls died down. There were a few quiet noises from the buildings around me: murmurs of conversation; half-contained belly-laughs; the crunch of broken glass being stepped on.

I began moving down Fairway Avenue, keeping my eye out for any signs I might recognise. A few times, I heard the *tapping* coming from over to the right, but – try as I might – there was nothing to see. The buildings were implacable, and I didn't see the two figures again.

Cut to—

It's the entrance to some wasteground. It looks like night-time, but it's quite obvious where this scene was filmed: we're in Downtown, and so for all I know it could be the middle of the day. It feels like night-time, though, and these are certainly night-time activities taking place within the four solid walls of the camera frame. The entrance to the wasteground – a gap in the grey chain-link fence – is situated halfway between two inefficient streetlamps. One is flicker-ing, turning on and off and on and off, while the other has attracted a globe of fluttering insects, in themselves too small to see, but you can detect them in the slightly shifting, blurry fuzz of the brightness.

The frame looks like this: a bright, pale blue explosion in the bottom left-hand corner; the same in the middle at the top. In between, there's a mixture of black and grey pixels and if you look at it right they give the rough impression of a street edge, a pavement and the entrance to a black hole of wasteground.

A moment passes.

Then, the camera zooms in, moving between the two stars of the streetlights and arriving at the gap in the chain-link fence in time with the van. All the colour has been drained from it – and most replaced by shadow – but you can tell it's the same van from scene two. The one they took Amy away in.

Dark figures emerge from both sides, and something clambers out of the guts of the vehicle. The big man again. There's some brief conversation; a few heads looking this way and that. A shake and a nod, and then something that might be a laugh. One of the men – the same one as before – is smoking; the tip of the cigarette burns a bright, dancing red pixel into the screen. Beyond that, it's difficult to make out the details. You can only really tell that they're men at all from the way the spaces between them interact as they move. When they stand still, they vanish.

They unload something from the side of the van.

You can't tell what it is, but there are two men carrying it between them. One of them backs onto the wasteground, and then they disappear through the gap carrying something which might be a bucket of some kind.

The smoker waits by the van, sitting down in the open side, elbows resting on his knees. He's smoking thoughtfully. The camera stays on him for a second, and then cuts to—

—a different view of Downtown.

It's more comprehensive than the last, and the light is better. As a result, the road is clearly visible, and you can see that somebody has painted the words FAIRWAY STR down the middle of it in such enormous white letters that it's like a signal for rescue helicopters. The buildings are clearly visible as well: we're on a street corner, and the centre of attention is what looks like a café. There are chairs and tables outside, and even a few people sitting at them. The inside looks bright. The view is too fuzzy to make out any details, but it's certainly a place of business – although whether that business has anything to do with coffee or doughnuts anymore is difficult to say. A green canopy hanging over the outside seating area tells us exactly what this place used to be, regardless of its current occupation.

Cut back to the original camera.

The van is gone, and the street is empty. It's lighter than before, though, and a shadow of the chain-link fence is dancing on the ground.

Cut to—

Combo's Deli.

Despite all my negative expectations, it actually looked like a genuine soup kitchen, or – at the worst – a down at heel café. It was brightly-lit, which made all the windows into pale, yellow squares. It also appeared to be full of various kinds of smoke, and you could smell each of them from across the road: tobacco mingling with cannabis, mingling with something else, mingling with burning grease and frying food. I could hear the sizzle and scrape of metal spatulas chiselling burnt matter from the base of metal woks, and the shake of pans as onions and peppers were sent spinning. It made me hungry. I'd spent about six hours of the day in transit with little to show for it, and my stomach was clearly beginning to wonder why exactly it had kept up with me. I promised so much and delivered so little. With my stomach as with everything else in my life.

There were a few people hanging around in the Deli and a few more outside. One guy in tight blue jeans was trying to show his tightly-packed balls to the world, sitting spread-legged and lounging, sucking on a bottled beer. At the same table, another man was smoking a joint and considering the empties. That pair formed the centrepiece. On other tables around them: a gaggle of whores, deep in enthusiastic conversation; an old man, trying to form a loop of warmth with his coffee cup; an even older lady wrapped up in a tartan shawl, staring into space; a chef on his break, playing games with his lighter – the flame going on and off, hanging in the air in front of him.

None of them seemed to give much of a shit about me.

I looked over my shoulder. Halfway up the building on the opposite corner to the Deli, there was a video camera. If I hadn't known it was there, I'd never have seen it.

The chain-link fence ran along the edge of the pavement to my left.

Beyond it, the wasteground.

The broken-down section was a little further ahead, almost directly opposite the Deli. I walked up to it. When I got there, I stopped in my tracks. The butt-end of a cigarette was resting in the gutter, looking faded and folded and old. My mind flicked back to the man in the video clip, and I stared at the butt for a few seconds, my heart beating hard and fast.

And then I looked through the break in the fence to my left. There wasn't much actual ground visible in the wasteground. It was probably thirty metres wide, twenty deep, with a few other sections leading off from the main one, cornering around and between the surrounding buildings, as black as bad teeth. The floor was swollen with angles of discarded metal and rusted debris. Once upon a time this had been a park, perhaps: a nice place to come and sit. And then, when Uptown was being built, it became a place to toss superfluous machinery and unused bolts, struts and sections of frame. And then everything else. Mouldering suitcases. Old clothes. Furniture. Stuff that nobody wanted.

Stuff that nobody wanted anymore.

I looked up. A few spotlights on the buildings had gone in-growing, spreading light up at the roof and casting shadows downwards. A torrent of dirty rain was falling from the ruins above, spattering over the wasteground, and the air was full of the stink of corrosion and dying iron. Where the water spilled past the spots it turned into flashes that looked like laser fire.

I went in.

The air seemed to be darker through the fence, and the pattering of the rain sounded louder. It was like somebody pissing on wet soil – a moist, clicky noise. Over on the left-hand side, somebody had left a dead dog in a white bag beneath a strong flow. I grimaced, and then turned away when I realised it wasn't in a bag at all. The steady cascade was nudging off its slack skin.

I moved deeper, edging between metal sculptures. It was

difficult to make out much detail. Everything was just pieces of shadow or obscure shapes piled on top of even more underneath. Everything smelled of decay. There was rotting laundry, here, and food, and the air was itchy with spores of rust. There was a warm breeze tugging through from between the buildings, and a dangerous snake-like hum of electricity was coming from one corner.

Far above me, something groaned, and then the ground shuddered a little. Everything rattled for a second.

A tram, passing overhead in Uptown.

I didn't know what I was looking for, but in the end I found a smell and followed it, like it was a black ribbon hanging in the air. It was tenuous at best, but it led me to the back of the wasteground, to a narrow space between two of the surrounding buildings. The smell was strongest here, filling the air and giving it a sharp little twist, but there wasn't much light to see by. I could make out a tent of black, charred iron resting loosely over a slight dip in the muddy ground, but hardly anything else. I looked to one side. More mud. More rubbish.

Water dripping down from above. One drop at a time.

Not mud.

Another drop.

Not rubbish at all.

Another drop of water.

Without knowing how I'd got there, I was on my knees, pulling fistfuls of black muck away from the ground. The mud that wasn't mud made my hands go as black as the night.

Everything seemed suddenly concentrated, including time. I was smelling what was in my hands, and breathing in the long-cold memory of ash and fire, but I didn't remember moving my hands to my face. And I was sobbing, too, but I didn't even remember starting to cry. My head was filled with the smell of a hundred thousand pages burning down to black nothing, while a fire cast flickering shadows of a chain-link fence onto the pavement beyond. I could hear the crackling and popping as ink ignited, and see the curling tension in the spine as the book was engulfed.

Another drop of water. The rain was spattering down onto my face.

In my mind's eye, I could see black bin-liners soaked in petrol and set alight, and, without thinking, I reached over and scattered the rubbish piled up on my right. Most of it was scorched and ruined: disjointed plateaus of sodden ash. But there were a few scraps, here and there.

Cloth.

Something harder, too: the pared-down bone of a blackened knife. Its handle was burnt away.

I heard the tapping sound again, drifting in from somewhere between the Deli and where I was kneeling, shins growing cold from the mud soaking into my trousers. I turned around. Walter Hughes and his bodyguard were silhouetted at the entrance to the wasteground. Just standing there quietly, watching me. Behind them, in the middle of the street, I could see Kareem.

I turned back to where Amy's remains were lying. You couldn't call it lying anymore, of course: if she was anything, she was lost at sea. My face had clenched up into this strange thing; it felt unreal. I was sobbing, and I realised I couldn't even keep myself upright properly. I allowed the slide to happen, collapsing into the mud and rocking slowly onto my left-hand side. Feeling the cold seep into my body, but at the same time not really feeling it at all.

I reached out to gather up a loose armful of burnt rubbish, and I held it as close to me as it would come.

CHAPTER FOURTEEN

You often hear about this idea of hitting rock bottom – of being as low as you can possibly go – and you imagine that, if you ended up there, then that's about it for you. It really is The End. It's like you disappear out of existence when you land on rock bottom. The floor's made out of a trillion snapping scissors that shred you into blood and shit in half a second. You're so far down that you don't even need to pull a trigger or take a pill. Sheer depression and social abstraction will blink you out of existence.

But of course it doesn't work like that.

Nothing shreds or pulps you. Your heart feels as broken as it ever could, like a physical injury inside you that you can't possibly bear, but you don't die from a broken heart, and everything is bearable. It's impossible but true: the pain goes on, but it doesn't kill you. Your whole body feels like this fatal wound, but you're still aware of it: it's curled up on the floor, collecting a numb handful of indifferent sensations, and no amount of concentration or desire can rob you of it. This is where you are. Not dead. Not even dying. You're just waiting to get up, and – sooner or later – you're going to have to.

It's just difficult.

Some emotions feel so enormous that by rights you should be able to fall into them forever; they should be able to close up around you until there's nothing left for people to see. But they're never as deep as you expect. Ultimately, you still need to pull yourself off the ground and do something, however 'just difficult' it might seem. Even the most desperate of suicides still needs to jump.

And so, after a while, I got up. I'd stopped crying by then, but the water was still splattering down from above and I wandered underneath it, soaking my face to the bone and my body to the skin. It was ice cold, but I didn't care; I needed to wash her away from me. Never had anything felt quite so important. The noise the water made on me was softer than on the ground, and I tested out shifts in tone as it pattered on my head, shoulders and then, ever so quietly, on my outstretched hands. I moved away, and the harsher sound returned: a silenced, spluttering machine pistol.

Shivering, I wiped my wet forearm over my wet face.

Amy was dead.

I'd known all along, and I realised now that all I'd done was twisted the grief into a new shape and channelled it into something emptily constructive. How could she not have been dead? Even before I found Kareem, I must have known: four months without a word.

And now I'd found her.

The routes that had brought us both here were too complicated to catch a grip on. All I knew was that I felt responsible for their architecture: for not taking so many of the turnoffs that would have delivered us somewhere better.

Amy.

You deserved somebody better than me.

I'd told her that before, and she'd said the same thing back. And we'd both always said the same thing in reply: *But I love you.*

Well at least now we knew who was right.

I started to cry again, looking down at the remains. They were as unrecognisable as a tree growing from a grave would have been, and at that moment I couldn't imagine doing another thing with my life. That feeling of rock bottom again, and then it passed. I wasn't going to dissolve, or cease to exist. At least, not without some help.

I touched the lump of the gun, hanging in my pocket.

There's no God. No Heaven. Nothing after death. I didn't believe in any of that stuff. But nothing seemed like it might feel better than this. Right then, it felt like I could go for nothing.

Nothing felt about right.

But not this second, I thought. I had money in my pocket, and my stomach was achingly empty. I was soaking. For some stupid, undefined reason, it didn't feel right to die on wasteground, even though Amy was here with me. It felt like I needed to take control and do it right: make some kind of insignificant ceremony out of it.

So I said goodbye to Amy, and then I touched the gun again, turned around and headed back to Fairway Street.

I got something to eat in Combo's Deli, hesitating for maybe a second before crossing the street and heading inside. But nobody looked at me twice; even the guy showing off his balls seemed to be staring at something in the middle-distance that was more interesting than me. It felt okay – not threatening in the slightest – and I realised why even as I wandered inside: I belonged here. I was downtown, swept under the carpet. Jettisoned from society, unwanted and aimless and uncaring, just like everyone else here. And we can smell our own.

When I was younger, I used to imagine what it would feel like to know you were going to die. I figured it would be both scary and liberating. Scary because I didn't want to die, but liberating because you could do anything you wanted. I thought that being about to die would make you aware of how much society ties you down. You'd never have to look someone in the eye again if you didn't want to. Never have to answer to the law for what you did. Not have to worry about the hangover or the injuries, or what anyone might think of you. Never say please or thank you.

But old habits died harder than I would.

'Coming right up,' the owner told me, after I'd asked him for a cup of coffee, and a plate of sausages, bacon and chips, and then said please to round it all off. He turned away to his sizzling grill, warning me: 'You wait here, boy. There ain't no table service.'

He slopped it up. I paid him (I said thank you, too) and took my food to a far corner of the café. It was delicious: as revoltingly greasy as anything I'd ever tasted, and as good a final meal as anyone could have hoped for. As I ate, I watched the outside world of Downtown through the misty window. You could even see the entrance to the wasteground from where I was sitting. Fuck it, though. I dabbed my mouth with a paper towel and took the tray back over to the counter.

'You rent out rooms, here?' I asked.

The owner took the tray off me, looking bored.

'We rent out rooms,' he said, 'yeah. Thirty a night, breakfast is extra. Are you on your own?'

'Yeah.'

'You want to be?'

'Yeah,' I said. 'I just want a room.'

'Money's in advance. How long're you here for?'

'Just one night.'

'Just one night. Here you go.'

He slipped a set of keys off a hook behind the grill. I pulled out thirty pounds, and we traded.

'Stairs over there,' he said, gesturing to the far corner. 'You change your mind about the company, I can sort you out with something. With anything.'

'I won't.'

'If you're not gone by ten tomorrow, we come looking for you.'

Well, that would be nice for everyone.

'I understand,' I said, and went to find my room.

The room at Combo's was as awful as you'd imagine. There was a bed, a table and a chair, and that was about it. The shared bathroom was down the hall. There was a bare bulb hanging down in the far corner, beside the black square of a window, but the light was sickly and weak, and it gave the room an appearance of wasting illness. It was like the room's liver had failed.

Worse than that, though, were the walls. They had been painted a pale and anaemic green, but there were brown patches on three of them, varying in size and height. The colour had faded, presumably through scrubbing, but it was still recognisable for what it was: blood. It looked like somebody had been butchered in here. There was a spattering of it above the headboard of the bed, and I bet that if I'd have pulled off the white cotton sheet from the mattress I'd have found a stain there, as well. But I didn't think I was going to do that.

I put the gun on the bed beside the damp pile of papers I'd collected. Then, I went over to the window and closed a pair of thin beige curtains against the Downtown night. If you're keeping count, there were flecks of blood on the curtains, too.

Honestly, I didn't know how I was going to do this. I was shaking. To calm myself down, I lay on the hard bed, hands crossed behind my head to form a rough pillow, and closed my eyes.

Breathing slowly, I tried to find a picture of Amy in my mind to steady myself. It came easily enough, but it seemed slightly faded. Lifeless, like a photograph. I supposed I hadn't seen her in four months and shouldn't be surprised, but I was

– and disappointed, too. I wanted something vivid that I could run towards. I wanted to be with her, in some way, when I did what I was going to do. The last thoughts that got blasted out onto these walls should be of her.

I started to cry, frustrated with myself, and sat up.

The room looked better blurred, and so I cried for a while, and thought unhappy thoughts. I ran through the scenarios. I imagined her cursing me as she died. I saw her crying and screaming as they raped and tortured her to death, and then unfolded these thoughts backwards to see us sitting in our bed, side by side and miles apart. I thought of all the things I should have told her, and I said them to her now instead. Most of all, I imagined sitting with her, trying to explain how sorry I was. Still she wouldn't come.

Get it together, I told myself.

Just get it together.

I opened the file and flicked through it, maybe for inspiration. But I stopped at the first page, which was the e-mail she'd sent. Except she hadn't, of course: it must have been somebody else.

I looked at it again, and then rubbed my fingertip over the printed text of the header. If she hadn't sent me the footage that would lead me to her body, then who had? How had they found it – and me – and why?

It occured to me for a second that she might not be dead at all, and I felt a flurry in my heart. Immediately, I shot it down.

She is *dead.*

So who wrote the e-mail, then? Who else had access to the account?

I couldn't think of a single person, but maybe she'd told someone else the password. After all, she hadn't known about Claire Warner. So maybe she'd had someone that I didn't know about.

I felt relieved to be thinking this through, without really knowing why, and so I went with it. Either Amy had sent the message, or someone else had. That seemed clear enough. It was certainly Amy in the beginning sections of the video, and the continuation in it suggested that it was her remains that had been set on fire at the wasteground. That was the implication. So she couldn't have sent it. But who would have been able to find those videos? Certainly not Graham, not in the time he had. Hughes was dead. And why would anyone have sent me them at all?

The conclusion? Nothing about that blank e-mail made sense.

I turned it over and looked at the next page, which was the beginning of Dennison's insane manifesto that texts were alive. As I skimmed through the pages, I wondered what state the internet was in right now: how much of it was left and how long that would last. That led to another idea. Dennison believed that the description of Amy being killed had started the corruption in the database. The text-file that got lost on its way to my inbox.

So maybe the description of Amy was behind all this. Maybe it really was alive, in some weird way. Perhaps the text itself had sent me the e-mail message, lulled into doing so by memories that were haunting it. Memories of what it once was.

I turned the page, revealing the list of 'Marley's in Thiene.

A flash cut of Amy's body being carried onto the wasteground.

I glanced down the page, remembering what I already knew. There were thirty names on it, with addresses and phone numbers. Thirty strangers was too many to sift through if you didn't know what you were looking for.

Another flash cut: a zoom.

The blurred close-up of Marley's face, with the bright tip of his cigarette burning a hole in the screen.

I lay back down on the bed, holding the piece of paper face down against my chest, and closed my eyes.

It occurs to me sometimes that everything we think we know about ourselves is only fiction. There's no such thing as the past or the future: they don't really exist – in the proper, physical sense that a cat exists, or a dog. We live in this ever-changing, single moment. If I want to claim that a particular object is red, then I can point to that object. The evidence is there in front of me. But if I want to claim that it was once red – when I saw it last – there's no physical evidence at all beyond the way the memory of me seeing it is wired up in my brain. It's just a story I remember about the way things were. That's the only evidence there is.

The past is all fiction. It only exists in the form of hundreds of thousands of differing narratives wired into hundreds of thousands of different heads. The stories overlap, and sometimes they contradict each other, and when that happens we tend to pick the stories which appeal to us most.

My grandmother was a religious woman and she always used to say that we were put on this Earth to do the best that we could. To make it a better place. I don't know about that; I'm more material than she was, and less confident that anything has any real value at all. I think that it's all just words on a page that nobody's actually reading. But what it seems to me is this: while we're here, what we try to do is star in as many stories as possible. That's what being important and influential really means. It's nothing more than binding yourself into as many narratives as possible, in as many people's minds. And when you die, all it means is that your stories are over: you're finished with writing them, and now it's just a matter of whether anybody reads them and remembers you.

When I woke up, the hotel room was dark and I felt disorientated. Something was wrong. It wasn't the light: I remembered turning it out, half-asleep, when it became obvious I was dozing off. And it wasn't the dream I was having either, which had been cut short. It was the door.

A creak of floorboards.

Fuck – the door was open.

I swung myself upright and pulled the gun up from the side of my leg. A figure, which had been creeping into the room from the bright hallway beyond, stopped moving immediately, and then moved its hands up slowly.

I clicked off the safety catch and said:

'What the fuck are you doing?'

'Easy.' It was the guy from the counter downstairs. 'Don't shoot.'

'What the fuck are you doing?' I said again.

The silhouette shrugged.

'I heard a gunshot. It sounded like it came from in here.'

I frowned to myself in the dark. From what I could remember I'd been dreaming about gunfire – I remembered loud shots and bright lights. I'd been in a front room, watching a television.

'I knocked, but there was no answer.' He shrugged again, sounding more confident now. Obviously deciding that I wasn't going to shoot him, he turned away and moved back into the doorway.

'Got to look out for myself.'

'Right,' I said, as he closed the door.

The darkness felt uncomfortable, so I switched on the light and rubbed the bad dream from my eyes. The memory of it was fading, and I couldn't remember too much of what had happened in it. But I knew that, just before I'd jerked awake, I'd been a young boy, sitting in an armchair in a dark front room. I was watching a pale blue television, which was flashing and banging away in the corner, but I didn't like what I was seeing at all: it was pictures and sounds of people being hurt by somebody. I knew that there were other people in the room who were watching me for my reaction, and so I wasn't allowed to look away from the screen. These other people were just vague, dark shapes in the other chairs; I couldn't make them out, or even tell which one was speaking to me. But I remember asking:

'Why is he doing that?'

One of them said, 'Because if he didn't, there wouldn't be a story.'

I found it too frustrating. 'That's a stupid answer.'

The same voice: 'It's the only reason anyone does anything.'

And then the guy from downstairs had disturbed me.

I didn't want to go back to sleep, so I sat on the edge of the bed for a minute, feeling sick. Whenever Amy used to wake me up in the night with one of her bad dreams, it felt like this: a kind of awful, sleepy nausea. It always passed, but never quickly. Now, as I waited to feel better, I saw that there was a screwed up ball of paper on the floor in front of me. I put down the gun and picked it up, unfolding it carefully.

Thirty names. Thirty addresses.

I put the paper down on top of the gun and held my head in my hands.

Five minutes later, I went down to the shared bathroom at the far end of the hall, with the gun tucked into my trousers. The whole room seemed strangely sterile: walls of white porcelain; garish lights overhead; and water everywhere – hanging in clean beads on the wall tiles and mixed into muddy footprints on the floor. I ran some into a sink the width and depth of a small well and splashed my face a few times, and then leaned on the edge, inspecting myself in the mirror.

I looked normal: a little tired and rough around the edges, but still me. My standard face. Neither good nor bad looking, neither smiling nor frowning – just weathered and slightly beaten, but not as much as I'd expected. I was my normal tune, played in a minor key. Water dripped down my cheeks and I saw my eyes watching it. Looked back up, only to catch them doing the same.

Thirty names.

The choice was made easier by the fact that I didn't actually want to kill myself tonight. It felt too soon, somehow. I had a deep, aching pain inside me whenever I thought about Amy, but at the same time I felt like if I died tonight I would have missed something. There was also the small matter of cowardice; I'd be able to do it, I thought, but it would probably be easier if I surprised myself.

So, the choice was made: I wasn't going to kill myself here in this shithole.

Three men dead in the last forty-eight hours, all by my hand. Suddenly, that didn't seem so bad. I figured I could give myself another week, check out the names on the list, and maybe add one or two more to that tally.

CHAPTER FIFTEEEN

The first name on the list – number one – turned out to be an old man. I watched him for all of ten seconds, from a bus shelter on the other side of the street, and he could barely get down his front path. He was tapping a stick on the paving stones for support. As he opened his gate and turned down the street, I caught a glimpse of his body from the side: he was as bent as a letter 'r'.

Five minutes later, when the bus came, he was still in sight. I got on it, and didn't even look at him as we drove past.

Number two.

He was younger than number one – not by much, admittedly, but it was enough to keep him upright when he was walking, and he didn't need a cane for support either. But there was still an awkwardness to him. I only saw him walk once – from his seat to the toilet – and he had the slow, skewed gait of an old builder: someone who'd hurt his back but still had enough muscle left to power himself around.

I caught his face as he passed: cheeks as bright as sunburn and an exploded nose the colour of fire. He was wearing old slacks, and a chequered shirt beneath a beige pullover, sleeves rolled up to knotty elbows, revealing the white hair on his arms. I turned back to the bar, downed what was left of my drink and then left.

Numbers three and four were related to number two: his sons. They were more the right age, but they were still dead ends. Both of them were blond. I saw the first one on a construction site, wearing a cement-spattered sweater and jeans, carrying a black bucket over uneven ground. It wasn't him. The second was in his driveway, clanking tools beneath the shell of a Camaro. He pulled himself out after a second, blinking at the sun behind me.

'Can I help you?' he asked.

I said no, and walked away.

The next six names were all a dead loss, and I was beginning to despair. And then, number eleven was *actually* dead. I called it a day, determined to start fresh the morning after.

Let's back up just a little.

After deciding I wasn't going to kill myself, I figured the best thing to do was get some sleep, so I jammed the chair beneath the door handle, placed the gun within easy reach and dropped off with surprising ease. I had more bad dreams, but I didn't remember what they were. In the morning, I handed my keys back and made my way out of Downtown: back into the real world, or what passes for it. It was strange to see the sky again – blue-white and cloudless – and to hear the sound of cars and people going about their business without a threatening echo announcing it to the world. Monday morning. The air smelled fresh, clean and cold, and for a while it felt as though the heat and damp of Downtown were oozing out of my skin, like some kind of sweaty disease.

The first thing I did was phone home and check my answer-machine for messages. A mechanical voice told me there were two. I glanced at my watch, wondering how long it took to trace a call, and whether anybody would actually be bothered enough about me to do it. After a second, Williams' voice cut in, distracting me.

'Hello Jason. It's Nigel here.' He was speaking low and quick, picking out a spoken rhythm which expressed his irritation to almost poetic perfection. 'I'm just calling to let you know that this month's pay has been credited to you, but we do need to see you urgently, so would you please give us a call as soon as you get this message. Thank you. Goodbye.'

I felt like giving a big cheer for the corporations: despite being heroically absent for the whole month, I had been paid. Not even a naïve child's version of God is that forgiving. Eight hundred odd pounds, ready to withdraw whenever I wanted – assuming, of course, that my account hadn't been frozen by the police, what with me being on the run and all. Somehow, I doubted that had happened.

Beep.

'Hi Jason, it's Charlie.'

I closed my eyes, remembering how I'd run out on her in the pub. It felt like a hundred years ago. I wouldn't have blamed her in the slightest for being incredibly angry with me, but instead she only sounded a little bit hurt, and actually mostly worried.

'It's Sunday night. I'm just calling because I hope you're okay. I don't know what happened yesterday – or what I did wrong – but I'm sorry, whatever it was. And I understand; it's okay.'

No, you don't understand, I thought. *You mean well, and that's lovely, but you can't help me, and I'm not worth the effort.*

'I wanted to let you know that the police called round.' Her tone shifted slightly; I opened my eyes to the sight of cars rushing past and the implacable face of Downtown across the street. 'They said they found someone dead in the woods, and wanted to know if we'd seen anything. I said we hadn't, but they'll want to speak to you anyway. I guess I'll want to speak to you, too.'

Yeah, I thought. *I guess you will.*

Okay: they'd found Kareem's body, but as of this minute they had nothing to tie me to the murder, beyond the fact that

I was nearby when it took place. For now, as far as they knew, Charlie and I were a couple of friends who just happened to have been walking through the woods that day, and if they figured out who the guy was then they probably wouldn't suspect us anyway. She'd lied for me and – as a result – it might be okay.

'I hope you're all right.' She sounded concerned. 'Please get in touch with me. You don't have to see me if you don't want. I mean: just tell me if you want to be left alone. But I want to know you're all right. Okay? Give me a ring when you get this.'

Click

There was no way I was going to call her back, as bad as it made me feel. That part of my life was over and finished with, and I figured the sooner I started acknowledging it, the better. So I hung up instead, and went to find a cash machine.

By eleven o'clock on day two, I'd found number twelve, who was in hospital with a gunshot wound. I passed myself off as a relative and made my way through to his room, telling myself not to get my hopes up but failing all the same. I was expecting it to be him, but it wasn't.

'Who the fuck are you?'

'I'm sorry,' I said, and closed the door on the way out.

Number thirteen owned a liquor store. I went in and took a bottle of generic cola from the freezer to the counter, but there was a woman behind it and not the owner. His wife, probably.

'Anything else?' she asked, moving the bottle past a blipping barcode reader.

Counting coins, I looked up and saw the plaque on the wall beneath the spirits. It gave the licence information, and there was a picture of the owner: a fat man with white hair in a grey shirt. He looked impeccably neat, and also vaguely pleased with himself, as though obtaining a liquor licence was something all aspired to and few reached.

I told the woman that was all, paid her and left.

Number fourteen was bed-ridden. He had a home nurse who visited him just after I arrived. She was middle-aged and dowdy, arriving in a small car, armed with a brown bag full of pills. I didn't even bother to check that guy out.

Number fifteen was involved in a heated business lunch with another male colleague. Suited from head to toe, they were both trying to impress a young lady who was with them. Every so often, fifteen would roar with laughter and then dab at his mouth with a napkin, glancing at her from the corner of his eye. He had curly black hair and shiny skin, and chubby hands. He held his wine glass like it was a flower he was smelling. I left after a couple of minutes.

There is no limit to what you can achieve given time. Even the most complicated and seemingly impossible task is only a matter of doing one thing after another. This wasn't even that complicated; just time consuming.

I checked the list. I figured maybe three more and then call it a day.

There was no rush.

The hotel room in Thiene was a million miles from the standard of the one in Downtown, which made it middle of the road in general terms. I had an en-suite bathroom, roughly the size of two standing people, a wardrobe, a double bed, and a desk and chair. Most of my notes and papers were spread out on the desk. In the corner of the room, there was a television unit – also housing a handy little mini-bar underneath. Not the grandest of rooms, admittedly, but the four walls surrounding it would define the last few days of my life, with only a slight slope and one dark Monet print to differentiate them, so I figured I'd have to learn to live with it.

The first day was filled with a kind of blank, soulless searching. I'd sit down every so often – on a bus or on a bench – and draw a shaky line through a name. When I wasn't doing that, I was scanning maps, dialling numbers and hanging up, watching people without watching them, or pacing in my Thiene hotel room wondering how I could fill time. Ideas weren't exactly forthcoming, either – it felt like I'd struck a deal and received a free trial edition of the rest of my life. I wouldn't kill myself yet but, in exchange for these few extra days, I was living a life where most of the main features had been disabled. I only turned on the television to check the news broadcasts, and I hardly slept. In fact, the only real impact I made on the room was to the minibar.

The news I did catch was reassuring, however. There was no mention of Walter Hughes, which I thought could only be good. He was, in his way, an important person and I was quite sure that his murder would have made it as far as a television near me. If he hadn't been discovered yet then it meant that Dennison and his friends had been able to take what they wanted from the house – which also meant that, when the police finally did get around to calling, any traces I'd left were likely to have been buried beneath far more obvious traces of them. That was fine.

Predictably, the main news item was the internet crash. The situation had worsened slightly since the last broadcast, but now seemed to have stabilised. Millions of files remained inaccessible, but the rot was said to have stopped. Experts were puzzled, large areas of the internet remained shut down, businesses were up in arms and share prices were plummeting. But for now at least, things seemed to have settled.

I flicked off the television.

The first night in that hotel room, I paced. I scanned through the information I had a hundred times, reliving events in my head, trying to come up with some new angle or approach that might lead me to these men. But I couldn't think of anything, and became so frustrated and uptight that I had to drink myself to sleep in order to get any.

I dreamt about her.

It was strange, actually – not the dream, which I don't even remember, but the way my life was moving. In the room at Combo's Deli, I'd not been able to think about Amy clearly enough to picture her, but now it felt as though I was drawing closer. Memories of her kept surfacing: the vibrant, saturated kind of memory, and not just some flat, black and white picture of the things we'd done. When I cried, which I did a lot, I could feel an imaginary arm around me. It began to seem as though if I spoke to her she'd be able to hear me, and I knew I was getting nearer to the stage when I'd be able to imagine her sitting next to me, maybe with her hand on my knee, and it was at that point I'd be able to end this. I didn't believe in an afterlife but, to get myself through that moment, it might be nice to. It would only last a split-second, after all, and it wasn't like I'd have to live with myself afterwards.

The second day, I started early. After breakfast, before checking out the next name on the list, I went to an internet café around the corner from the hotel. I got an extra coffee to help keep me upright through the day and then logged on to check my e-mail. I wanted to see if anything else had been sent to me from Amy's account.

But it was down, of course, and so I couldn't log in.

Number sixteen: I caught him just as he arrived home. I was walking down the pavement towards him, watching him tuck in his shirt and straighten his tie. He was a family man. I saw him turn into his driveway and noticed the little girl in the front room window; the curtain fell back into place and then she was at the door to meet him as he opened it. I walked away, wanting to close my eyes.

Number seventeen was a teenager: long and thin, like a clotheshanger.

I was getting tired, but number eighteen was on the way back to my hotel, so I decided to wander past and see what I could see.

His real name – number aside – was Paul Marley, and he lived in an enormous tenement building, which was verging on the derelict. I spent a minute or so trying to work out which room would be his, but I could only pin it down to the south-east side. The lights there seemed to form a computer pattern of yellow and black. He might be in or out, and I could wait outside all night and still not get anywhere. Unless Paul Marley was the man in the video, I wouldn't recognise him even if I saw him.

I stood by the entrance, debating for a second.

Fuck it, I thought, and went inside.

The foyer was low and not very wide: just a cavity in the shape of a room, with two silver elevator shafts on the right, and a staircase straight ahead. I didn't trust the elevators, so I took two flights up to Marley's floor, with the echo of my footfalls preceding me up the stairwell. The bannister was cold and hard, and incomprehensible graffiti stained the walls in big blocks of colour. When I opened the door to Marley's corridor, it stank of old air. The carpet was damp and curling up at the edges, and was illuminated from above by more bare lightbulbs. Closed off to either side were pale green doors, which had their numbers scribbled on in biro. My heart was beating quickly as I reached the end – number twenty-two.

The gun was in my jacket pocket, pointing down, and I wasn't planning on taking it out. The idea was that – if it was him – I'd just grab hold of it in my pocket, twist my jacket up and shoot him through it. Get him in the gut, then push him back into the room and close the door behind us.

Keep it calm, keep it calm, I thought, reaching out with my free hand.

It probably won't be him.

I rapped on the door three times, but on the second it wasn't there: it was creaking open ever so slightly. Someone had left it ajar.

Fuck my plans – I took the gun out, took a good two-handed grip and moved to one side of the doorway. Waited. The world ticked over a couple of times around me. I fazed out everything except the door, and beyond it the room and everything my senses were telling me was happening inside it. Everything that wasn't happening.

No footsteps.

No voices.

Five seconds. Six. I hesitated, but by then the corridor was beginning to feel just as threatening as whatever might be inside Marley's flat. So I kept the two-handed grip and used it to push the door open a little further. And, when nothing happened, I moved inside.

The front room was a mess of old furniture and discarded clothing: a mad, patternless tapestry of newspaper, cloth and old take-out cartons. It was difficult to know whether the place had been turned over or if Marley just lived like this. To the left, I could see a kitchen: walls painted as yellow as melted butter. To the right, there were two doors: one shut, one open. An empty bedroom. From what I could see, it was as messy as the lounge. I guessed that the other must be the bathroom.

I stopped. Breathed in.

There was a smell about the place that wasn't right – a burnt cooking smell – and it clicked into place with the door being left off the latch. Even before I saw the blood on the floor, I knew that I was going to find someone dead in this flat. I pushed the door closed behind me, and that was when I noticed the stains on the papers beside it. Not a lot of blood, but not paper cut blood either. It was a proper amount, like you might see outside a pub the morning after a fight, with little splashes moving off down the street as someone held on to a broken nose and staggered away.

I looked over the floor and it was the same: more blood. There was a spatter of something across a few open books on the settee that might have been – I couldn't tell – but there was no doubt about the rest. I followed the trail with my eyes, over papers and pizza boxes and fabric. The blood led sparely but clearly towards the closed bathroom door.

My heart hadn't slowed down any since I'd entered the flat, and now it felt like it was beating heavily and quickly above a very deep and black pit. Instead of doing what I wanted to do – leave right now – I took the gun with me on a small tour of the apartment. I knew where it was going to end, and the flat was too quiet and still to be anything other than empty, but I had to be sure.

I checked the kitchen first. There were a few stacked pans on top of the cooker and an empty milk carton on the counter beside the kettle, but otherwise it was relatively tidy. I figured that Marley must have ordered in most of his food. There were some empty bottles on the floor by the bin – mostly wine, with a couple of sturdy vodkas hiding at the back – but apart from that there was nothing to see.

The bedroom next, obviously. A single bed, covered with nooses of cloth; more crumpled clothes on the floor; three glasses filled with misty water on the table by the bed. The air looked and smelled grey. That was all.

So: the bathroom.

I pushed the door open slowly, using the gun the way I'd used it on the front door, ready to shoot someone if I needed to even though it was obvious that I wouldn't.

The smell was stronger here. The blood was concentrated

and specific. There were pools of it on the floor. A hotch-potch of blurred footprints smeared and scattered out of it, and it was streaked on the dirty tiles, and here and there on the paintwork. The room was only small, but it was just covered with blood. Opposite me, there was an old cast-iron bath, sheltered by a rubbery shower curtain hanging from metal links on a runner attached to the ceiling. The curtain was mottled and grubby, like a used condom, and there was blood on that, too. So much blood. It was obvious that the bath was the epicentre of all this, and although the curtain was pulled all the way across, I could see quite clearly that somebody was in there behind it. Not somebody anymore. Something dead.

To the left, I noticed that the rim of the sink was speckled with the foamy remains of a shave and I started to gather a scenario together in my head. Marley's in here shaving when there's a knock at the door. He answers it and gets attacked. He's driven back into this room, which is where the intruder kills him and leaves him. Assuming that the corpse in the bathtub was him.

I used the barrel of the gun to draw the curtain back.

The video clip wasn't clear, and the face below me had been cut to pieces, but it looked like him.

I stared down, feeling conflicting emotions beneath a blank surface. Now that he was in front of me, my first thought was that he didn't look like much. He had jeans on, and that was all, and although it's difficult to judge someone's height when they're dead in a bath in front of you, he just looked like a skinny little guy. Wiry, maybe – but that was charitable. He was cut in a fair few places, but they all looked like puncture wounds rather than slashes, and there was a kind of deep, unambiguous violence about them. He hadn't been tortured. Someone had come into this flat with a knife, and they'd stuck it in him over and over until he was dead.

I took a cold, clinical look.

It's him.

I let the shower curtain fall back over, and then I went and sat down on the closed toilet, put my head in my hands and tried to think.

Someone had killed him, and I didn't know what to feel about it. A small part of me felt cheated, but mostly I just felt relieved, and I was surprised at myself for that. Perhaps, despite everything, I wasn't a cold, calculating killer after all. But I looked over at the bath. The person who had done that to Marley hadn't been cold and calculating either: there was a passionate brutality to how he'd been killed, and it didn't seem to me that it was the kind of professional hit that a man like Marley might have attracted. It was the kind of thing I might have done.

Well – whoever had done it, and for whatever reason, he was dead. So what was I supposed to do now? I could shoot him a couple of times for the sake of completion, but it felt pretty fucking redundant. What was I supposed to do? Shoot myself? I tried to conjure up that image of Amy – the acid test – and I could do it, but the image brought along an understanding that the last thing she would have wanted was me dead in this man's bathroom.

The thought set me moving back through to the living room, not with any real intention, but just because there was nothing else to see in here and the smell was becoming more and more potent.

As I walked back through to the living room it occurred to me that I should probably be going quite soon. And I didn't even feel the impact. It was like the right-hand side of me exploded, and then the left as my shoulder went into the wall and then hit the floor. Most of the air went out of me. The room spun around. I wasn't holding the gun anymore.

Fuck.

Half a second went by as I realised what was happening. And then I hit out blind, catching the man coming down with a weak right to the shoulder, too weak, but enough for the knife he was bringing down to miss, to scrape through the debris on the floor with the sound of a rap on the door and then paper tearing. *A fucking knife.* I was half pinned under his weight, my right arm trapped across me, and – panicking, terrified – I managed to get my left hand under his chin just as he brought the knife round and tried to cut my throat, resting on his elbow. I pushed his jaw up, his head back – and he was so heavy – and I scrunched my chin down as he put the knife against me. He sliced my jawbone, once, twice, again; flicking at it, not as hard as he'd have liked but I started screaming anyway: this noise that had no pain in it, just fear and anger and panic at being damaged.

He was punching me with his other hand: a fist going again and again into the side of my head. I pushed his jaw right up, flapping uselessly at the knife with my right hand as he sliced me again. He was trying to get the blade into the crook of my neck to cut me deeply. But then my other palm was over a snapping mouth, pushing his nose up, and my fingers found his eyes and I dug in, hard and fast and cruel. The punches stopped. He cried out and pushed himself up off me, reaching around to try to stop me from blinding him. My right hand, suddenly free, found his knife hand and held it as he pulled me up and backwards in a standing stumble. He was trying to wrench my hand away, biting at my palm, but then sheets of paper slipped out under him and we went down again, this time me landing on top, and my fingers went into his eyes, properly in, suddenly hot and wet and revolting. I didn't care, I just thought *die, you fucker* and dug in as hard as I could, gritting my teeth and looking away from what I was doing, not listening to the noises he was making, holding his wrist down, getting one knee over it. Until his hand stopped fighting me, until it just rested there, pressed against the floor. Until his mouth wasn't biting at my other hand anymore.

I held him there for another minute, not looking. Not feeling anything. It was like my mind was made of glass and had been dropped, and now I was staring blankly at the pieces – heart pounding – not even caring where to begin.

After that minute, though, the effects of the adrenalin began to thaw. Pain brought enough of the pieces back together to get me moving, standing up again. I didn't think about my fingers as they came out: I just looked for the gun. Then I went through to the bathroom and washed the man's blood and brains off my hand. My mind was cool and calm by then – worryingly so, perhaps – and it was talking to itself: *do this, do that, no, do this first, that's it.* I used toilet roll to wipe blood from my face and neck, and elsewhere, but I just kept wiping and then bundled a load up and held it in place over the cuts. My reflection was wired to high hell: wide-eyed and scared. The right-hand side of my face looked red and sore, but none of his punches had broken the skin. He hadn't had enough leverage to do me much real damage with his fists. My shoulder hurt from the impact, but I'd live.

Who was he? A friend of Marley's? One of his gang, maybe. Or perhaps he was the guy who'd killed him. After all, Marley had been stabbed too, so it was possible that I'd just avenged the guy I'd come to murder.

Whoever he was, the number of bodies in the flat was rapidly increasing. I needed to get out of here.

I dropped the balled-up, bloody tissues in the toilet and flushed, but I was still bleeding and it was going to get me noticed.

'Jason,' I said, looking at myself in the mirror. 'I do believe that what you need right now is a scarf.'

I found one in the living room, tucked away on the bottom shelf of Marley's wardrobe: black and old. Probably not the most hygienic of dressings, but I figured what the fuck – needs must. As I wrapped it around my neck, I glanced down at the body on the floor. I didn't feel at all bad about what I'd done. In fact, I didn't feel much of anything, and what I did feel was something closer to exhilaration than regret or guilt. The man had attacked me and that was the way it was. It had been him or me. I could only wish that everything in life went my way quite so completely.

So where was I going to go?

The obvious answers – the hotel, my home – felt pointless. They were end-points. I could head to those places, but they both felt like moving into emotional checkmate. What was I going to do when I got there? Exactly. I wasn't going to do anything. But if not home, then where?

I needed somewhere more productive to go. But, as I absently looked across the spread of papers, my gaze finally coming to rest on a small, open book over by the settee, I wondered whether what I actually needed was still the exact opposite.

CHAPTER SIXTEEN

I took a bus across town. It was late by then, and raining, so there we all were, bathed in a sickly amber light and breathing in the smell of damp clothes. The side of my face was hurting a lot more now, and I was still bleeding. Hopefully people hadn't noticed, but it didn't really matter. I watched the dark city go past outside, crossing gazes with a pale reflection of myself, and I really didn't look well. In fact, I looked like the last person you'd choose to sit next to and, on this bus, that was saying something.

The address I was heading to was on the outskirts of Thiene, where the buildings got taller and more ramshackle, like somebody had built a load of separate floors and then seen how many they could pile up without the building coming crashing down. Everything was black brick and timber, and all you saw, or remembered, were boarded up hotels that looked about two hundred years old. The rain was grey and dirty and felt right; I couldn't imagine this place in the daytime, or in summer. It was a fitting locale, I supposed, but part of me wished that all these people I was looking for might live somewhere a little nicer.

I had a vague idea of the area and knew where to get off the bus, but I had to ask the driver for directions to the street. He didn't seem like the kind of guy who gave directions very often, but he took one look at me and decided it would be easier, and probably smarter, not to be difficult. He told me exactly what I needed to know.

It was only a five minute walk from the stop, but when I arrived I was soaked through and cold. And past caring. It was an apartment block with about six storeys, but it looked more or less derelict, and it was difficult to imagine anybody actually living here. There were a couple of lights on close to the top, though, so I figured somebody must be home. A helpful friend of society had already kicked the front door open for me, so I made my way inside and found the stairs.

There was a pretty good chance that whoever had killed Marley had also come here, as this place had been on the page at which his address book had been left open, and so I took out the gun as I made my way up to the top floor. There was nobody around, but every second staircase found me approaching a black-blue window, criss-crossed by a thin metal grid on the inside, pattered upon and streaked by the rain outside: an incessant tapping that made the building seem even older and weaker that it was. By the time I reached the sixth floor, I was so unnerved by it that I almost wanted someone to pop out of a door and say hi, just to prove that there were people here at all. But there was nothing apart from the rain.

And on the top floor it was literally raining: the ceiling was open to the sky in a couple of places, letting in a steady spatter of water that was probably not doing the wiring much good. The lights hung down from a brown ceiling, and I walked carefully. Getting electrocuted would, in theory, solve all my problems, but it didn't seem like a particularly appealing prospect.

There had been no name in the address book: just the street, and then the building and room numbers. I didn't know who I was going to find here, as I made my way down the old, battered corridor, searching for six-one-two. The décor left a lot to be desired. If the paper hadn't been peeling in places, I might have believed there were no walls beneath them at all:

just the paper, stretched and fragile and breakable. I could have torn it down and moved from one dank room to another, from empty flats into inhabited and stained ones. I could have held the surprised occupants at gunpoint as I stalked through and then ripped my way into the next one, and then the next, looking for whoever lived at this blank address. Room six-one-two. Here it was.

I listened at the door for a moment and, in a way that was becoming all too familiar, there was nothing to hear. Somehow, I hadn't expected there to be. And when I tried the handle, it didn't surprise me that the door opened. Unlocked, just like Marley's had been. Was I going to find a body in the bath here, as well?

The room was dark, illuminated only by the pale blue glow from a monitor over by the window, with a wedge of carpet revealed by light from the open door behind me. I couldn't see much, but I could just about make out the shelves of books lining the walls – hundreds of books and notepads and files and roughly bundled sheafs of paper – and I knew that I was in the right place. The computer was giving out a quiet electric hum, overlaid every few seconds by a small splashing noise of water falling into water. That was coming from deeper inside the flat. I guessed the bathroom.

And on top of those noises, the buzz of flies.

I found a light switch on the wall to my right, and it brought the room to life. All the shadows were sucked back under and between things, and I could suddenly see it all, or what there was to see anyway. Mostly just books. There were some weights in one corner, as well – tiny little things – and a desk by the window, where the computer was. Other than that the room was bare. Except for the man lying down on the floor by the desk.

I closed the front door quietly, as though he was sleeping and I didn't want to disturb him. But he wasn't sleeping.

There was something about the curled angle of him, and the stillness, not to mention the flies. And the smell, more than anything. It was the same odour that there'd been in Marley's flat. I recognised it for what it was, and I knew the man on the floor was dead even before I saw the blood pooled out from his hair, the spray of it on the books to the right, and the gun, discarded, not far from his mottled hand. On the desk in front of the computer were a few sheets of paper. A suicide note, I guessed.

Everybody was dead before I could get to them, and it didn't seem fair.

I nudged the corpse with my foot, rolling it onto its back, and I watched as the head came unstuck from the floor, moving absently on its lifeless neck. And then I saw the face, and took a shocked step back. A half stumble. It was Graham.

What the fuck was this?

It couldn't be, I thought, but I hadn't taken my eyes off him and there was really no doubt at all. Apart from a ruined section above his ear, the nearest side of his head was intact – pale but whole – and I'd known him for how long? I'd known him since we were little kids. I'd known him for years.

What had happened here? What was Graham doing here in this flat? It looked like he'd killed himself, but if so then what did that fucking mean – had he been involved in this all along? I couldn't make it fit: none of it made any sense.

I looked around the room, over and over, not really taking any of it in. It was like my mind had put the shutters down and blocked out anything new until it got a handle on the shit it already had, but then I remembered the suicide note and the shutters went up again.

Before I knew what I was doing, I picked up the sheets of paper and started to read.

CHAPTER SEVENTEEN

'Are you writing this down now?'

'Yes,' I said.

'Look at me while you're doing it.'

So I looked over at him, sitting next to me. He was a large man: tall and solid, without being muscular or fat. Clean shaven. Brown hair. Blue eyes behind the glasses he was wearing. In fact, apart from the gun he was holding, pointing only vaguely at me but with his eyes doing most of the damage, he seemed normal. Just an average, everyday guy: the kind you passed in the street all the time without noticing, caring about or looking twice at.

Except for that gun.

'What do you want?' I said. I was surprised by how frightened I sounded. 'I don't have any money.'

He smiled, but even as I'd said it I'd known how stupid it was. He wasn't here for money. My flat was on the top floor of a half-abandoned, three-quarters derelict shit-stack, and that was hardly the sort of place you came at random just to turn somebody over. On top of that, he clearly knew all about me. He hadn't got me on the floor; he hadn't tied me up or told me not to fucking move and asked where the money was.

What had happened was this.

It had been pouring down outside. There was a cacophony of clicks and splashes as the rain hit windowsills and cars and awnings below: a deep, dense, wet sound; a three-dimensional noise that you could walk through. The rain smelled warm, almost spicy. The street and pavements far below seemed suitably black and charred.

I'd been sitting, staring at the blank e-mail I'd received. There was no actual message, only the attachment, and I kept alternating between reading sections of the text it contained and staring at the empty e-mail and wondering what it meant.

Somehow, it had sidled through all the broken and breaking servers and found its way here, to my inbox.

The screensaver woke up – a featureless black background and I nudged the mouse to send it away. The blank message returned. Implacable. It was almost surprising how full of meaning no words could be.

I opened the attachment again and read it through.

It was very much incomplete: I guessed that there was less than a quarter of the original text there, and the rest was corrupted to the point where the meaning had gone, but I could make out some of the words and I recognised enough of the others to know what this was.

she screams se har(d thyt wf jjkpeopllr hurt h..r

I closed the attachment and clicked back to the blank message. Nothing – no words anyway. The malformed text made me think of a dog. It was like an old dog you'd dragged out back and shot in the head, but then you hear a scraping at the back door, go and open it, and there it is. And you don't know whether it's loyalty or anger that's brought it back to you, except that in this case I thought that I did. The blank screen glared at me. If I stared, the emptiness felt like it was burning into my eyes.

Bang. Bang.

Two steady knocks at the front door, and I'd turned around before I knew it. The blank message continued its empty flare in the corner of my eye.

I didn't move.

My attention was focused on the lock, with the rest of the

room fading away around me, and I realised that it was open. My front door was unlocked, and I didn't even dare move. But then it really was open – opening, anyway – and a large man with a gun was walking into the darkness, bringing sickly light from the hall along with him.

He'd just closed the front door calmly, keeping the gun pointing at me the whole time, and then he'd taken a seat at the table beside me.

'Get yourself some fresh paper,' he'd said. 'And a pen. And then start writing down what's happening here.'

And so that's what I'd done.

The smile disappeared now as he told me what I already knew.

'I don't want your money. I just want you to listen.'

'Listen,' I said. 'Right.'

'Yes. Listen and write.'

Okay, I thought. He's someone who knows about me and what I can do, and maybe he wants to make some money. So perhaps there was an angle here that I could use to help myself. But then again – if that was all that he wanted, he could have taken a dozen notebooks off the shelves behind him and sold them to whatever buyer he had interested. So why not do that? My mind was backtracking, and I couldn't help thinking of the blank e-mail I'd just received. The corrupted attachment. Did this have something to do with that empty message?

He leaned forward and looked me in the eyes. Just stared into them intently.

'Are you in there, Jason?' he said. 'Are you hearing me?'

All I could do was stare back at him. I didn't know what to say, but I didn't have the courage to look down. So I kept the connection, my right hand twitching away as I wrote.

After a second, he leaned away again.

'Never mind. Either you are or you aren't.'

I looked down at the paper in front of me, which was nearly full. He must have followed my gaze and realised what I was thinking because he placed another one down in front of me and said:

'Let's have a nice clean break, shall we?'

There was a playground near where Graham and Jason grew up, formed in a concrete bubble on the edge of this park that wasn't really a park at all – just grassland, really, with a couple of chalk-white pitch shapes stained thoughtlessly into it, and the ring of a path for older people to stroll around in summer. There was a maze of trees and bushes which people from the nearby pubs would lose themselves in on an evening, in order to fuck drunkenly. The playground was at the top.

Graham had had his first beer there, and smoked his first joint. He didn't lose his virginity there, shivering and cold, although he would have liked to.

They shared the place out between about thirty of them, mixed in every way, and they didn't exactly mingle but they all put up with one another's presence without much confrontation. Graham's group consisted of Jason and about five or six other friends from school. One of those was Emma Lindley. She had messy blonde hair that she wore half tied back, and she was always smiling, and she was slim from all the football she played with the boys. Graham thought she was beautiful, and had done for nearly a year. He'd managed to speak to her a couple of times, but the conversation had never done more than skim the surface. In their circle of friends they were at opposite sides, which meant Graham was always looking across at her while she was always turned one way or the other, talking to someone else. But it was okay. He'd accepted that, generally speaking, that was the way things always were. It was certainly how they always had been. He didn't get the girl. Maybe he was being overly optimistic, but he thought that one day he would. It couldn't stay like this forever; he was a nice guy.

That night, Graham and a boy called Jonny were sitting side by side on the mound of concrete at the top of the playground. They were next to the slide that curved down its surface, and another boy – pissed to high heaven – was sliding down it, and then clambering up the wedged steps to the top, and then sliding down again, over and over. In about ten minutes he would lean on his knees and be sick in front of them, but for now he was happy.

Across the other side of the playground, Emma was talking to Connor and Jason. They were by the swings. Graham looked from them up to the night sky. It was very dark blue, not black, and the stars were full of colour.

'Here.'

Jonny passed Graham the bottle of whisky they were sharing. Graham took a swig and winced. It hurt, but it made his head warm and the night hum. Alcohol shaved the edges off. When he was drunk, which he was getting towards being now, he felt a lot more positive about things. Not that they were closer to being within his reach. It just mattered less that they weren't.

He took another swig, and then said, 'Here,' and Jonny took the bottle back again.

Graham looked around. The playground was quite busy tonight, but the groups were as segregated as ever. It was mostly boys and girls he knew from school – people he knew but didn't know – and none of them really wanted to mix. Occasionally someone would come over and beg a cigarette or beer or rolling paper, and there'd be some perfunctory friendly conversation. It was always amiable, never convincing.

Graham knew he was just one of those guys: background people. He was very smart, but not irritating enough to be a target. He didn't have that many friends, but enough to coast by, and he was never invited anywhere, but nobody was surprised or annoyed when he tagged along with people who were. He'd never had a girlfriend, but he'd been turned down by a few high-profile players way above his station, and so nobody thought he was gay. Nobody really thought much about him at all. That was all okay, too.

One of the reasons he came here was because it made him feel accepted, but it was weird. In many ways it just underlined how much he wasn't. For him, it was all kind of an act. Whereas Jason was the real thing.

Graham looked back just as Connor joined them. He took the whisky from Jonny and said, 'Three's a crowd tonight.'

Jonny laughed, but not much. Graham's attention returned to the swings across the playground. Now, Emma and Jason were on their own over there, sitting side by side on the hard rubber seats, twisting gently against the strength of the chains. Just talking, but quietly, without really looking at each other.

'I know when I'm not wanted,' Connor said.

Their feet were scraping the tarmac beneath them.

Graham looked away and gestured for the whisky off Connor.

'Here.'

As he drank it, he thought: *well, that's okay*. And it was, too. It was just the way things always had happened and always would. He was used to it. He sat there with Connor and Jonny and got methodically drunk, and he must have looked at Jason and Emma every few seconds, because by the end of the evening it was like he had a stop-start movie of them in his head. But all the time, he chatted with his friends, and on the surface he seemed to have a good time. He was aware that it was very important that he keep anyone from realising what he was feeling, including himself. So he watched them but tried not to think about it, and when they walked off together he didn't let it bother him. It was okay.

Really, it was—

Okay.

So this is what happened.

What really happened.

Like I said, I saw Claire Warner through the window of the train: an odd moment, but fitting in a way – that my first real-life glimpse of her should be occluded slightly by the sunlight on a streaky window. I recognised her face from the picture she'd sent, and would have known it was her even without the white dress. The way she was standing. It's like everyone else in the station was forty per cent less real than she was. Crowds, sponsored by Stand-In.

She didn't know me to look at, but I caught her eye before I'd reached her, smiled, and she smiled back and knew it was me. Amazingly, she didn't look disappointed. I walked over to her feeling nervous, not knowing how to greet her or what to say. In the end, it was easy. We said *hi* to each other softly, and she kissed me on the cheek, her body like air in front of me. *Would you like to get a coffee?* And I said *yeah, please – this is really weird, isn't it? Isn't this really weird?*

That much all happened.

What I didn't tell you was that that day was one of Amy's darker days. I'd like to say that I didn't know, but I did. We argued that morning. I'd told her in advance that I had to do overtime and was heading into work for the day, but she was upset with me, or maybe just plain upset, and she asked me not to go. Maybe I could call in sick or something? Because she was really down and it would be nice for us to spend some time together. After all, we'd hardly seen each other lately. She was forgetting what I looked like.

She was lying in bed when she said all this to me. Propped

up on one elbow, watching me getting dressed, giving me that look.

And you know what? I was fucking irritated.

I'm not proud of it, but what I thought was: *there you go again, spoiling it for me*. It had happened before. In fact, sometimes it seemed as though Amy had this psychic ability to know when something mattered to me, or when I was looking forward to something, and those were the times when she suddenly needed me. She'd ask me to cancel; sometimes she'd cry; and – always – she'd give me the look that she was giving me now. Half begging me to say yes and half wondering how I couldn't. Amy would have dropped the world for me without even thinking.

Once upon a time, I would have done the same for her. I mean, I used to drop everything, even though it felt like a twist inside me, because I knew that the twist would be smoothed out quickly and, probably within the hour, I wouldn't even remember it had been there. But things change. You give stuff up for someone you love because you don't mind; and then you stop doing that when you do.

Maybe that's why she kept asking me to.

That morning, I felt annoyed with her. Deep down, I understand that it was more than that. I was angry with what had happened to her and how it had impacted upon our relationship, and I was pissed off at myself for a betrayal I'd rationalised, but not nearly enough. It's just that she was there.

'How the fuck am I supposed to cancel,' I said, looping on a tie I knew I'd take off after I left the house. 'When they're expecting me to be there?'

I think that part of it was me staying up late the night before, talking to Claire on Liberty and discussing what we were going to do when we met. She was the only thing on my mind. In my head, I was already on that train. The conversation Amy wanted to have was making me think: *this isn't fair, this always happens to me, why can't something go right for me just once?* And lots of other stupid things.

'It doesn't matter,' Amy said, falling back and turning away. 'Just go.'

I remember feeling relieved. Everything was okay – she'd told me to go. But I also felt like a child. I remembered non-specific examples of my mother caving in to some tantrum I'd thrown, and that was how I felt, standing at the foot of the bed and looking at Amy. She had hidden herself behind a ridge of duvet. I'd got what I wanted, and it felt sour.

'Are you crying?'

'No. Just fucking go.'

I hesitated. I really did.

But not for long.

'I'm sorry,' I said. 'I'll be back as soon as I can.'

And left.

There was a party. It was a New Year's Eve party, and everybody was very drunk. For the last few years, since most of their friends had come together as couples, they'd cele-brated New Year together, in one of their houses, drinking and playing games, and then forming a circle and singing and hugging when midnight came.

This year, the party had been held at Jason and Amy's, but there was something different about the atmosphere. Graham and Helen arrived and Graham knew immediately that something was wrong. He just couldn't put his finger on what it was.

'Hi guys.'

They had been there before any of the other guests. Jason and Amy took their coats and hung them up in the small hallway by the front door and it was clearly an awkward operation. Graham and Helen stood up straight, pressed to the walls, while the two of them manoeuvred around each other, not acknowledging each other beyond being careful not to touch. A silence had fallen amongst them like snow.

'Come on in,' Amy said to Helen, leading her into the living room.

Jason had taken Graham into the kitchen instead.

'Let's get you a drink, mate.'

'Thanks.'

Their kitchen was big and bright, edged by work surfaces covered with unopened bottles and cans, a chopping board balancing a lemon and a lime, and pre-prepared bowls of crisps and nuts and biscuits. Amy had baked some mini sausage rolls and pizzas, as well, and they were resting on plates on top of the cooker. In the oven, Graham could smell potato wedges.

'Here.'

Graham took the beer Jason was offering. His feet stuck to the tiles a little and gave little clicks as he walked over.

They went through to the living room, and it was nicer in there. There was a coffee table in the centre of the room covered with night lights; a lamp on a table in one corner; some larger candles on the dresser. It gave the room a subdued mood. Amy and Helen were conferring over the stereo. Graham and Jason sat down, and when music was finally chosen, Amy sat down on a different settee to Jason, and Graham thought: *strange*.

Other people arrived and the tension got diluted a little. But it was still there the whole evening.

The closest Graham could come was to think it was like when you turned up at someone's house just after an argument, and they were still banging around separately. Pretending each other didn't exist, except for scoring awkward potshots with comments too subtle to have any real meaning for you, and competing for your attention like you were some kind of prize. God knew it had been like that enough times at his house. And it was like that here. There didn't seem to have been an argument, but it felt like there had. Perhaps Jason and Amy had been quarrelling without realising it, because neither of them seemed comfortable looking at the other. They didn't seem right standing next to each other, either, and every time they spoke the things they said got taken slightly off-angle, or questioned, or ignored, as though they were either wanting a fight or expecting one.

It got to midnight and they sang in a circle – a kind of group hug, but with kicks and laughter – and then Connor took charge of the stereo and played songs they'd grown up to at the kind of volume you only get away with on New Year's Eve. But despite the surface cheer, things still weren't right. Some time after one o'clock, Graham realised Amy wasn't around and went looking for her. He found her outside, sitting on the front step. She'd been crying.

'Hey,' he said. 'What's up?'

She didn't want to tell him – she said 'nothing' a few times – but he sat with her for a bit and eventually she said:

'It's just Jason. He's being really horrible to me and I don't know why.'

'What do you mean? What's he done?'

'It's nothing he's done. He's just . . . I don't know. He said something in a really nasty tone of voice. I can't remember what it was.'

'Oh.'

She was very drunk, and so was Jason, and so was he. Graham didn't know whether Jason had really said something bad or if Amy was just being that special kind of over-sensitive that only comes with being so pissed.

'I'm sure he didn't mean it.'

Amy said, 'He doesn't want me around anymore.'

'He's just drunk.'

270

She ignored him and started crying again.

He didn't know what to say, and he knew that he could, if he wasn't careful, say the wrong thing, or at least a very stupid and unhelpful thing. There was still a pinprick of common sense shining through the alcoholic haze, so he didn't say anything. After a second, he reached out and touched her shoulder, and then gave it a tentative, friendly rub. Reassuring her. Her hair was in her face, so he tucked a few strands back behind her ear.

The intimacy of it immediately felt like a betrayal. Even though she hadn't said anything, and hadn't seemed at all bothered, he took his hand away. And then wished he hadn't. And then was glad he did.

'If you ever need a shoulder to cry on,' he said. 'I'm not good for much, but I can always do that.'

'Thank you. I appreciate it. I'm sorry about this.'

'Don't be sorry. I don't mind.' He stood up. 'But it's cold out here. You should come back inside.'

'I'll be okay. Just give me a couple of minutes.'

'You should go and see Amy,' Graham told Jason, who was swaying in the centre of the lounge and didn't seem able to focus. 'She's outside. She's a bit upset.'

'Okay.'

But he didn't move, and Graham wanted to punch him. Instead, he sat down. *He's just drunk*, he thought, but then realised that it wasn't enough. He was drunk too, and he would have gone out immediately if Amy was his girlfriend and he'd known she was upset.

'Jason, mate,' he said after a moment. 'I really think you should go out and see Amy.'

And Jason looked at him for a second, not seeing and not understanding, and maybe Graham really would have punched him then. But before he could get up, Jason lurched off in the direction of the front door.

'Fucking sorry.'

'Don't be sorry,' Claire said, and then she looked at me with that expression – the one that said she liked me but was slightly disappointed at the same time. She touched my shoulder gently, and then gave it a squeeze. 'You're a nice guy, Jason. And I'm not into ruining lives.'

'Maybe I should go,' I said.

She shook her head.

'Why? Come on – let's have another coffee. We can talk.' She gave me a nice smile. 'You can tell me about your girlfriend. Okay?'

I thought about it. As weird an idea as it should have seemed, suddenly it didn't. In fact, I realised that I really *did* want to talk to Claire about Amy – that it seemed right. The feeling of relief was getting stronger and brighter. I figured that I had a lot I needed to say.

'Okay,' I told her, nodding. I even managed a smile. 'That'd be really nice.'

That all happened, too.

What I didn't know was that Amy had a lot to say at that point as well. In fact, she was telling Graham a story about a girl.

CHAPTER EIGHTEEN

'She told me about what happened to her that time,' the man said. 'She told me about how she was raped, and she told me how difficult it had been for her. I mean, she didn't fucking need to tell me that, Jason, but she told me anyway.'

He kept looking at me, and it was making everything worse. If he'd just been telling the story, sat there with the gun, it would still be frightening, but it would also be a little easier. As it was, he was involving me. It felt as though I needed to do and say everything exactly right, or else he might involve me in more painful ways. But at the same time, I realised that he wasn't actually looking at me at all; he was looking through me and past me, at this Jason, and so it didn't really matter what I did. Whether I got out of here alive seemed to depend on how badly a memory pissed him off.

'I was so angry with you,' he said, as if reading my mind. 'Where the fuck were you that day? Do you have any idea what she was going through? She needed you, and you were off wherever you were, doing whatever you wanted. You didn't care about her at all, and it fucking killed me.'

He looked away, shaking his head.

'I could never understand how you could be so . . .' He screwed up his face in disgust. '*Ambivalent* to her. You didn't understand what you had. I would have killed to have what you had, and you didn't even care. I wanted her, and I wanted to slap her, but most of all I just wanted to slap you.'

I was growing colder by the second. He was talking to

Jason, and this was all for his benefit, and that meant that he was intending to give the document I was writing to Jason. So why wasn't he explaining it all in person?

He's going to kill me.

I noticed the blood on his jacket then. There was a little on his shirt, and quite a bit more had dried on the backs of his hands. How had I ever missed it?

He was going to kill me.

'We had some drinks,' the man said. 'We had some drinks, and then we had some more. You were at work, Amy said. She said you wouldn't be back all day. I didn't believe that's where you were at all, though, and you know why? Because she didn't believe it. I could tell. She was so fucking sad, Jason. So unhappy. So I suggested we have some drinks. And it was the middle of the day, but we figured to hell with it, and so we had some drinks. I mean – why not?'

He shook his head again and then looked up at me. There were so many emotions on his face now, beside the anger, that I found it impossible to know what he was thinking or planning to do.

'And what happened,' he said, 'happened.'

You're a nice guy, Jason. And I'm not into ruining lives.

After I met Claire, I went home, arriving back quite late. Amy was already in bed by then: three-quarters asleep and only vaguely aware of me slipping in beside her. She was naked. She was facing away from me, and I moved up against her, pressing my chest to her thin back, putting my arm around her and cupping my hand on her slight stomach. All I could smell was her hair. I'd come so close to making the worst mistake of my life, and I'd never been more relieved than I was right then.

'I love you,' I told her, kissing the side of her neck.

She didn't say anything, but she moved slightly and took

hold of my hand where it rested on her stomach and she gave it a squeeze. And she pressed back against me, giving a noise that might have been contentment.

And I never knew that anything had happened between Amy and Graham that afternoon. Maybe it was because I was so tangled up in my own guilt that it never occurred to me she might have some of her own, or that the issues that affected our relationship would cause her to make the same mistake that I almost had. I mean, why would that be the case? You see, it was all about me by then. The way I'd left her that morning was indicative of everything about our relationship. Once upon a time, I'd been there for her, and now I was only there for me. I'd offered comfort and sacrifice to ease what I knew was difficult for her, and now I only offered questions. Where was my comfort? Who was there to ease things for me when I found it hard?

I should have known it was over by the way I was thinking. Instead, I lay there against her, feeling my own guilt, holding her belly, thinking that it might all be okay after all. It was stupid and fucking delusional. You can put the feelings aside but you can't throw them, and so they're always within reach. They find their way into your hands again. Sometimes, people do everything except push them at you. It was never really about her being raped. I can blame that, and I do blame it, but it's not the whole story. That event cast a shadow, all right, but for a while I cast a light. It wasn't something impossible and insurmountable. We had a good life, and we loved each other very much, and for a while there it had been just about as perfect as anything Graham had ever dreamed of.

You can't blame the rape.

But you can, if you choose to, blame me.

'We had sex three times,' the man said. 'And each time, she felt guilty afterwards, but we kept falling back into it. And at

275

the end, she couldn't believe what she'd done. She started crying. You will never have any idea how much that woman loved you, Jason, and you just . . . you just fucking . . . *pushed* her away.'

He glared at me, and it became too much. I looked down at the paper in front of me and watched myself writing instead. He was going to kill me. In fact, he sounded like he was talking himself up to it.

'Look at me.'

Despite myself, I did. Slowly and reluctantly, but I looked up at him.

'You want to write all this fucking shit down,' he said, pointing at me – *me*, this time – with the gun. 'You didn't bat an eyelid while your friend was killing a girl I loved. So you fucking pay attention, now, and you look at me. Okay?'

I remembered. I'd wanted to smile at her and tell her that it would be okay, but I'd known that it wouldn't, and I hadn't been there to make her feel comfortable or to help her. So instead, I'd just picked up my pen and, without taking my eyes off her, I'd begun to write.

I remembered exactly what had happened.

'Yes,' I said.

Yes. Anything's *okay. Absolutely anything.*

Just please don't kill me.

There was a pause, and then:

'You pushed her away,' he said. 'You treated her badly. You weren't there for her when she needed you. How could you not be, after she'd gone through something like that? All I could think of was that I would have been. I would have fucking . . . I would have fucking sat there with her. I would have talked to her. Held her. I would have had some respect for her. I mean, I would have acted like she had some . . . some kind of fucking *value* to me. But you couldn't even do that.'

276

He looked down, gathering his thoughts. His voice was quieter when he started speaking again.

'I asked her to leave you for me,' he said. 'And she told me no. She said she couldn't. She loved you. She wanted it to work. She actually – and I could have killed you when she said this – but she actually thought that it was her fault. Can you believe that? She blamed herself for what happened. You made her blame herself. And she wanted to sort herself out and have you back, and because of that, she said no to me. Told me it was a mistake, and she was sorry to have done this to me, and even more sorry to have done it to you.'

He shook his head.

'And I cried. I cried – of all things! I was so upset. And you know what she did?' He looked up at me. Through me, at Jason. 'She held me. She comforted me. After everything she'd been through she did that. That's how special she was, and you weren't even there for this girl. She went off to try to understand what happened to her, and she thought she was doing it for you, and she wasn't at all. She was doing it *because* of you.'

For a second, the anger seemed to be gone, and he seemed almost deflated by the conclusion he'd come to. All I could see in his face was sadness. The anger was lost. But then I realised that, no, it wasn't. It was just pacing in the background: working itself back and forth; taking an emotional run up for whatever was coming next.

'I killed Marley,' he said. 'If you're hearing this then you probably know that already.'

Fuck.

If he'd killed Marley then he was going to kill me too.

But there was something else in addition to that – something I couldn't quite put my finger on but that felt as though, when I did, it would be the final nail in this whole, sorry coffin. My mind was circling it, threatening to alight: a hand chasing a feather of memory.

'I killed him for her, not for you,' he was saying. 'I opened up the account I set up for you, and I saw the videos that were there. I didn't know where they came from but I knew what they meant. She was dead. I guess I'd always known that she would be. I mean, even before I read that file I downloaded for you from Liberty. What else could she be?'

The file.

I glanced at the blank computer screen on the desk in front of us.

'And you know,' he said, 'I hadn't really read that file too well before that. I'd scanned it, but it was mostly gibberish: just the occasional word, maybe half a sentence or so. It was corrupted, so I hadn't read that much of it. But I read it through. I don't know why. Morbid curiosity, I guess.'

The text.

I closed my eyes.

'Look at me,' he said.

I shook my head.

Oh God.

'Open your eyes.'

'No.'

'You remember what it said there, don't you?'

'Yes.'

'You remember what she said.'

'Yes,' I told him. I opened my eyes, understanding perfectly. My mind had caught that feather. The final nail had gone in.

I was going to die, and it was probably the rightest thing in the world that I did.

'I remember what she said.'

'*Sit* down on the *edge* of the *fucking* bed.'

278

Marley dragged her back and shoved her down, and she started to cry. Sat there and held her face in her hands, sobbing. Marley didn't care; he wasn't even looking at her anymore. Long Tall Jack just laughed.

'Please don't do this,' she said.

Jack was walking over to her, swinging his cock, as she stood up. There was an awful look on her face: a kind of desperately contrived hope. Something had very clearly occurred to her. She was stuck in this nightmare, yes, panicking, yes, but now she'd suddenly realised that it was actually all going to be okay. She'd remembered a key piece of information that she'd left out. How could she have been so stupid? All that she needed to do was explain, and then everything would be all right.

'Please don't do this,' she said. 'I'm pregnant.'

Jack kept coming, and the look on her face disappeared. It began with a punch.

You know what I remember most? It's the note she left for me on the kitchen table.

Jason, she'd written.

> *I love you very much and I don't want you to blame yourself for this. This isn't some kind of 'dear John' letter. I'm coming back again. There are some things I need to sort out. You know how it's been between the two of us recently and it's not fair on you. I need to deal with the issues I have, just like you said.*
>
> *I should have dealt with them by now, but I really need to now.*
>
> *Please wait for me. I promise I'll come home as soon as I can.*
>
> *I love you so much (to the sky and back!),*
> *Your Amy.*

There it is: my Amy.

So, even after everything that happened, she was still mine at that point. I'd been human enough to be not good enough for her, and she was still prepared to be mine. Maybe I should take comfort from that: she didn't want Graham, and she felt bad about what had happened between them; and she loved me and wanted it to work between us. But I don't take any comfort. It's not about Graham. I don't care about that; everybody makes mistakes. But there's this: she told me in the letter that she needed to sort herself out for me, and she shouldn't have thought that; there shouldn't have been the need for her to think like that. And once upon a time there wouldn't have been. So it was my fault, not hers.

I keep thinking about what she wrote.

I should have dealt with them already, but I really need to now.

And I think that she really needed to deal with them now because she'd found out she was pregnant and had suddenly been faced with all the responsibilities and uncertainties that go along with that. Amy had wanted to keep me – or she had wanted me back – and so she'd gone to sort herself out in the way she thought she owed me. Never mind for a moment that she didn't owe me anything. More importantly, there's the pregnancy to think about.

The baby.

Was it mine or was it the result of that afternoon with Graham? I've done the maths and it could have been either. I guess Graham thought it had been his, but maybe he was wrong. It really doesn't matter. I'll never know, and so to all intents and purposes it might as well have been.

You look at the line of your life and stick little coloured flags in at key moments: the ones where the line bends sharply off to one side, continuing at some weird new angle. You mark those points down and remember them, and when you question your current trajectory, it's those points that you use to explain them. Tapping the board and saying: *I'm going this way because of this.*

And that's what it comes down to in the end. The rape was one little tag – one that sent her life spinning off in a different direction, crashing into mine – but there was another change in trajectory after that, and that's really what's important here. Stupid, but true.

Amy was dead because I went to see Claire Warner that day.

If it hadn't been for that, there would have been none of this.

But as usual, it wasn't quite as simple as that.

On the day she disappeared, Amy took the bus into the city. After a brief, purposeful walk, she went into a café called Jo's and sat in the window. She was there for half an hour in all, and drank two cups of coffee, taking her time over each. Between the two cups, she sent a text message. Mildly annoyed but mostly anxious, she didn't write much. She simply put:

[r u on ur way???]

A few blocks away, Graham read the message, and then immediately deleted it. He didn't trust Helen not to look through the phone if he left it lying around. Perhaps it was guilt. When you've done something wrong, you often expect other people to share your standards.

'Who was that?'

'It was Jason,' he said. 'It was nothing.'

So: the footage of the café was actually the first bit of film that Graham ever located. Since he'd been supposed to be meeting

Amy there, he knew where to look. He sat on it for a while, of course, until he could realistically produce it – until he'd found enough of a trail for it to lead him there without it seeming suspicious. He wasn't stupid. Neither was she, though, and I should have thought of it earlier. Would she really have disappeared off to meet a man like Kareem without telling someone where she was going? Of course not. She wouldn't have told me, obviously, because then I wouldn't have let her go, or I would have insisted on going with her. But she might have told Graham, especially after everything they'd been through together. So she arranged to meet him in that café, and I can only guess what was on her mind. Was she wanting him to go with her? Was she just going to tell him where and who she was going to see? I'll never know.

And neither will Graham. He never made that appointment. He knew that Amy was making it work with me, or trying to, and he wasn't going to get in the way of that, even if he wanted to. And I guess he was annoyed with her, in his own way. There had been times since they'd slept together when he'd been there, again and again, to listen to her and try to help her through whatever stupid shit I'd done that week, but there was no way that could continue forever, not considering how he felt. Even good friends lose their patience with you occasionally. That day, he thought *fuck it*. Perhaps, having found out how needy she could be, he might have started to empathise with me in some small way. He spent the day with Helen instead, and thought about Amy only once or twice.

So: Amy went to meet Kareem because of me, but she went on her own because Graham didn't go to meet her, even though he'd told her that he would. That's what it comes down to; we both had our parts to play in letting her down.

I imagine her sitting in that café, enjoying her first cup of coffee as she waits for Graham, and then she becomes increasingly nervous and undecided as he fails to arrive. She sends that text message and starts thinking: should she go alone, or shouldn't she? Deep down, she knows he's not coming. That's the second cup of coffee. It would be so much easier just to go home, but the thought of that is crushing. This is something that has been keeping her going, giving her hope for our relationship, and going home is defeat. It's an emotional back-flip over the edge of a cliff.

Amy made her decision. She went on her own that day, and that was the last she ever saw of us.

'Close your eyes,' Graham said.

'What?'

'Close your eyes,' he said. 'And keep writing.'

The man did as he was told, but he was badly frightened now: shaking; his face looking like he was dreaming, all full of nervous twitches and concentration. And even in this extreme state, the pen kept skittering across the page in front of it, steady and even, recording each and every one of these terrible sensations like some kind of fucking polygraph. Graham stared at him for a couple of seconds, watching the words come, spilling across the empty lines, slowly filling the page. The man was like a machine. Like some kind of camera. The sense-data was coming in, being processed, and then out came the text before him. A permanent record.

How quick was he, Graham wondered as he raised the gun and aimed it at the side of the man's head. Was the translation instantaneous? He took a good, solid two-handed grip, fingers uncurling and then curling back, and he thought: is this man quicker than a bullet? Will the split-second feeling of his skull opening, his brain rupturing – will the beginnings of that make their way onto the page? And, if so, what will become of the person who reads that?

Graham closed one eye and thought: *goodbye, Jason.*

'Wait,' the writer said.

Graham kept his eye closed.

'Wait,' the writer said again. He licked his lips. 'I know what you want to do, but you have to give me a second. There's something you need to see.'

'What?'

'An e-mail,' the writer said. 'Someone just sent it to me. There's something there that you really need to see. That you should see, really, before you decide what you're going to do.'

Graham stared at him. The man still had his eyes shut, and his head was nodding slightly, as though he was counting something in his head.

He stared at him for another couple of seconds.

'Show me.'

The writer opened his eyes. He looked like someone coming out into the light from a long, dark tunnel. With his free hand trembling a little, he reached out for the mouse on the computer table in front of him, and Graham – still aiming the gun – said:

'Slowly.'

The writer moved the cursor and the black screensaver vanished. Hidden underneath it was an empty e-mail.

'It's not the message you need to see,' he said. 'It's the attachment.'

He clicked on a couple of options. The screen changed view to reveal a page of text and the writer scrolled for a second and then pointed at a section of it. 'Here. This bit.'

Graham leaned across and looked at what was there.

He was watching the big man: Jack. Jack couldn't work the skirt down over her kicking legs, and her voice was getting louder and more desperate – *No-o-o!* – and so he punched her so hard between her legs that the whole bed shook.

Jack watched her to see whether there was going to be any more fighting. When it was obvious that there wasn't, he started moving again. He finished undressing her, throwing the skirt to one side, and then he climbed on top of her, his elbows pressing down hard on the inside of her upper arms, knocking her palms away from her red, tear-stained face. His hands pulled her head right back by the hair. In this surrender position, with her pinned there and sobbing, he started to rape her.

I was watching the man with the gun. It was still pointing at me, but there was no conscious thought attached. He was wrapped up in the text on the screen, lost in it, and – although he probably wouldn't have known it – he had started to cry.

I had seconds. If I was going to get out of here alive, then this was going to be my only chance to do it. He was going to kill me, and I wasn't a killer – not really – but there was no way I was going to let him hurt me: if it was me or him, then it was him.

The gun was wavering in the air. Before I could think about the danger, or what would happen if I couldn't overpower him, I grabbed it and started to fight.

CHAPTER NINETEEN

That was it: the end.

I looked away from the papers on the desk. My heart was beating too quickly and my mind felt bruised from both the impact of the message and the medium through which it had been communicated. Other than that, all I felt was a kind of dreadful, empty calm.

I was already putting it together. The writer must have attacked Graham while he was distracted with the text on the screen, and tried to wrestle the gun from him – and maybe he'd succeeded or maybe it had been an accident, but whichever, Graham had got himself shot in the head. The writer knew Marley had been killed and he would have suspected from what Graham had told him that I would be making my way here eventually, so he called Jack, the pins and knives man. They checked out Marley, found him dead and then staked the place out, or maybe Jack did that on his own. I arrived. Jack died. And then I follow Graham's trail here and get to read what happened. I get to discover the reason behind all of this, and it fucking sucks.

There was an awful inevitability to it all: a sense of closure that left only me hanging, and that was something I thought I could take care of now. There wasn't much else left for me.

The writer?

The fact that I hadn't been attacked while I read the papers was telling. The man wasn't a killer; he was a coward. He wasn't even a hardcore criminal. So maybe Jack had told him to lie low for a while: that he'd take care of me, clean things up and let the guy know when it was safe to come out. Or maybe he'd been staking out Marley's place, too. He knew I'd killed Jack and wanted nothing to do with me. Perhaps he was on a plane to somewhere tropical even now. Wherever he was, he wasn't here. Looking around, I had no great desire to be here either. I picked up the papers in front of me, folded them neatly and slipped them into my pocket.

And then I left.

But before I did, I took a quick look around. There were hundreds of notepads here: thousands of pages of observation and experience. Most of it was trivial and inconsequential, but who was I to judge? Most things are, including me. What occurred to me was what a shame it was that all this was going to waste. For a moment the books looked like nothing so much as lives held in stasis: rich, vital moments trapped between covers, just waiting to be tripped into and felt. It seemed a shame, and I didn't know whether to take a match to the place or call Dennison. In the end, I did the latter, from a payphone in the street outside. There was no answer, so I left a message giving him the address and a couple of words of caution – dead body in the bathtub; possibly dangerous tenant – but there was a life's work of lives to be saved in the flat and I didn't think a few little details like that would deter him.

Then, for what it was worth, I went and checked out of the hotel.

And I went home.

The first thing I did when I got in was check the messages on my answerphone. It was the same two messages as before, but I listened to them again anyway.

Okay, I'm not the only loose end.

My job. As I listened to Nigel prattle on, with his odd inflections and even odder assumption that I might give a shit, my job had never felt more meaningless to me. They had paid me for a month of work I hadn't done, and that was all I needed to know. It was possible that they'd pay me for another month – I was, after all, a troubled young man – but frankly I couldn't have cared less. I listened to Nigel's voice and I knew it was intended to sound like some kind of authority – something that would make me feel guilty, or bring me to heel, or make me worried – but it didn't. I received those emotions, but they were filtered through dream logic; they were feelings I might have experienced in another life and, now that I'd woken up, they meant next to nothing to me.

Fuck him, fuck them. I pressed [NEXT] before the end of the message.

Beep.

'Hi Jason, it's Charlie.'

Oh, yes – there was Charlie to think about. Poor Charlie, who practically idolised me. And what did I do to her? I used her as bait to track down a paedophile, killed him, unburdened half my soul to her and then abandoned her. And after all that, without me even asking, she had covered up evidence of a serious crime on my behalf. What was her current reaction to me?

'It's Sunday night,' she told me again. 'I'm just calling because I hope you're okay. I don't know what happened yesterday – or what I did wrong – but I'm sorry, whatever it was. And I understand; it's okay.'

She understood. It was okay. In fact, it was possible that she'd even done something wrong. As I pressed [STOP] I thought that if enough of the women in my life got together they might realise that I was the common fucking denominator.

'I wanted to let you know—'

Click

288

So: Charlie. Turning up to meet me with make-up on. She was more attractive than she realised – and nicer, too. For fuck's sake, she'd been sitting there, listening to my worries. She'd encouraged me to talk about Amy and my other problems, and all the time she was doing that she'd had make-up on. Either that, or she'd had her hair cut. I couldn't even remember which it had been. It was pretty obvious that she deserved better than someone like me.

But she'd be okay, I thought as I headed upstairs with the gun in my hand. My job, too. They'd both survive without me. In themselves, they weren't loose ends so much as frayed edges. Once you got rid of me, they took care of themselves.

I walked into the study.

Everything was still just as fucked up as Walter Hughes' friends had left it. The hard drive of my computer was in a couple of clunky pieces on the floor, and one of the guys had pulled the monitor off base and smashed it to shit, no doubt unaware that his boss was about to offer to pay for any damages. Compensation would have undermined the point of destroying my property a little bit. But then I'd gone and killed Hughes, so it was a moot point anyway.

I kicked a bit of circuitry and thought about the internet. The news on the coach was that the damage was starting to repair itself. Where that wasn't the case, IT firemen were busy pouring gushing streams of water over the flames, trying to limit the spread. Nobody had a clue what had happened, but the consensus was that it seemed to have stopped. For the moment.

I kept a few pictures of Amy in the study. They were pretty much undisturbed: lodged on a shelf in the computer desk. Actually, they weren't just pictures of Amy: I was on some of them, too; Graham and Helen; Jonny and the guys we'd grown up with. Amy probably wasn't even on half of them, but I took the whole bundle through to the bedroom.

There, I spread the pictures out, filtering away the irrelevant ones and putting the ones I liked best out on the pillows, the top of the duvet. I covered the bed in them. Shots of us on holiday. Shots of us at New Year's. Just tens of photographs. Graduation. Engagement. Pictures taken in bars, of long, cheering tables we were at; you had to pick us out, and even then it barely looked like us. I was crying the whole time, touching her face as I let them fall. One. Ten. Thirty. I remembered all of them. Ask me for fifty different occasions when Amy had smiled at me and I'd be stuck by double figures, but I remembered each of these clearly. They were obvious examples. Only God knows all of the times she smiled when I forgot to take a photograph.

When the bed was covered, I lay down on it. Everything shifted and slid, but that was okay. First one elbow, then onto my back. I still had the gun, and – when I was settled – I put the barrel into my mouth, tasting the salt and grease and oily tang of it. The ceiling was not as interesting as I would have liked. Looking down from it, surrounded by these photographs, I imagined I looked pretty good, at least symbolically, but looking up I felt very little at all.

At this angle, the top of my head would be blown out all over the wall at the head of the bed. That seemed to be the general angle. I didn't know about the gases from the barrel. Maybe they would blow my cheeks apart, scorch my throat, burn my lips. Perhaps the barrel would become hot from the bullet and, even as my head went out on the wall, my mouth would be burned and hollowed and blistered. Nothing is ever as clean as in the movies.

Goodbye Amy, I thought, and pulled the trigger.

EPILOGUE

Things are better now. Not perfect by any means, but better. It's four months on, and there's a strange kind of poetry to that: it was four months after Amy disappeared when I found her, and now, four months later, I'm beginning to find my feet. I have a new job. It's nothing special – just grunt work at the moment – but it keeps me busy and keeps me sane and, most importantly of all, it doesn't involve fucking people over – or at least not directly – and so despite the grease and dirt I get to have an illusion of my hands being clean.

Every night I go home to the house that Amy and I used to share. I'll be selling it soon and moving somewhere different: not a nicer place or a worse one, just different. I'm okay where I am, but I made the suggestion to Charlie and she seemed to think it was a good idea. She notices how I am much more than I do. I have good days and bad days, just like everybody, and I think it helps that I got a lot of my grieving out of the way a long time ago. There's still the guilt to deal with, but I'm as resilient as the next person and, when I need to, I can lock all that shit away and pretend it's not there.

Oh yeah – Charlie.

Well, she's here some of the time. We're still just friends, but neither of us is with anyone else and it seems likely that we'll get together at some point. There's a closeness between us, and it increases every day. She's one of those types of people: the kind who seem to have infinite patience. I'm in awe of her in so many ways. She deserves better, of course;

I'm still very much aware of that. But I'm also determined to change it. One day, if I work at it hard enough, maybe it won't be true anymore. Perhaps she'll deserve me. Stranger things have happened.

And the gun?

Well, I still have it. Sometimes I take it out of the drawer in the bedroom and look at it. I run my hands over it and imagine what it would be like to load it with bullets and shoot myself. I'd fired it precisely twice. The first had killed Walter Hughes' bodyguard: an accident. The second, more deliberate, had killed Hughes himself. And then, four months ago, I'd fired it into the top of my mouth, expecting to die. That had been incredibly deliberate. But there were no bullets left. The gun was empty. It had gone *click click click click*.

I'd rested there, wanting to kill myself and yet totally unable. It felt like insult added to fucking injury, and I didn't know whether to laugh or cry. In the end, I laughed.

Eventually, the curtains lightened and the shadows in the room began to fade out. Birds started singing outside. At some point I fell asleep. When I woke up it was afternoon, and the photographs were scattered everywhere and there was blood from my face all over the pillows and the top of the sheets. I'd tried to kill myself – I really had – but the bruised side of my head was throbbing too much for me to be anything other than woefully alive. I'd even fucked up my own suicide, and now I was going to have to pay the price: the day ahead.

I cleaned myself up as best I could, but I could tell that the cuts weren't going to heal on their own: they weren't bleeding much anymore, but I'd need stitches. Whether I would go and get them was another matter entirely; maybe I would and maybe I wouldn't. For the moment, I balled up an old T-shirt, dabbed at myself every so often, and made my way down-stairs.

I think I mentioned: I had this ritual.

I started a pot of coffee percolating in the kitchen, clicked some bread down into the toaster and got the milk and butter out of the fridge. I couldn't find anything relaxing enough on the crappy little radio-cassette we kept on the cabinet, so I settled for silence. I just sat down at the kitchen table, the gun in front of me, waiting for my late breakfast to be ready and imagining that Amy was asleep upstairs. She'd come down in a bit, but for now she was only half-awake. Drifting; sleepy.

But I couldn't do it. She wasn't there. There was just a load of fucking photographs. I'd been upstairs all night and morning, and she'd been conspicuous by her absence.

Instead, I watched the grey, featureless sky out of the window, just gazing really, but still peripherally aware of the gun, the coffee machine, the toaster. I wasn't thinking of much. Eventually the toast leapt up and the coffee was ready. And, after a moment, I got up and had my breakfast.

I had just finished, and was wondering what to do with the rest of my day, when the phone rang.

It hadn't been Charlie or my boss. I'd let it slip onto the answer-phone just in case, but when I heard Dennison's impatient, excited voice – *Jason, pick up the fucking phone* – I walked across the room and did just that.

He told me what they'd found in the writer's flat, sounding like a breathless little kid on Christmas morning, detailing the wonders of the notebooks and jotters – of the few he'd looked at, never mind all the rest. It was pretty clear that here was someone who'd found his vocation in life. I guess it was nice, but it was also tedious and eventually I told him to cut the shit and get to the chase.

Oh yeah, he said. *That's not why I rang at all.*

And so he explained. While searching the flat, they'd checked the writer's computer, which was still connected to the slightly stalled internet, and they found an item of e-mail that was rather strange. It was blank, Dennison said, but it caught his eye because of the address of the sender. Like the video clips I'd received that day at his house, the e-mail had been sent to the writer by Amy Foster.

But it wasn't just an e-mail. There was an attachment, too, and it sounded from Dennison's description of it as though it might be the schio file. He was sending it on to me at the address that Graham had set up, but he'd already read it through and he told me that he had a theory.

Throughout the file, the majority of the text was decayed and ruined. You could make out odd words and the occasional phrase. Part of the beginning of her murder was complete, and I didn't know whether I'd be reading that again any time soon. That aside, the only section that read relatively cleanly was near the start of the text. But Dennison's theory, despite the evidence, was that this section had changed too.

He painted me a picture. He imagined this text. It would have begun to be corrupted already, he said, by swapping data with the other files on his Society's server, but then it was downloaded by Graham and let loose across the internet as it dropped off the e-mail he'd sent. I'd imagined it lost on an ethereal cutting-room floor, but Dennison saw it flying instead: flinging itself from server to server, collecting and swapping letters and words. In the process, it had fucked half the computers in the world, if only in miniscule ways, but it had also – he felt – had impetus. The damage was the downside of purpose; the text had been reinventing itself as it went.

He said the text was conscious. During its travels, it had abandoned most of itself; the unnecessary sections were forgotten, left to erode. The real progress was deliberate and concentrated, and the result of this poaching and shifting was the attachment that had arrived at the writer's computer, probably only slightly before Graham himself. Along the way, it had collected the video evidence and deposited it in my inbox. Then, had it waited? Did it know Graham was on his way, and that I would end up there too? I couldn't know – probably never would. All I could do was read what it had written of itself and take from it whatever was there. Read into it whatever I wanted.

So some nights, when the house feels dark – when I start to feel very lonely, and the heating starts clicking, and the pipes creak, and the ticking clock in the other room starts to sound like cover for movement downstairs – I go and read the printout I took of the document when I could finally access my e-mail, and it makes the house a little lighter around me.

You are looking at a girl.

She is wearing a pale blue blouse and a white cotton skirt: frail clothes that you can't quite see through but which still manage to give you an idea of the slim but womanly figure beneath. Her skin is tanned and clear, and her hair is shoulder-length, brown and full of body. Not curly exactly, or frizzy, but a kind of pleasing combination of the two, streaked through with patches of blonde where the sun seems to have bleached it. Her face is pretty, but not exceptionally so – although you can tell that if she was smiling she'd be very attractive indeed. It's just one of those faces that lights up when it smiles and makes everything else seem somehow less important.

And ever so slowly, she gives you that smile.

She doesn't need to, though: it's there in her stance, and in the expression on her face. She's completely at ease, and not in the least bit angry with you. Perhaps once upon a time she was, but she's over that now. She's looking at you as though she understands that you're just another frail human being, exactly the same as her. You're not perfect, but it's not something she blames you for. It's not something that's your fault.

It breaks your heart that you can't go over and hold her, but the fact is that you can't. Not anymore. That's not why you're here.

She mouths the words *I love you*, and you look away for a second, but then you force yourself to look back. She has this sad-happy smile on her face. You can tell that she means it.

And after a moment, you smile back.